I0780789

JAKS STOOD AND TURNED. HIS EXPRESSION was stony and resolute. "Mayfield, take our guest and find an appropriate accommodation for her, then send out the alerts. In five minutes, I will send an alert and notify the Elder Sons."

"Understood," Mayfield said, his jovial manner all gone. He pulled at Zurah, forcing her to move with him.

"I didn't do this. I swear," Zurah said as they moved past Jaks.

He turned to stare at her, his eyes glowing with a cold green light, which spread like web-like veins across his face and down his neck. "Get her out of here."

Zurah threw one last look at the Old Mother's quiet body. Blood had begun to pool around the old woman's head, turning the edges of her jumpsuit along her shoulders dark and slick.

The woman who had come to help gently picked up the crystal and placed it back in her bag. "The Old Mother is dead. Long shall the Elder Sons watch the divide."

#sciencefiction
THE EMBEDDED UNIVERSE
The Three-Fold Suns Series

The Rapscallion

Project Clear Sight

The Diplomats of Dar

The Secrets of Epo-5

The Celestial Light

The Black Gates of Objer Series

Abandoned Echoes

Echoes of Revenge

#fantasy
Scattered Worlds

Burning of the Shrouds

#minithology and **#scatteredstories**

The Secret Lives of Crazy Dragon Ladies

Fairies in Jars

A Most Unusual Garden

Moonlit Wings

Holidays Afar

Daughter of Spring

Scion of Summer

Heir of Autumn

Child of Winter

The Dream Spider

Echoes of Revenge

The Black Gates of Objer
Book 2

by

ELIZABETH KNOLLSTON

LEWIS BROS PRESS

Copyright © 2025 Elizabeth Knollston

Echoes of Revenge
The Black Gates of Objer Book 2
All Rights Reserved

This book, or parts thereof, may not be reproduced in any form without permission.

This is a work of fiction. All characters and events in this book are fictitious. Any similarity to real persons, living or dead, is coincidental and not intended by the author.

ISBN Paperback: 978-1-959159-19-3
ISBN Ebook: 978-1-959159-18-6

Cover Art and Interior Design © Elizabeth Knollston
Editing by Red Adept Editing Services

Published by Lewis Bros. Press
PO Box 261
Larned, KS 67550

www.elizabethknollston.com

for those who
so selflessly give of themselves
to support others
in times of great need

Grains of sand rolled across a desert landscape, moving to the endless rhythm of a wind that didn't exist. Tan sand dunes crowded against each other along the horizon in every direction. Time had ravaged this place, and the planet was a silent graveyard of long-past ambitions, deceit, and sorrow. The dunes held the last echo of a world teeming with life, now consumed and forgotten. The twin suns traveled across a cloudless sky, marking the passage of time, though there were none to witness and none who cared to remember.

Then one day when the suns were at their zenith, the air above a sand dune shimmered. The faint lines of iridescent light twisted and grew into a glistening diamond. The edges rippled with blues and reds bleeding into the clear light of the diamond's outline.

A void as black as the darkest depths of the universe appeared in the center of the diamond. Gradually, twinkling points of light appeared, until there were thousands of endless possibilities. The void's surface rippled, and its image shifted to a bleak landscape—a world that had been cut off from the sands, abandoned and forgotten.

The void's surface rippled again, and a fat, metallic object moved through the void, kicking up clouds of sand as it raced across the dunes before disappearing on the horizon. The object reappeared, sweeping the area once more. Then it stopped, suspended in the air directly in front of the strange diamond. Static filled the silence for a moment, then a burst of chatter spewed out from the object.

"All clear. We are a go," a voice from within the void said. A series of lights flickered off and on across the object's body, then it floated back through the void.

As the lights dimmed along the diamond, gradually receding until nothing remained, the sand ceased its movement. The forgotten world was shrouded in absolute silence until something exploded up through one of the sand dunes. Grains of sand rolled toward each other, building on top of one another until a fragmented form appeared. The edges of the figure were not well defined, as if it couldn't quite remember what it had once been. A half-formed head turned its eyeless sight to where the diamond had appeared as if waiting and watching for the shimmering light and its cavernous mouth of endless possibilities to appear once again.

When the light did not reappear, the figure gradually dissolved, but as it disappeared, a swirling maw of sand whipped around its feet. What had been forgotten was remembered.

1

Laughter and good-natured jests filled the room, but that did little to lift Zurah's spirits. The goliath-class cargo ship, which had been scuttled and half buried after transporting the teams and equipment to Objer, had been heavily modified to meet a wide variety of needs for the scientists, researchers, and security individuals who had signed on to work for the enigmatic Finn and Alex Goldsmith. In the mess of tables and chairs—which had once served as a dining hall and was now undergoing hasty renovations to become a rec room—Zurah sat alone as she finished her third glass of whiskey. Her thoughts were focused on Nissa and Dr. Ordotham. Both individuals were tucked away in the main medical bay, several decks above Zurah. Though fragile, Nissa's medical status remained stable in the stasis pod, while Dr. Ordotham's status was unknown, despite various attempts over the past several days to ascertain whether the Neetho doctor was alive or dead.

The whiskey helped dull the edges of her anger as Zurah replayed the events of the last few days. *If Mexa had only ignored the request for transport from Finn… If only Nissa had turned down Finn's offer… If Finn had been forthcoming with intel…* And more potential scenarios swirled through Zurah's thoughts.

A shout went up from the crowd as a man swaggered through the room, smiling and throwing around "you're welcome" and "you bet." His olive skin shifted colors under the neon lights, and despite everything that had happened on Objer, Alex Goldsmith—heir to the Goldsmith Consortium—appeared as relaxed and unfazed as ever. He spotted Zurah and waved. When she didn't respond, he made his way toward her.

"Given it a try yet?" He jerked a thumb over his shoulder to point at what had the crowd so excited.

Zurah shook her head.

"Aw, come on. You know you want to," Alex teased as he made his way around the maze of tables and chairs surrounding Zurah and squeezed into a seat beside her. "It's a brand-new version, not even released at market yet." He reached for her drink as a devilish grin spread across his face.

"Hands off, Goldie," Zurah said, swatting his hand away. "And no, I don't want to, because if I did, you know I'd beat your butt, and I don't need your sour face trailing me when we go through the gates."

Alex's grin faltered for a moment. "You still have time to change your mind. No one will think any less of you."

But I'll *think less of me*, Zurah wanted to tell Alex but couldn't get the words to come out. Instead, all she could manage was a whispered "Thanks." She gulped the last of her drink and set down the glass, slowly twisting it back and forth. "But having seen what happened… after experiencing what the cryrot is capable of, I have to see this through. I have to make sure that—"

Alex reached out, cupped his hand around hers, and gave it a small squeeze. "I know. I understand," he said quietly.

A smidgen of her anger evaporated with Alex's presence, and Zurah decided she needed to try and shake off her malaise. "But you know, if you're going to insist at a round, then by all means, lead the way." *Maybe all I need is a good distraction.*

Zurah hadn't been surprised by Alex's last-minute addition to the supply list. What had surprised her was Finn's silence on Alex's little project. The two cousins were polar opposites—Alex was lighthearted and good with individuals, while Finn was stoic and kept everyone at arm's length. But after learning of Finn's true identity— the sister of the Emperor of Old Earth—Zurah had a somewhat better understanding of the notorious woman.

The moment the long-hauler had returned—only one day later than Finn's nine-day estimation—the crates had been shuttled to the surface of Objer. And before Finn or anyone could double-check the manifest, the Neetho arcade wall had been installed. If there had been a betting pool, Zurah would've gambled on Finn putting her foot down on such a frivolous item, but the thundercloud that was Finn had been oddly silent.

"You're on." Alex slapped the table and stood. "Ten to one?"

"I'll take those numbers," Zurah said, following Alex to the makeshift bar. She chose a neon-green dart, expertly flipping it back and forth. Darts, any variation of the game, had become her go-to for earning credits after her parents had left.

"You know what? I'll bet you twenty to one with a half-down stinger on top," Zurah said. "And I'll give you a bonus round."

"Confident," Alex said as he grabbed a handful of darts. "I like that. But you should know—"

"Excuse me, ma'am?"

Zurah turned, the moment of levity gone. "Is it the doc?"

A woman dressed in mechanic coveralls coated in grime bit her lip. "No, ma'am. I'm here because there's a problem with the stasis pod. I was called in to—"

Without waiting to hear the rest, Zurah pushed past the woman and raced out of the rec room. Her boots pounded against the metal flooring as she ran up to the deck where medical was located. By the time she reached the doors to the medical bay, her lungs burned from the unexpected cardio. The half-buried ship Finn and Alex used as their base of operations on Objer was massive.

"Slow down," Alex called out, only a few steps behind her.

Zurah didn't wait. Sucking in stale, recycled air, she burst into the medical bay, heading toward the back where the stasis pods had been moved. There was only one active pod at the moment.

"What's wrong?" Zurah asked frantically as she wiped away condensation on the glass view port. Even though Zurah had seen Nissa lying in the stasis pod more than a dozen times, each time she took in Nissa's pale skin and shallow breathing, it was a shock.

"We're not entirely sure," the mechanic said as he stood and wiped his hands on an old rag. "Everything reads clear, but that warning light won't flip off."

Zurah tore her gaze away from Nissa to look at the blinking red light just below the control panel. "And why the hell don't you know what it means? Aren't you all supposed to be the best of the best?" She reached for the control panel, ready to pop it off and start a hack to determine what was wrong with the system.

Alex laid a hand over hers and gently pulled it back from the pod.

"Jason, what's up?" Alex asked calmly. "Run it down for me."

Zurah bit her bottom lip and glared at Alex as she shrugged off his hand, but she stayed silent.

The woman who had interrupted Zurah and Alex in the rec room appeared, winded and visibly annoyed. "If you had let me finish before running off, I would have told you we suspect a malfunction in the nutrient containers."

Jason threw the woman a reproachful look. "Sir," he said, addressing Alex, "it could just be a typical issue with this generation of stasis pods. I've read about these bugs in a few of the tech-support docs. And if so, then it really isn't something to be too worried about at this point, which I stressed to Opal. We're going to switch out the containers, one by one." He turned his attention to Zurah. "But in order to do so, we need to shut down the main power to the pod—only temporarily. For less than a minute, really. Normally, this would be a quick in-and-out job, but we've got orders to let you know about any maintenance and that you're supposed to give us the go-ahead for anything like this."

Zurah blinked. "What?" Her fear-fueled anger vanished quickly. "Who told you that?"

"Finn," Opal said with a shrug. "Said you have authority over what happens with this pod."

The gesture from Finn was unexpected but welcomed. "And you're sure there won't be any lasting damage by doing this? Having to shut it down? Nissa is not in good shape at all."

"No, ma'am," Jason said. "We're just double-checking the pod before it's scheduled to leave. We'll run a detailed diagnostic list for the maintenance crew and the docs."

Relief swept through Zurah, and she stepped back and nodded. "Fine, go ahead and do what you need to."

Jason and Opal got to work. Zurah moved out of the way, pulling a chair out from one of the workstations so she could watch.

"Everything will be fine. Nissa's been cleared of the cryrot, and I've made sure only the best docs will be looking after her. You have my word," Alex said softly as he pulled up a chair next to her.

Zurah believed him. And despite having had a hand in helping destroy the cryrot—the strange crystalline entity that had impersonated Alex and infected several individuals, forcing them to do the cryrot's bidding—Zurah couldn't fight off her lingering anxiety. She knew Nissa was going to be well cared for, but the tangled web of emotions surrounding her boss created a knot in Zurah's chest. There were so many questions rolling through her thoughts that she needed answered. And the woman inside the stasis pod held several of those answers. But more than that, Zurah wasn't sure she could withstand losing Nissa.

Nissa had been a good boss and an employer who had taken a chance on hiring Zurah as a security hack for a small three-person team. The team had worked well together, and over time, Zurah had discovered how much she had wanted to trust Nissa. Yet when Nissa accepted Finn's offer of a simple shuttle job, everything Zurah had thought she'd known about her relationship with Nissa had been turned upside down.

Finn's request of a simple transport mission to Objer had turned into a nightmare. Nissa had been severely injured, and Mexa, their pilot, had bravely sacrificed himself to give Zurah and Nissa a fighting chance against an impossible enemy. An enemy no one fully understood—yet.

Zurah closed her eyes, a memory from several months ago pushing to the forefront of her thoughts. The lights on Nissa's small ship, the *HighTail Flyer*, had been dimmed to simulate evening. Mexa had been curled up in the pilot's chair, dozing off and on as the auto navigation kept the ship on course to their next job. Nissa and Zurah had settled in the back of the ship to play a friendly game of Moon Fish. Zurah had been up by five points, waiting as Nissa took longer than usual to study the cards in her hand.

"When I was a kid, my folks stayed away from the gaming houses. Thought they rotted a person inside out." Nissa laughed, then she puffed out her chest and lowered her voice. "What have I told you? Crack open those books, girls. Learn your numbers." Nissa shook her head. "Dad meant well. He came from a hard life of scratching and had seen too many individuals waste their lives away on a game-house dream."

"He was a scratcher?" Zurah asked.

"One of the best," Nissa said. "Worked on Nibulous Prime. Became a level-three dig-man. But that kind of life takes its toll on the body. There are some things humans, flesh-and-blood individuals, can do better than machines. And knowing how to read the signs of a mine is one of them. He saved lives multiple times in his career. But he made it clear he didn't want his children to follow in his footsteps. Pushed us out into the schooling branches." A look of regret flashed across Nissa's face as she laid down a live-bait flush. "Didn't work out the way he wanted, though. For any of us, it seems."

Zurah played her next hand, hooking the bait, and stayed quiet. Nissa rarely opened up about her past, and Zurah didn't want to spook her by saying the wrong thing.

"If I could go back and change things, I would. Believe me. But I'm doing the best I can, trying to make up for those mistakes I made." Nissa abruptly laid down her cards, face up, throwing her hand to

Zurah. "That's all we can do. Learn from our mistakes, make amends, and move on."

"We're finished, and everything is green," Jason said, interrupting Zurah's memory.

"Zurah? Did you hear that?" Alex leaned over and gently touched Zurah's arm.

Zurah shivered and nodded. "Yes. Thank you."

Alex stood and maneuvered Jason and Opal away from Zurah, their voices low and hushed. For a moment, Zurah continued to stare at the pod. *Make amends for what? Were you trying to tell me something? Apologize for something? You should have told me who you really were. That you are my aunt. And then you should have told me what happened to my parents.*

Medical personnel moved through Zurah's field of vision, cutting through her thoughts. She watched them walk by, noting how each of them skirted the edge of what had once been an open depression in the medical bay's flooring. The outline of the circular area was visible even though it was now sealed shut. *Another unbearable heartache.* Inside that sealed depression was Dr. Ordotham. The Neetho had trusted Zurah and ultimately sacrificed himself in order to keep her safe. And now, she had no idea if he was still alive or rotting away beneath the floor.

A flush of irritation washed through her, and she stood, turned, and marched out of the medical bay.

"Hey, talk to me," Alex called out after her. "What's going on?"

Zurah whirled around. "Why are we just sitting here, wasting our time, playing dumb arcade games, and drinking? We should be going through the gates and hunting down the rest of those creatures. Making sure whatever threat is out there is dealt with. The longer we wait, the greater the chances of more individuals getting hurt… or worse."

Alex reached out to grab Zurah's shoulders, but she took a step back. He let his hands drop to his sides and shrugged. "You know as well as I do that we can't go through until Finn gives the green light."

"Which should've happened the moment the supply ship was unloaded and the gear sorted," Zurah snapped.

"Finn's being cautious. Can't say I blame her. If we step through the gates without being prepared—"

"I know." Zurah huffed and moved so she could lean against the wall, her fingers running along one of the seams. "It's just… I don't know how much more waiting around I can take. I thought with what we'd figured out from dealing with the cryrot and the information we were given on how to use the gates, we would have been prepped and ready to go within a day or so of getting our supplies."

"Then your wish is reality," a voice said.

Zurah turned and watched as Finn approached them. Her dark hair had been braided and wrapped around her head like a crown. The black suit she never seemed to take off moved with her like a second skin, and Zurah once again felt a shiver of envy at what Finn could do with the advanced piece of tech. No doubt there were programs and coding tucked away within the suit's hardware, which had never been released on the market. Being the sister to the Emperor of Old Earth had its advantages.

Zurah's gaze swung back to Alex. Not only had she gotten tangled up with the emperor's sister but the heir to the Goldsmith Consortium. Her life had turned upside down in a matter of days, and Zurah was working with two of the most notorious people in the known worlds. She wasn't sure she found anything comforting in her situation.

"The data's been sorted, and there's a briefing in half an hour to finalize the last-minute details." Finn said. After a split second of hesitation, she added, "Nissa?"

"Fine," Zurah replied. "Thanks for what you did. Giving me authority and all that."

Finn stared at her with little emotion. "You are her relative and therefore have the legal right to say what happens." She turned slightly toward Alex. "You've got an incoming priority-one call. I'd say your father wants a word."

"Shit," Alex muttered and stalked past Finn.

There was a moment of awkward silence before Finn turned and left, leaving Zurah alone in the corridor. Zurah eventually followed after Finn but made an impromptu decision to head outside before the briefing. She needed a moment alone, just to think and sort through the jumble of emotions coursing through her.

At the small station that marked the main entrance and exit for the ship, Zurah activated her suit's helmet and double-checked the readout. Everything was in working order. With a courtesy nod to the guard, Zurah let them scan her HalfLife chip then stepped out as the door opened to reveal a desert-like landscape permanently encased in an eerie darkness.

Objer was a planet shrouded in mystery not only in its history but in its position in space. Lost in the dead zone, the solitary planet had no fixed star to dictate its orbit. A rocky landscape dominated its surface, with huge megalithic stones clustered in the area where the ship had been half buried. Zurah glanced up, knowing the security grid was there—invisible but still there. She scoffed. *Little good it did to protect anyone.*

A security grid was made to keep things safe. But thanks to the cryrot, nothing had been safe. In Zurah's life, she had come across a wide range of species that inhabited the known worlds, and while she had found their cultures fascinating, she hadn't given much thought to the diversity in the universe. Her focus had been continually improving her skills as a security hack and being a valuable member to whichever team she was working with.

But since having landed on Objer and getting tangled up in its mysteries, Zurah had begun to wonder what exactly was out there. She certainly never would have imagined encountering the cryrot, a life-form composed of crystal—or so the science and biology teams currently believed. Nor would she have guessed she would ever come across a human being who had been turned into some type of sand creature. But the strange crew members from the lost ship, the *Eagle's Nest*, had become just that. Except for Angelina.

Zurah walked a few meters away from the ship. *Now, there's a woman who is more mystery than anything else.*

Angelina claimed to have been the second-in-command of the *Eagle's Nest*, which had been lost to the dead zone more than three hundred years ago. Angelina had been found in an escape pod, claiming to have no memory of what had happened. Shortly after her pod had been found, it had been bought by Alex, who believed Angelina.

I'm living a jute-store story.

A tiny blue light blinked on the bottom left of Zurah's helmet's visor, and she raised her arm to touch the control screen embedded in the arm of her suit.

"You are to report to command at fifteen hundred hours."

Zurah closed out the message and continued walking away from the ship, her gaze drifting to the megalithic stones. Within those stones was a technology beyond anyone's understanding. The technology to transport an individual to a strange new world. Of course, there had been the ill-fated Zap'N'Roll tech years ago, but that tech had been scrapped due to molecular breakdown of the individuals who used it. But as Zurah had dug through reports from the teams working on Objer, this technology appeared to have fixed the flaws in the Zap'N'Roll. Exactly how that had been accomplished, no one knew.

Questions rolled through Zurah's head as she wondered who had built the megalithic structures and why. She flexed her fingers, desperately wishing for a simple problem she could unravel, like a straightforward security hack, where she could see all the variations of coding, understand how the programs worked together, and find the weaknesses to exploit. But the mysteries surrounding Objer were far more complex, and so far, Zurah wasn't finding a way to sort through the information in order to reveal the answers.

Walking a few more paces away from the ship, Zurah knelt and scooped up a handful of dirt. She rolled it around in the palm of her hand. The suit automatically sampled the particles and produced a readout of its composition. Everything was tagged green. Even though Zurah hadn't the faintest clue about geology, she knew green was good. Green was normal. She let the dirt and the few rocks tumble through her fingers, then she stood and brushed off the remaining particles.

"What in the world makes Objer so unique?" Zurah asked herself. She was under no illusions as to the nature of being a security hack or the teams she had worked with. A handful of jobs had been legit, but the majority had involved stealing or "selective acquisition and redistribution of goods," as Mexa had called it. Each job's objective had been for something of value. Maybe not to the crew but to the individual who had hired the crew. *So what makes Objer unique? Or rather, what's on the other side of the gates? Why would the* Eagle's Nest *or the emperor send a team to go through the gates? What was the high-value target?*

The tiny blue light returned, and with a sigh, Zurah turned around. As she headed back to the ship, Zurah was sure of one thing. Traveling through the gates was going to test her beyond anything she had experienced, but she wasn't going to let it destroy her. She had picked herself up after being abandoned by her parents and learned how to be the best security hack she could be. This situation wasn't going to be any different. She would watch and learn, study what she needed to, and figure out how to survive.

2

Zurah slipped into the conference room, surprised at the number of individuals who had been requested to attend. Squeezing between the last two rows of chairs, she settled into a spot in the back. She recognized a few of the faces: Dr. Manath, a biologist; Dr. Panish, an engineer; Montgomery, the head of security; and a handful of others Zurah had bumped into. But there were more she didn't know, and the crowd made her nervous. Finn stood in the front, deep in conversation with Alex. Neither one looked particularly happy.

"Don't worry. They always have it out before one of these, but ultimately, they do know how to work together," Angelina commented dryly.

A flutter of unease rose in Zurah's chest. Angelina had been nothing but professional and polite, but Zurah knew the truth about Commander Angelina Adeyemi. Angelina professed to have no memory of how she had been separated from her ship and her crew, and in Zurah's experience, people who claimed not to remember things were often hiding the dark truth of what they'd done.

"You should've all had time to read the command packets I distributed to each one of you," Finn said, turning away from a sour-faced Alex.

I did, and once again, you're a little light on the details. Zurah had tried to ask for clarification, but Finn had dismissed her concerns, telling Zurah she would be given more information at a later date. Zurah had believed this briefing would provide that information.

"We have," a middle-aged man said as he stood. "And we disagree." Heads nodded around him. "You owe us more than being left behind, begging for scraps of information. You hired us to unravel the science and purpose of the gates, and now you're just leaving us here?"

Zurah frowned. *They're not coming with us? What the hell is Finn playing at?*

"How do you expect us to do our job?" another voice called out. "We need raw data, and we're not going to get that by staying behind."

"Not to mention a security detail," Montgomery added. "You're traveling into unknown territory and, from what we've learned, more than likely hostile territory. Yet you aren't going to—"

"This isn't up for discussion," Alex said. His entire demeanor had changed. No longer pouting, his expression was just as stony as Finn's.

Zurah straightened up in her chair and felt another

flutter of unease. *This* was the heir to the Goldsmith Consortium—a man who was valued at an impossible number of credits and whose family pulled the strings of governments across the known worlds. This was how she had expected a Goldsmith to behave—cold and commanding.

"The assignments in those command packets still stand," Alex continued. "This meeting is to address any questions pertaining to those assignments. If you feel you aren't able to fulfill your duties, then we will be forced to renegotiate your contracts."

The tension in the room shifted, and Zurah watched several individuals pull back. They crossed arms against their chests or began to fidget, throwing nervous looks back and forth.

"We aren't… I mean, we're not trying to get out of our contracts," the man who had originally spoken said as he sat back down. "We're simply trying to voice our concerns—"

"Which have been duly noted and considered," Finn said. "But right now, we have one objective. There is an enemy out there who is more than capable of toppling the known worlds. Production of an inoculation is progressing, but the timeline has been forced to be reconsidered—"

Finn's eyes met Zurah's for a split second. And in that look was a shared sense of grief. Dr. Ordotham was not only a friend but an important key to their ability to develop the inoculations against the cryrot. This was due to his unique biological makeup as a Neetho as well as his brilliant skills as a doctor and scientist. But until the nest in the medical bay was opened—either through brute force or the doctor's command—he was sealed inside. And Finn hadn't wanted to risk opening the doctor's nest in case his recovery was dependent on a sealed environment.

"We have weapons and tools to fight the cryrot on Objer, and production has already started on multiple worlds," Finn continued. "But it takes time to ensure the worlds are protected. And so we are going to the source to destroy it before it has a chance to infect other worlds. You have your orders, and I expect them to be carried out. You were all selected for a reason and have specific clauses in your contracts."

There were a few low murmurs of annoyance, but the majority of individuals nodded.

"Blackmail," Zurah muttered. She'd never cared for the tactic but had seen it used time and time again.

"The gate is on standby, and the team will be leaving... now," Finn said.

"What?" more than a few people called out, Zurah included. *Leaving now? What the hell?*

"Well, that's one way to do it," Angelina commented dryly.

"Do what?" Zurah demanded. "I need to pack my gear, double-check my suit's systems, and receive the final briefing."

"To prevent myself or anyone else from sabotaging the mission," Angelina said.

Zurah bit her bottom lip. She hadn't considered that angle, and Zurah felt like a fool. Of course Finn would be playing it safe; there were too many unknown quantities and too many layers of secrets between Finn and Alex. The immediate concern was the cryrot. Despite their best efforts, no one was willing to declare the ship or personnel a hundred percent clear of the threat. Then there was the unanswered question of what the Emperor's team was doing on the other side of the gates. Not to mention the startling discovery that some of the *Eagle's Nest* crew were more alien than human now. In Zurah's opinion, the teams were now mini reactor cells, waiting for the right ignition source to explode.

"Are there any more questions?" Alex asked.

There were a handful, which Finn and Alex dealt with, and once the majority of individuals were satisfied, the group was dismissed. Only those who had been selected to go with Finn through the gates remained.

Zurah followed Angelina to the table and took a seat across from Montgomery.

"If you have anything left that needs to be taken care of, then I suggest you get it done within the next fifteen minutes. At which time, I want you at the security checkpoint," Finn instructed.

"What about our gear?" Zurah asked.

"It has been taken care of," Finn said. "Everything you requested is prepped and ready to go."

"That's not true," Zurah replied. "I know my suit and the gear I requested is in my hab unit. I haven't done the final—"

Finn turned to stare at her. "Your gear is prepped and ready. Are you telling me you no longer wish to accompany us?"

"No, she's just—" Alex started.

"Let her speak, cousin," Finn snapped.

Zurah took a few deep breaths to quell the rising panic, reminding herself who Finn was. She wasn't a friend or someone to bicker with. *She isn't Nissa.* "I understand. I'll be there."

Without waiting to be dismissed, Zurah stood and left. *Fifteen minutes. Shit.* Zurah had planned on spending time with Nissa in the hours before leaving. But now, by the time she reached medical and could record the message she had been composing in her head, there wouldn't be enough time to get back to the security checkpoint. *Damn her.*

Zurah triggered a countdown with her SeeClear tech as she headed to the nearest hardwired comm system and plugged in. She tagged the file under her personal network and labeled it *Read Only in Case of Death.* She stared at the screen, debating if she should change the file name. Her suit flashed the current time, and Zurah knew she didn't have the luxury of trying to compose the perfect message.

"Hey, so this is Zurah. Obviously. I mean… this is Zurah Winters, recording a message for Nissa. Shit, I don't even know your last name." Zurah had to stop and choke back the tears threatening to overwhelm her as the reality of what she was about to do settled in.

"Look, what I really want to know… what I feel like I deserve to know is why you never told me you were my aunt. Why did you hide that from me?" Despite her best efforts, Zurah was crying. She swiped her hand across her eyes, trying to clear her vision and her thoughts. *Suck it up. You're not a little kid.*

"Who would've thought I would be the one to go off on some half-assed crazy adventure? Not me. That's for damn sure. But here I am, teamed up with Finn and Alex Goldsmith." Zurah paused for a moment, unsure what to say. "Look, Nissa. You missed out on a lot. And I'm sure when we can safely get you off Objer and the medical treatment you need, you'll wake up and get a debriefing. But things aren't great. At least not yet. I'm hoping we're going to be able to take care of things and get life back to a normal routine. All that's to say, I hope that everything gets back to the way it was… working with you and a small crew. Doing odd jobs here and there and dreaming about better days. Despite what you haven't told me, you were… no, you *are* a good boss. And I appreciate that. And I'd work with you again in a heartbeat."

If I ever return. The odds are I won't, and I'll never see you again. That harsh dose of reality shifted Zurah's thoughts. "You take care of yourself, and go find another lost girl and save her. Be the boss to her that you were to me."

Zurah signed off and, before she could change her mind, sealed the file. She rubbed her hands across her face, trying to erase the evidence of her tears, which didn't seem to want to stop. Sniffling, she stood and slapped her hand against the wall in frustration. *Get a hold of yourself. You don't want to be crying when you check in. Come on. This is another job. Just a job. You get in, do the work, get out, and get paid. That's all.*

Biting her tongue and focusing on the pain in an attempt to quell the tears, she slowly made her way to the security checkpoint and arrived with thirty seconds to spare. The guard at the station waved her past into a small room off to the side, where emergency suits and equipment were stored. Finn, Alex, Angelina, and Montgomery were already there, each one in a various state of undress.

"Your suit is over there." Finn pointed to a suit identical to hers hanging against the wall.

All Zurah's fears and anxiety fled as she touched the fabric.

"Get dressed," Finn said. "We don't have much time."

Zurah didn't have to be told twice. She quickly shed her old suit, double-checked the integrity of her under-suit, then got dressed. The suit fit perfectly, and the feel reminded her of the ArmorTex Flex and Hold. Once the suit was sealed, she paired its system with her SeeClear tech. Grinning like a fool, she scrolled through the wide variety of options.

"Comms check." Finn's voice came through loud and clear.

Everyone checked their comms and gave the all clear.

"This will be our central comms. Label it Comm 1. I want everyone on the same channel. Back banter is fine, but not when it comes to sharing intel. Clear?"

"Clear," Zurah said as the others echoed the same.

A request came through Zurah's SeeClear tech from Finn. When she acknowledged the request, Finn said to Zurah, "This will be our private comm channel. Route in through my internal storage attached to my SeeClear tech, then pair it with yours. I want you to report directly to me. Not Alex. You're to be my eyes and ears. Like any other job as a security hack. Keep your systems hot and wide. Any disturbance or anomalies, you alert me first."

"Yes, sir," Zurah replied, the excitement over the newfound tech quickly disappearing. *Finn's the boss now. Just like I would do with Nissa. Remember that.* Zurah half expected Alex to chime in and request a private comm line with her as well, but he remained oddly silent.

"Last check, pair up and make sure your suit is secure," Finn ordered.

Zurah turned to see Alex moving toward her.

He took hold of her arms before she could protest and checked the readouts on the embedded screens. "Good to go." Then he double-checked her suit's seams, helmet lock, boots, and gloves. "All clear."

Zurah quickly did the same for Alex and turned to join the group, but he held on to her arm.

"Zurah, be careful. Finn isn't interested in getting us killed, but she has her priorities," he said.

Zurah narrowed her eyes as his voice came through over the Comm 1 line, but no one else turned to watch them. Not even Finn. She glanced at Alex. His eyes watched her intently then shifted down to stare at his hand. When Zurah looked down as well, she noticed his thumb was placed directly over the screen on her left arm.

"A chameleon?" she asked.

Alex nodded. "Just between us. Tap into the system with your SeeClear tech, then tag it however you want. But this will allow us to communicate without the others knowing."

"All good?" Angelina asked as she stepped toward them.

"All clear. Just double-checking the seals." Alex let his hand drop.

"Then it's time to go," Finn said. "The rest of our gear has been loaded and taken to the gates."

They left the security of the ship and climbed into the rover assigned to transport them to the gates. The driver nervously tapped the steering wheel while they waited for everyone to hop in. Once the group was seated and buckled up, the driver kicked the rover into gear. Then they were off to the Black Gates of Objer.

<h1 style="text-align:center">3</h1>

The Black Gates of Objer loomed on the horizon as the rover raced toward the imposing megalithic structure. Zurah leaned to the side to gain a better view and blinked to run a scan. Information flooded her vision, and she removed the files tagged as fringe whispers. The gates were constructed from a type of metamorphic rock that long-range sensors flagged for inconsistent readings. Each gate pillar was built from five different megalithic blocks, all slightly rectangular, with each block slightly smaller than the one below it.

Numerous scientific papers discussed the theories as to who or what had engineered the gates, but no consensus or overarching hypothesis had been reached. As Zurah sorted through the information, the ideas increased in absurdity. All the information available to the general public boiled down to the fact that no one knew the purpose of the gates or who had constructed them. The only hard fact everyone could agree on was that the *Eagle's Nest* had vanished in the dead zone, and popular theories tied its fate to the gates.

Shutting down the search, Zurah stole a glance at Angelina. Zurah couldn't help but wonder what was going through the woman's mind. Zurah wasn't naïve. Angelina possibly remembered everything and knew exactly what the team was facing. *Could that be why Finn is so distrustful of Angelina? That Finn suspects Angelina is lying? Or that Finn has proof she's lying?* But those questions always led to the opposite possibility—that Angelina was telling the truth and was in the dark like the rest of them.

As Zurah continued to weigh both sides of the argument, she leaned toward the second possibility. *When Alex and I got to the bridge of the ship so I could hack the systems and use the ambient noise against the cryrot, Angelina had been shocked to see her two former crewmates—an impossibility that they were still alive, just like her. Of course, they're not really human, though, are they?*

They'd been changed into some kind of sand people, and Zurah believed that seeing those men still alive—if not entirely human any longer—must have taken its toll. But Zurah couldn't pick up on anxiety or trepidation from Angelina. *Note to self: don't play poker with the woman.*

If Zurah's intuition was sure of anything, it was that no one was telling each other the whole truth. That was a great way to get everyone killed.

The rover rolled to a stop a few meters from the gates, where a temporary worksite had been established. Three large tents were nestled off to the side, and a handful of mobile workstations alongside generators and other pieces of equipment dotted the rest of the area.

"Everyone out," Finn ordered.

An alert to proceed with caution popped up on the bottom left of her helmet's screen, advising Zurah she was three meters away from another security field. The alert flashed red then shifted to green before Zurah had time to ask Finn whether to proceed or not. A series of numbers and letters scrolled across the bottom, and her suit informed her she was cleared.

The team followed Finn's lead as she headed toward an individual stationed in the middle of the site. "This is Dr. Yumi," Finn said. "Updates?"

"Energy levels are holding steady, and we're well within the safety zone from the information you provided. Whenever you and your team are ready, you're cleared to proceed." Dr. Yumi's voice rolled through Zurah's suit.

"Montgomery, double-check the rovers. Alex and Angelina, those crates over there need to get tagged and bagged," Finn said. "Zurah, come with me."

Zurah threw a nervous glance at Alex, but he shook his head and made a small shooing motion for her to get going. Finn moved to one of the workstations, the scientists quickly moving out of her way. She brought up an encrypted file and entered a string of codes to open it.

"Everything your friend Gregori provided," Finn said.

Can't say he was my friend. Zurah wisely kept the thought to herself then reconsidered. *I should've worked up the courage to ask Angelina about him. Did she work closely with him on the* Eagle's Nest? *Or had he simply been another crew member on a list?* Zurah blinked, realizing Finn had continued giving instructions, not noticing—or not caring—about Zurah's moment of distraction.

"All of the notes and extrapolations from our teams have been compiled since working with this new information. Download the file packet. You and I will take this information with us; it might turn out to be useful on the other side." Finn paused then switched comms. "Your primary goal on this mission is to be my security hack. There may come a time when I need you to hack a system without question. To shut it down or destroy it completely. Clear?"

Zurah nodded. "That's my specialty. But a heads-up on the types of systems would be appreciated. I can do prep work now."

Finn reached out and touched Zurah's suit. "This is all you'll need. Learn the suit's systems. Its strengths and weaknesses."

"Are you telling me I'll need to be able to hack our own suits?" Zurah asked with a sinking feeling.

"I know what you're thinking, and currently, the answer is no. I'm not asking you to be able to hack Alex or the others. Although I'm assuming you can do that." Finn took a few steps away from the workstation, turning her back on the camp. "Your suit is one of mine. They are as close as I could get to the types of suits the emperor's teams were equipped with. My brother—" Finn stopped and appeared to struggle with what to say next. "The emperor's team is after tech they believe can be used to create the ultimate weapon. A supersoldier."

"What?" Zurah asked, staring at Finn. "And you're only telling me this now? Do the others know?"

"I can't operate on the idea that Alex doesn't know. But no, this information isn't widely known. The balance between worlds right now is tenuous, and my brother erroneously believes humanity's influence is slipping and that creating these supersoldiers is the answer."

Zurah took a step back, as if Finn had physically pushed her. This was not what she had expected, but if she was honest with herself, she should have. She had witnessed numerous power struggles between rival gangs, individuals vying for a higher position with a crew, and local governments throwing fits over not being able to throw their weight around.

"What I'm telling you is to be kept strictly between us," Finn said. "Is that clear?"

Zurah nodded.

"I need to hear it," Finn said.

"I understand," Zurah replied weakly.

"Good. Your secondary goal is to ensure nothing can go through the gates that we don't want to. While no one fully understands this tech, I'm asking you to study these files and find the weaknesses that can be exploited, just like the suit. If we have to destroy the gates in order to protect the known worlds, then that's what we do.

"When we're over there, I need someone I can rely on. I've done the background checks, and while it might appear to be a foolish idea to let you tag along, you have the skills I need. Plus you have no other loyalties other than to Nissa. And seeing as how you've held your own these past couple of weeks, I know you've got what it takes.

"This mission isn't just about ensuring the cryrot—if there really is more of it out there—doesn't come through the gates. While that alone is a nightmare in the making, we have to make sure that if there is advanced tech out there, my brother doesn't get ahold of it. Humanity can't survive another war, not after the devastation of the Cricade Wars. And that means if the crew of the *Eagle's Nest* is out there and has that knowledge, we can't let it fall into the wrong hands. They will have to be stopped. No matter what. Which might involve cracking their security systems and destroying everything if we have to. Am I clear?"

Zurah swallowed and nodded. "Yes, sir." The confidence Finn was putting in her was overwhelming. But she should have realized why Finn would've agreed to let her come with them through the gates. "What about Alex?"

Finn grimaced. "Alex's loyalties may be divided. While I trust him more than most, he is still a Goldsmith, and his father is—" Finn stopped. "Stay focused on your assignment. You'll be free to do whatever you need to do. Alex and I will do the scouting, while Montgomery is tasked with keeping an eye on Angelina." Finn turned, moving over to Dr. Yumi, while the others finished making sure the rover was secured and ready to go.

As the information transferred to her suit, Zurah took the opportunity to work through the suit's interface, changing various options to fit her own needs and embedding codes to make her suit's network secure. The last few days had thrown Zurah and the others together, making them rely on each other to defeat the cryrot, but that didn't mean any of them were best friends. Not even with Finn appearing to share the truth with Zurah. She knew she would have to be careful with the web of lies, secrets, and divided loyalties if she was going to survive what was coming. And Finn's appearance of looping Zurah in on what the emperor was really up to made Zurah nervous. Zurah was well aware of the fact that Finn didn't share anything without careful consideration.

The files finished downloading, and as she was about to sign out and signal Finn, an alert popped up. *"The sands aren't safe, even for those who have pledged loyalty to the tribunal. Not even the Old Mother."*

"What the hell?" Zurah muttered. She backtraced the alert and found a jumble of codes, none of which made sense. When she attempted to sort through the first clumping, the codes vanished. Nothing she tried could retrieve the codes, but the message remained, scrolling across her helmet's screen. Motion caught her eye, and she turned away from the workstation.

Zurah watched as dust kicked up for a brief second then settled back down. *That's impossible. There's no wind on Objer.*

"Gregori," she whispered. Out of the three crew members from the *Eagle's Nest* whom they had encountered on Objer, Gregori had been the only one who had actually tried to help Zurah and the others.

"Everything okay?" Alex's voice broke through.

Zurah ignored Alex and replied through the group channel. "Finn, I'm finished. But I've got something you need to see." Part of her wanted to keep the message private, to have time to puzzle it out, but Zurah wanted to survive. She knew she was navigating a complicated mess of relationships, but with any other job, this was intel that needed to be shared. And the message wasn't a part of the intel Finn had just shared, and therefore, Zurah reasoned it was fair game.

Finn looked up then motioned Zurah over. "Show me."

Zurah copied the message, along with its coding, and passed it on. She watched Finn's eyes track back and forth then settle on her.

"Work on unraveling the coding then report in." Finn turned back to Dr. Yumi.

Zurah tensed, switching over to the private comm with Finn. "What about the others? Shouldn't they know about the warning? Maybe they'll have some ideas on what it means."

"And what if it was one of them who sent it? Can you assure me that Montgomery or another individual isn't working for my brother? Someone who wants to scare us off this mission?"

Zurah huffed in frustration. There were too many entanglements to keep track of for her liking. But she didn't press the matter with Finn, and for a moment, she debated ignoring the woman altogether and sharing the message. The others were aware of Gregori and the sabotage the long-lost crew members of the *Eagle's Nest* had done to stop Finn and Alex from using the gates. As much as she hated it, Zurah knew Finn had a point. The message might not have come from Gregori; it could have come from the other lost members of the *Eagle's Nest*. Angelina had said Ethan Johnston—one of the two men who had been on the bridge of the ship—had been their chief engineer, and he would have had the necessary skills.

Zurah understood the chain of command, and Finn was the boss. But Alex had been more forthcoming through the whole mess with the cryrot than Finn had been. If it hadn't been for Finn's secrecy, perhaps Mexa would have survived, Nissa wouldn't have been severely injured, and they would have completed their mission and left before everything had gone wrong. Zurah was under no delusions that Alex was sharing everything either, but out of the two, Zurah was inclined to go to Alex first.

With a sinking feeling that no matter which decision she made, it would turn out to be poor, Zurah opened up the private channel between her and Alex.

"Alex?"

When he didn't respond, she glanced in his direction. Alex was leaning against the back of one of the rovers, facing Montgomery.

"When you have a chance, we need to talk," Zurah said.

"We need everyone to gather behind the security grid," a voice interrupted through the comms. "Gates are going live in two minutes and fifteen seconds."

Zurah moved to stand behind Finn, watching the scientists scramble back and forth between workstations. She turned on her SeeClear tech and started recording, gathering as much information as possible. Even if she didn't understand half of what she was seeing, she knew the data was important.

"Last chance to back out," Finn said as she turned to Alex.

"Fat chance." He winked. "Think I'd miss out on something like this?"

"Not really. Just remember the massive amounts of paperwork your father has forced me to sign," Finn replied.

"Lawyers," Alex quipped.

"We're seeing an increase in energy levels," one of the scientists reported.

"Still within safety?" Finn asked.

"Yes, sir."

"Yumi, what's the load tolerance?" Angelina asked.

"Two hundred and sixty," Yumi responded. "But we can withstand a surge of thirty percent and still be within acceptable levels." There was a pause as she consulted with another one of the scientists. "All right, heads-up. Here's what we're all here for."

"Green line or blue?" Finn asked.

"Green this time," Dr. Yumi responded. "Wasn't expecting that, not after a solid turn of numbers."

Are they speaking gibberish? Zurah had studied all she could about the gates, but the sheer amount of knowledge required to understand even a fraction of what the gates represented was daunting.

"This is where you are going to hop in and take a look. No actionable hacks or walk-throughs. Simply record what you can, experience what you can. These small interfacing discs will integrate with your suits.

We reverse engineered the specs you were given. You're going to see, feel… even taste. There should be no physical damage, but if there is, now is the time to experience it before you actually walk through the gates. If everything stays green, we'll give you the all clear. If not, we'll cycle the gates down, readjust, and try again," Dr. Yumi said.

One of the scientists moved through the small group, handing out the discs.

Zurah took the proffered disc and spun it around between her fingers. *I could back out. Give them my apologies and join Nissa. She'll heal, then we'll leave all this behind.*

The memory of Mexa's face abruptly took over, and Zurah's heart ached. He had sacrificed himself so Zurah and Nissa had a chance to get free. *I should leave and honor Mexa's sacrifice… No, I'm not backing out now.*

Zurah plugged the disc into her suit, and Mexa's face disappeared, only to be replaced by the ruined body of Dr. Ordotham. *This is my job now, and I'm going to see it through. I won't run. I won't let anyone else get hurt if I can help it.*

The disc's systems integrated with the suit, and the effects were instantaneous. The campsite and the scientists were all gone. As Zurah turned, unsettled by the abrupt change, she noted Finn and the others were still visible and standing next to her. None of the other members of the team were sharing intel, but they simply stood staring at the gates. Zurah looked and gasped.

Suspended between the twin pillars was a tangled ball of green lines, reminding Zurah of Slurpy Noodles that some fool was desperately trying to unravel. The vibrant lines shifted back and forth, straining against each other at times, but at the same time looped and twisted together to form a tight knot.

Zurah's suit was a self-contained system, filtering contaminants and recycling her body's waste products. But as powerful as the suit was, it wasn't able to keep out the overwhelming stench of... *Flowers? How is that even possible?*

Alarmed, Zurah double-checked her suit's readouts, but everything was functioning as expected. No reports of a malfunction in the air filtration system. Nervous, she licked her lips and was startled to taste the tang of iron. On jobs that went well, Zurah rarely saw action, but there had been a few jobs where things had gone sideways and she'd ended up having to join the fight. She remembered the punch in the jaw that had filled her mouth with blood. It was a taste she would never forget.

Cautiously, she took a step forward and checked her suit's telemetry. When no alarms went off, she stepped forward again. The others were in various stages of cautiously moving toward the gates.

"This is base checking in with the alpha team." Dr. Yumi's voice crackled through the comms.

"We read you," Finn replied.

"Everything is reading green. You're a go."

"Roger. Initiate the second phase."

"Second phase to be initiated in T-minus two minutes and thirty-four seconds."

Zurah watched the strange green strands of energy twist and turn, zooming in with her SeeClear tech. She was startled to realize there were things moving *inside* the strands. Magnifying her vision again, Zurah had the sneaking suspicion she was witnessing bits and pieces of an alien language system. Or at least a coding system, moving through the strands. The longer she watched, the more repeating patterns she found. *That's helpful at least.* Leaving the recording tech running, she moved to the base of one of the pillars in order to get a better angle, curious to see if the strands touched or moved through the pillars or were simply suspended between them.

Gotcha. A strand touched then appeared to move into the pillar, and Zurah caught a brief flare of the same type of symbols running vertically down the side of the rock. *Control nodes inside? Would make a lot of sense. But where was the original power source?*

The scientists had rigged up a series of generators around the base of the pillars, but as far as Zurah could detect, there wasn't a power source located anywhere on Objer. She took another step closer, carefully looking at the rock.

The ball of yarn abruptly stopped moving and began to pulse. Zurah hastily backed up and walked back to stand beside Alex. She watched as it pulsed, mentally counting the pattern. *Three. Five. Three. Two. Four. Two. One. Three. One.* The ball of yarn burst into a thousand cascading bits. Zurah's suit adjusted for the flash to protect her eyes. When the visor cleared, she gasped.

A small tear had appeared in the void beyond the gates, wide enough to let Zurah catch a glimpse of something on the other side. It looked like a desert with a fierce wind kicking up the sand and twin suns burning brightly in the sky.

"Everything is still green," Dr. Yumi said. The comms were filled with more static this time.

"We're a go." Finn confidently stepped up to the gates, with the others following her lead. "Rovers on autopilot until we clear the gates. Then Montgomery and myself will take control."

When Zurah took her turn to move through the gates and step across the impossible to another world, she glanced up at the peaks of the pillars. A strand of the strange green energy came shooting down and pierced her straight through the heart.

4

Voices drifted through the comms as Zurah blinked, trying to get her bearings. Static obscured the individual words. Confused and disoriented, Zurah attempted to sit up. Two dark shapes stood a few meters away from her. The tone of conversation abruptly exploded into anger on both sides. The shadows waved their arms, and the taller of the two turned and left. For a heartbeat, the other shadowy figure stood still, seeming to watch the other one walk away.

The figure was wreathed by the gentle glow of an outdated vid screen. Framing either side of the screen were several potted plants, each one genetically enhanced to help improve the quality of recycled air. The shadow came in and out of focus before finally revealing a middle-aged woman with her dark hair twisted up into a bun. She lingered there for some time, staring at the vid screen, then moved to a bookshelf tucked back into the corner of the room. The woman reached out, and her fingers hovered just above the spines of the ancient tomes.

"Momma?"

The shadow turned, and the woman slowly made her way to Zurah, who was sitting at the kitchen table. Tablets had been spread out across the deeply scarred secondhand piece of furniture.

"Have you finished reading Dr. Manuela's report?"

"No."

"Then you'd better finish it before supper." The woman's face came into focus, her amber eyes glistening with tears, as a hand reached out to brush Zurah's hair out of her face.

"Momma?" she asked. "Where did Dad go?"

"Hush, child. Never you mind on that. Everything will sort itself out."

"But what about—"

"Zurah? Can you hear me?" a male voice interrupted. "She's not responding. Grab a med—"

The woman's face faded then disappeared altogether.

"Momma? You can't do this. You can't leave me. Do you know what I went through?"

"Zurah? It's me, Alex. I need you to respond if you can hear me."

Grief and pain bubbled up to the surface, threatening to overwhelm Zurah as she relived one of the last times she'd seen her mother. The arguments between her parents had gradually increased until Zurah fled the room each time they started to fight. She had often tucked herself away in her bunk, huddled under a mound of blankets, silently willing her parents to stop. She had worked hard to bury those memories, unwilling to dwell on the past. But now, the heartache of not understanding why her parents had left or what had happened to them threatened to overwhelm her.

"Why did you leave?" Zurah whispered. A wave of dizziness washed over her, threatening to cause her stomach to twist and churn. She squeezed her eyes shut, trying to regain control. When she opened them again, a very concerned-looking Alex was squatting in front of her.

"Alex? What happened?" Zurah whispered, the memory and present reality an uncomfortable mixture.

"Your suit recorded a massive energy spike as you came through the gates." Finn's voice cut into Zurah's memories. "You're lucky it didn't fry."

"Lucky?" Zurah mumbled as Alex helped her sit up. "I'm not sure that's the word I would have chosen." She closed her eyes and forced the memory back into place, buried deep within her where it wouldn't bother her again.

"Your suit needs a reboot. Angelina is grabbing the kit," Alex said as he sat down next to her. "Nothing to be worried about. All of our equipment is designed to withstand a lot of trauma. They're a unique combination of Goldsmith engineering and Finn's paranoia."

Zurah turned to look at Alex, and the wry grin on his face did nothing to banish the concern in his eyes.

Angelina crouched next to her. "Zurah, I need access to the left port, just under the screen."

Zurah glanced at Finn, who gave her a tiny nod before she turned and walked away. "Montgomery, report."

"Everything reads clear. I'm making the final circuit and will be back in position in three minutes," he replied.

"Understood," Finn replied.

As Angelina worked on Zurah's suit, Zurah looked over at the rover, which had been packed with supplies. A makeshift tent had already been set up, and a few of the crates had been opened. The equipment they had brought with them stood out against the unending horizon of sand dunes. As she took stock of the area, Zurah noted there were no corresponding gates or megalithic structures, nothing physical to indicate a correlation between Objer and this planet. *Yet this is where the gates took us.*

"How long was I out?" Zurah asked.

"Roughly thirty minutes," Angelina said. "But we needed you conscious to do a reboot or else risk shutting down some of the emergency med systems. Hang on… There. Can you take it from here?"

Zurah glanced down and nodded, easily working through the reboot and double-checking her suit's integrity and security coding. Angelina stood and moved toward the rover, pulling another crate out of the back. Zurah half watched as she worked through the myriad of questions the suit threw at her, choosing a few more customizations than she had before. Angelina pulled a small generator out of the crate along with a portable shield console.

"You're setting up base camp here?" Zurah asked

Alex. The sand dunes wouldn't provide any type of shelter or relief from the twin suns of the planet.

He shrugged. "As good a spot as any right now. We've got a programmable set up, so once we get everything in place, we'll map and record it. Then it'll be a breeze to take down and move somewhere else if we need to. But for now, we're staying next to where we popped out."

Zurah remembered reading the stats report on the probes. Dr. Yumi and her team had conducted fifty-three different tests. They would activate the gates, send through the probe, and close the gates. After a random interval of time, the team would reactivate the gates then ping the probe's location, recalling it to Objer. The gates opened in a variety of different locations but all within a roughly four-hundred-meter square.

Zurah recalled that in one of the briefs, several of the scientists had debated on leaving the portal open for the team. But eventually, it had been decided to shut down the gates and reopen them after thirty-six hours. The amount of energy it would have taken to maintain the portals was too great a strain on the resources they'd brought to Objer, and too many of the scientists were concerned about the potential for a cascade failure within the gates themselves. The consensus was that the gates had been designed as a transport hub, to be switched on and off as needed.

Despite knowing this was going to be the situation, Zurah felt an uneasy twinge in her chest at the thought of being stranded who knew where in the universe. The probes had mapped the night sky, but nothing had matched any star charts.

The second rover came into view as it crested one of the sand dunes, spewing sand behind it as it sailed down the dune and returned to base camp. Montgomery climbed out of the rover. "Perimeter check completed. But we'll have to do some visual inspections on the rovers. Further analysis of the sand indicates some highly corrosive elements, nothing like what the probes picked up on. May have to figure out an alternative mode of transport."

"I'm not waiting that long," Finn said. "Find a solution."

Montgomery had no issues challenging Finn, and Zurah tuned out the rest of their conversation.

"You said you needed to talk?" Alex asked quietly as he sat down next to her.

Zurah glanced down and noted he'd activated their private comms. "I got a strange message right before we left." Zurah sent Alex a copy of the warning. "I shared it with Finn, but as usual, she wants it kept quiet."

He read the message then frowned, looking up at Zurah. "Where did this come from?"

"I'm not entirely sure, but it happened after I transferred the file packet from what Gregori provided. You wouldn't have had any anomalies pop up on your end around the same time? Before we went through the gates?"

"No, but hang on and let me check." Alex was quiet for a minute then shook his head. "No, nothing."

"Think Finn might have?" Zurah asked. "And she was lying to me?"

Alex stared at Finn for a second too long. "I don't

know." There was a sharpness to his reply which made Zurah uncomfortable. She was walking on the edge of a knife between the cousins.

"I warned you I don't want to play games," Zurah said quietly.

Alex pressed his lips together then looked away for a moment. When he turned back to Zurah, his expression had softened. "I know you don't. Unfortunately, Finn and I don't know any other way, and old habits are hard to break." He stood and offered Zurah his hand.

She grabbed hold and let him help her to her feet. "What do you think it means?"

"Not a clue, but we knew this was going to be dangerous." Alex turned to face Zurah. "Thanks for trusting me with this. Finn and I might have differing agendas, but staying alive is something we can all—"

The sand beneath their feet shifted, threatening to topple Zurah. She grabbed Alex's arm for support then watched in horror as the sand undulated—as if a giant rock had been thrown into a sea of sand. The ripples were moving outward until they hit the rover Montgomery had crawled underneath to service. There was a sickening cry of pain through the comms then an explosion of chaos.

"Montgomery!" Finn shouted. "Do you read me? Montgomery, respond!"

The comms filled with static as Montgomery tried to respond. "I'm… tangled… Can't see… Suit is showing war—"

"Hold on. We're coming," Finn said. "Angelina, the grappling hooks!"

Time appeared to slow as Zurah watched Finn and Angelina move. Their bodies were tilted forward, but with each step they took, Zurah couldn't see any progress being made. She was trapped in another nightmare.

"Stay here," Alex said as he took a step forward.

"Oh, God." Montgomery's voice crackled through the comms. "The sand… it's…"

Sand shot up toward the sky where it had swallowed Montgomery and the rover, painting dark clouds across a clear blue background. Zurah threw up her hands to shield her face, but when nothing happened, she slowly lowered her arms. The other three team members were scrambling to set up the grappler unit, but Zurah had a sinking feeling nothing could be done to save Montgomery.

"I don't care if it's not fully charged. Any shot is better than none," Finn snapped at Angelina. "Get the coordinates set."

Alex had made his way to Angelina's position and leaned over the machine to help.

"Montgomery, hold on. We're coming," Finn said, then she turned around. "Get it done!"

"Grappler set," Alex replied. "We've imputted the coordinates and Montgomery's HalfLife chip. Release in three… two… one."

The grappler shuddered then spit out a long, thin rope with a drill tip on the end. It arced through the sky then plunged into the sand.

"Three meters. Ten. Seventeen meters now and slowing," Angelina reported. "No contact."

"Pull it up and try again," Finn ordered.

Even at the distance, Zurah caught the swivel of helmets as Angelina and Alex looked at each other.

"Retracting," Angelina said as the grappler wheeled in the line. "Release in three… two… one." Again, the grappler fired, burrowing through the sands.

"Five meters, fifteen, eighteen and slowing," Alex said.

"Push it," Finn ordered.

"Twenty," Angelina said. "Now twenty-one. Twenty-two. The drill has stopped. No contact. Initiating a scan."

Zurah made her way down to the grappler, peering over Alex's shoulder. The system was scanning the area, but it wasn't picking up on anything. No residual biosigns or any signs that the rover was down there. *What the hell?*

"Well?" Finn demanded.

"Nothing," Angelina said. "It's as if Montgomery and the rover weren't ever here. There isn't any trace at all."

Silence fell over the group, and Zurah turned to stare in disbelief where Montgomery had been minutes ago.

Alex stalked forward, and Finn started to issue orders. "Angelina, run the scan again. That simply isn't possible. Alex, I want you to run a full-spectrum analysis of the area. Zurah—"

"I'm not reading anything," Angelina responded. "None of our equipment is picking up on anything. Not even my suit. Montgomery's biosigns, his suit's homing device, HalfLife biochip readings—it's all gone."

"That's not possible. A cave-in or sand trap are the likely causes," Finn replied. "And in either case, Montgomery could be trapped just below the surface. All of the geological readings came back with the same conclusions.

The sand is no more than seventy-five meters thick, with bedrock and clay beneath the sand." She moved to the grappler unit. "This has enough line to reach the bedrock. Something must be blocking the feed."

"I don't claim to understand what just happened, but I'm telling you that there aren't any readings," Angelina said, moving toward the spot where Montgomery had vanished.

"And wouldn't that just be convenient for you," Finn said. "Losing our security detail? Did you think that losing him would give you the upper hand?"

"The upper hand for what?" Angelina challenged.

"This whole charade," Finn replied. "You claiming to not remember a thing that happened. I find it difficult to believe the amount of funding the Consortium has put into this project based on the information from a woman who doesn't remember anything."

Angelina shook her head. "Believe whatever you want. But I've told you the truth. I'm here to find out what happened to the *Eagle's Nest*. Whatever hidden agenda you think I have—Forget it." She huffed and turned her back on Finn.

"The sands aren't safe," Alex whispered, and Zurah's head whipped around to stare at him.

"Surely not. Surely, the message didn't mean—" Zurah felt beads of sweat break out along her hairline, then she looked down at the sand beneath her boots.

"Stop!" Zurah called out.

Angelina froze in place. All three remaining members of the team turned to stare at Zurah.

"Did you get a ping?" Finn asked.

"No," Zurah said. "I just… Surely, it isn't safe. She shouldn't—"

"It's all right," Angelina said. "I've changed the focus of my suit to monitor the sand and any potential disruptions. Everything is currently reading normal. If there's a chance he's down there, we have to do what we can." She turned toward Finn. "Despite what you think, I'm not interested in anyone dying."

Zurah hadn't known Montgomery, only having said a few words to the man in passing or in the briefing sessions. But the abrupt loss of yet another person brought up a surge of anger, which ripped through her. "Angelina isn't the problem. You are." Zurah pointed at Finn. "You and all your damn secrets. We were warned the sands weren't safe."

"What warning?" Angelina asked sharply.

"When I downloaded—"

"Zurah, we need to stay focused on—" Finn started.

"Hell no," Zurah said. "If you weren't so damned secretive, then perhaps this could have been avoided."

"What's she talking about?" Angelina asked.

"I received a warning. I don't know from who, but—" Zurah sent the message to Angelina. "We should've paid more attention to it."

"What is this?" Angelina hissed. "Why didn't you share it with us?"

"I told Finn, but she—"

"Knows the importance of understanding the difference between your friends and your enemies," Finn said. "Do you know how many death threats I've received throughout my life? How many hoaxes have been generated in order to intimidate me or sway me toward one political alliance or another? I've survived as long as I have because I'm careful."

Zurah closed the distance between them. "You're right. *You've* survived, but how many others haven't? How many have died because of the secrets you choose to keep?"

"Zurah, that's enough," Alex said quietly. "Both of you have valid reasons for doing what you do. But I think right now, the four of us can agree we need to share intel. Finn?"

"And will you keep that agreement, cousin?" Finn asked.

"Yes. While we are here, yes."

"So be it." Finn whipped around. "Zurah, log in to the rover's systems and expand its search radius. I want to make absolutely sure Montgomery isn't down there before we move on."

"How can you be so calm?" Zurah asked. "Montgomery is gone. And we don't know what kind of threat we're facing. How long until we're all swallowed by the sands?"

Alex moved to her side and gently placed a hand on her shoulder, but Zurah shrugged it off.

"Go, let me talk with her," Alex privately told Zurah.

"You're always making excuses for her," Zurah snapped.

"I'll agree that I do on occasion, but right now, losing our tempers isn't going to help the situation. We need to stay calm and focused."

Zurah shook her head. "Whatever. Do what you want."

"I'll give you a hand," Angelina said.

Zurah slid into the passenger's seat and paired her suit's network with the rover's. Overriding a few of the codes didn't take long, and together, she and Angelina completed three more scans of the area.

"Montgomery was a good man," Angelina said quietly. "I read his personal files. He would've been my top pick for security chief as well."

Zurah wasn't sure how to respond; she hadn't bothered to read his file. "Did he have family?"

"Yes. But he and his wife were divorced some years ago. They had two sons and a daughter."

Will they ever know what happened to their father? Zurah couldn't stop her agitation, and her right leg bounced up and down.

"I read your file too," Angelina added. "You're good at what you do, but you've never been a part of something like this, have you?"

Zurah shook her head.

"Something you're taught in command is that loss is inevitable, even on the most benign of missions, and that everyone who serves under your command understands that fact. Some learn to harden their hearts, to sweep the horrors of loss into a sort of mental lock box. Others let the loss affect them too strongly and find their ability to make decisions compromised. When you're in a leadership position, doing what we do, we have to know that sometimes, our orders will mean death."

"How do you live with yourself?" Zurah asked.

"By remembering the faces of everyone I've served with," Angelina replied. "And losing quite a bit of sleep."

"How are you even able to function? At first, living with the loss of the *Eagle's Nest* and everyone you must have known. Now, knowing that somehow, there were survivors?"

"It was hard, harder than anything I've ever done. But after seeing the others, hope keeps me going," Angelina replied. "Do you think the message was from Gregori? Or one of the others?"

Zurah knew she was changing topic and didn't push. "I'd suspect Gregori. He's been the only one who's been helpful. The others seemed pretty worked up on not letting us get access to the gates."

"Sounds like a solid theory. I'm not seeing anything come through. You?"

"No."

"We're not picking up on anything," Angelina reported. "Throwing you the data now."

Finn and Alex shared the data from their scans, each one having cautiously moved around the perimeter of where Montgomery and the rover had disappeared.

"Same," Alex said. "There's nothing. No traces of any metallics or biological life signs. They've completely vanished."

"How is that even possible?" Zurah asked, leaning back against the seat. "How do they completely vanish?"

"How does any of this technology work?" Alex replied. "We're dealing with a level of technological sophistication which is well out of our understanding."

"Which is why we need to understand what my

brother is trying to do," Finn said. "The scans are conclusive, agreed?"

The others nodded.

"I want verbal confirmation."

Alex gave his, with Angelina trailing after, but Zurah couldn't help but hesitate. Having to verbally agree that a member of the team was lost wasn't something she'd had to do before. If someone got hurt, injured, or worse, it was on the boss, not on the others. Zurah squirmed under Finn's gaze and gave in, confirming the scans showed nothing.

"Then we are in agreement. I will program one of the probes to stay behind and record an update and warning for the teams back on Objer. If we're not here when the gates are activated, then the probe will be recalled." Finn took a step toward the rover, then she stopped and turned toward Zurah. "You're right. The secrets I've kept have helped me stay alive. I can't tell you how many have died because of that. This is how I was raised, how I was taught to survive. But it doesn't mean I am impervious to each loss." There was an unreadable expression on her face when she turned to pull out the probe.

The anger Zurah had felt still simmered but was challenged by a twinge of empathy then frustration. *But will I be one of those people?* As she watched Finn fiddle with the probe, downloading the results of their scans and recording a brief update, Zurah was sure of one thing. *I don't know if I will, but dwelling on the what-ifs won't help me survive.*

"Angelina, do you have any idea what the tribunal or the Old Mother are?" Zurah asked.

Angelina paused then shook her head. "No. I'm not sure."

"Did any of your crew members worship a deity called the Old Mother?" Alex asked. "Or did you conduct discipline through a tribunal system?"

"What religion any of the crew members ascribed to would have been personal and not any business of mine," Angelina said. "So they definitely could have. But as to the tribunal? No. We followed standard disciplinary procedures as outline by the Council of Standhaven in 2234."

"There are seventy-nine different religions which have references to the Old Mother," Zurah said, running a search through the rover's database. "The majority of religions reach back hundreds of years, which provides us with too many possibilities."

"But perhaps we're thinking about this the wrong way." Angelina leaned forward and pulled out one of the small portable screens from underneath the rover's dashboard. "Let's work on the assumption that the message was sent by Gregori. I'll pull up his personal files. Perhaps there might be a clue in there. Or the Old Mother might not be anything religious. Could be a member of the crew who took charge, which would infer that Captain Ujthout didn't survive or lost his status as captain."

Zurah and Alex both leaned in to scan through Gregori's personal files, but as Angelina neared the end, no one had seen anything that might be helpful.

"There is another possibility," Finn said.

Zurah jerked back. So engrossed trying to find a hint as to what the warning had been about, she hadn't realized Finn had moved to stand beside the passenger's door.

"Do share," Alex drawled.

"My brother and his team. I have a reasonable guess as to who he sent out here, and she followed the old ways."

"I can't believe he'd let her leave the palace. Didn't she have a hand in one of the assassination attempts?" Alex asked. "I thought he threw her in prison."

Zurah tried to interrupt, to figure who in the worlds they were talking about, but Finn responded before Zurah could ask.

"I'm slightly concerned your intel is so out of date," Finn said. "He pardoned her a little over two years ago. She became a Shadow."

"A practice which was outlawed over fifty years ago," Alex replied. "But then again, why am I not surprised your brother would see fit to reinstate it."

"Reinstate what?" Zurah asked.

"The Shadows were the silent hands of the emperor, often tasked with assignments that took them outside of the law. Eventually, the pressure from other worlds forced the program to be shut down. Until my brother decided otherwise."

"And you don't think that this information was important? You should have told my father at least," Alex said.

"I did. But it turns out he was more interested in hiring a Shadow or two himself than making sure my brother followed the laws."

Alex's face turned red, and he stepped away from the rover. "He wouldn't."

"Of course he would, and he did," Finn replied. "Don't act naïve."

"I'm not—" Alex almost shouted as he spun around.

"Enough," Angelina broke in. "This is a family discussion for a later time. Finn, who is the Shadow?"

"Suen Kailani, my mother."

"Your mother?" Zurah asked.

Finn nodded. "One of the many reasons I left Old Earth. I may have been trained in the ways of my family, but it doesn't mean I chose to follow in their footsteps."

"If Kailani is here, on this world…" Alex started but shook his head. "At least she is a known quantity. And if it's really her your brother chose to lead the team, then we know what type of team she would choose."

"Yes," Finn said. "We need to move, and we need to assume nowhere is safe."

Zurah snorted but didn't say anything. She was already assuming nowhere was safe. Not here and not on Objer. Not anywhere, really.

"All the theories in the world aren't going to move us forward. Not without more information," Finn said. "We need to get moving."

Quickly working together, they reprogrammed the rover and their suits to continuously run several different scans of the area in hopes of providing enough warning to escape a fate similar to Montgomery's. Once complete, Finn released three more probes, two spaced out in front of the rover and the third behind them. And while Alex and Angelina finished packing up the site, Zurah fiddled with what was left of the coding behind the strange warning.

"Any luck?" Finn asked as she slid into the driver's seat.

"No. The work was clever, but the codes have been arranged in a way I haven't seen before. If the original back dataset hadn't vanished, maybe I could figure out a work-around. But as it is, I'm working with only half the puzzle."

"Then return to focusing on the gates' systems."

"To what end?" Zurah asked. "I'm not an engineer or technician. And we don't have access to the gates on this end."

"I'm aware. But if we're followed through the gates, then we need a way to shut them down. Permanently."

Zurah nodded. "I understand." Zurah had been chewing on this since Finn had given Zurah her orders. "I want to try and create a blind for the system. Then set up a rotating schedule of melting codes with a cascading effect."

"As long as the gates shut down before someone can undo your handiwork," Finn said.

That was an assignment Zurah was confident she could complete. And it gave her mind something to focus on rather than stewing on all of the unknowns they faced. She slipped into one of the back seats as Angelina and Alex packed the last of the equipment into the rover. Pulling up a skeleton program, she started the first step to building the blind, sorting through her custom-built coding options.

"All finished?" Finn asked Alex.

"Just about," he replied. When Alex was done, he

hopped into the back with Zurah, pulling out a security harness for her.

Zurah shook her head and stuffed it under her seat. "Don't want to feel trapped."

"I get that," Alex said with a tight smile.

Zurah tried to return his smile but found it difficult. With Montgomery's death having happened within hours of coming through the gates, Zurah was unsettled. The conflicts between the others were pulling her in too many directions. And Zurah didn't want to contemplate the implications of their internal issues for the success of their mission. Instead, she returned to her work as Finn engaged the rover and they took off.

5

Zurah blinked, trying to clear her vision after staring at her screen for too long. The base for the blind was almost finished and was, thankfully, to the point she was able to trigger a few automations to complete the process. Glancing up, she noted the landscape hadn't changed. The endless sea of sand dunes continued to stretch across the landscape. The twin suns had made significant progress in their journey toward the horizon, and Zurah checked her suit. The temperature had started to drop.

"How cold do you think it'll get?" she asked.

"The data from the probes indicated the average nightly temperature is just around freezing," Angelina replied.

Zurah shivered despite the suit's ability to maintain a constant temperature of her choice. Temperature fluctuations were one of several reasons she preferred artificial environments. She hated trying to match the appropriate amount of clothing with potential temperatures. Working on ships or stations with artificial environments beat any day jaunt planetside. Except for when those artificial systems broke down or were junk to begin with.

The four days Zurah had spent holed up on Zeb's Emporium were four days she would never forget. Zeb's was an old space station that had been decommissioned by the Glipglows and refurbished as a knockoff Rockerton's. After Zurah's last job with the Needles, she had needed some place to lie low for a while before considering taking on a new position with a new crew. With the few credits she'd been able to save, she'd taken a one-way ticket on an old freighter—upgrading the security systems in exchange for a fifty-percent reduction in fare—to Zeb's.

And not a minute too soon. A few hours after disembarking at Zeb's, Zurah's suit had shut down. The tech had been old and outdated, and despite her best efforts at tinkering with its systems, the suit had simply worn out. Cursing her luck on several levels, Zurah had scouted out the most affordable shop she could find. That had meant spending two days either freezing to death or feeling like she was going to melt into a puddle of goo.

The station's temperature swings were enough to drive any space-born individual crazy. While the station catered to the different needs of its diverse population, the station's environmental controls were just as old and outdated as her suit had been.

Glipglows preferred warmer temperatures, but their

area of the station was freezing, while the Telts were dealing with the opposite problem—melting to death due to an out-of-control heating coil when their species preferred cooler climates.

Everywhere Zurah had gone, shoppers and store owners grumbled and moaned over the inconsistent temperatures. She'd even witnessed a confrontation between the head of maintenance and a particularly agitated Glipglow. Zurah hadn't been sure the head of maintenance was going to survive—quite literally. After her experience on Zeb's, Zurah couldn't fathom how humanity had survived before technology.

"Check your suits. I'm getting a fluctuation in the sands roughly fifty-seven meters to my right," Alex said.

Zurah glanced down at her suit. "Confirmed. And I'm picking up another one sixty-three meters to the left as well."

"The rover confirms," Finn said. "Sending one of the probes to investigate. But so far, I'm not reading anything straight ahead. Maintaining our current course."

Zurah tracked the probe's progress, and using her SeeClear tech, she zoomed in on the site with the most activity. The probe hovered above the area and sent the recording back to their systems as a live feed. The sands shifted in a different pattern, zig-zag ripples coursing through the sand in a roughly ten-meter-square area. With each subsequent pulse, the waves of sand grew in size, until a sudden vortex opened up and the sand fell away, revealing a dark chasm.

"Are you seeing this?" Zurah asked, incredulous.

"Yes. I've never seen anything like it," Alex replied.

"Doesn't look like we're picking up on anything inside that vortex. No biosigns or energy signals."

The vortex remained open for just under a minute before it closed and the sands returned to normal.

"The faster we get this done, the better," Alex commented.

"It would be a lot easier with some sort of directions or at least a target," Zurah muttered. "Instead of aimlessly wandering around."

"We're not," Finn replied. "We do have a target."

"What?" Alex asked. "Don't tell me, another one of your—"

"No. But as stated in the briefings, we're searching in a prearranged grid pattern, with our systems marking off each section as we go. I have no desire to stay here any longer than necessary. And if our search doesn't yield any information, then we return to Objer and regroup, returning with more equipment."

"We might not have to," Angelina remarked. "Stop the rover."

Zurah braced for Finn to argue, but she didn't. Instead, she brought the rover to a stop and turned to stare at Angelina.

"Look at the data from the other probe."

Zurah pulled up the intel, and a chill ran through her body. Another vortex had appeared, similar to the one they had been busy watching. Except this vortex was still active, and something was moving in the darkness. The hairs on the back of Zurah's neck rose, and her flesh was covered in goose bumps despite the warm recycled air of her suit.

The sand inside the vortex shifted, shaping itself into a lump. Then it moved again, and the lump stretched in all directions until it resembled a crudely formed human. It had no mouth, eyes, or nose, though. There were no discernible features other than the rough outline of a humanoid shape.

A strange humming filled the air, and Zurah minimized the feed and checked the readings. Multiple energy spikes were being recorded, with fluctuations varying so wildly, she couldn't discern any type of pattern.

"Shit," Alex breathed.

"Exactly. Remind you of anything?" Zurah said quietly.

He glanced over at her, a haunted look on his face. "You don't think…?"

Zurah reached out and gave his hand a light squeeze. Remembering the feeling of the cryrot's voices in her head left an unsettling feeling in her gut. Alex's experience had been even worse.

"Could be. The species or the cryrot who built those platforms had to have come from somewhere," Zurah reasoned. "We're working on the assumption that the smaller portals and the gates were built by the same species, right?"

"Yes," Finn replied. "And assuming the species had a home world, or at least a world which was their base of operations, it could stand to reason this is that world. The gates are large enough for a ship, while the others appear to be designed for limited transport."

"But you're forgetting that Johnston and the others weren't composed of crystals but sand," Angelina said.

"The fact that they weren't a part of the cryrot makes me consider the opposite. Everything we know is that the sand entities and the cryrot are enemies. What makes you think the cryrot would have developed on a world which is largely composed of sand?"

"Then perhaps we've been looking at this picture the wrong way," Finn commented. "If the two are opposed"—Angelina started to disagree—"*if* they are opposed, we don't know anything for certain, then this could be the base or home world of the sand entities. Which could lead to the conclusion they are responsible for the portals and gates."

The strange hum intensified, and Zurah winced, adjusting her suit to tune out the sound but also making sure to record the noise.

"I think we've just discovered one solid lead," Alex said. "The cryrot used music just like we're hearing now. I have a hard time believing that's a coincidence."

Angelina pointed at the sand figure. "Coincidence or not, that entity may be our first and best clue in understanding what happened and what is currently happening." She opened the door and got out of the rover. "If we were going to spend our time theorizing, then we should have stayed on Objer. We came here for answers, and sitting here isn't going to get us any closer to the truth."

"Angelina, get back in the rover," Alex said, an edge of panic to his voice.

Zurah glanced down at her suit's screen, tapping into Alex's vitals. His heart rate was elevated, and his breathing was slightly labored.

"This is why we're here," Angelina said.

"But we don't know what its intentions are," Alex said, leaning forward. "What if it tries to take over like the cryrot?" His hands gripped the back of Finn's seat, his fingers digging into the material.

"Alex," Zurah said quietly through their private comm. "Just breathe."

"I can still hear the echoes of those screams… those voices," he whispered. He switched back to the shared comm line. "We need to back up, slowly," Alex said on the shared comm line. "I don't like this. It's too similar to what Zurah and I experienced with the cryrot."

"Angelina, get back in the rover," Finn ordered. "We'll observe for now. Let it make the first move." She put the rover in reverse, waiting for Angelina to comply.

But Angelina took a few steps forward.

The strange entity rose higher, sand continually overflowing like a fountain where the figure's feet met the pillar. Its strange body rotated a full three hundred sixty degrees, and when it faced the rover again, Zurah was certain it was watching them. Even with the entity having no discernible eyes, Zurah could feel it studying each one of them.

"We need to get out of here," Alex said again. "Angelina, get back in the damned rover."

"No," Angelina responded. "We came here for answers. I came here needing to understand what happened to the *Eagle's Nest*. To all of those individuals I served with, who I was supposed to help protect. I *need* to know."

"And what if it was their curiosity which caused the

physical change?" Finn asked. "What if contact with that entity is what happened to them?"

When Angelina took yet another step forward, Finn put the rover in park and jumped out. She leaped over to Angelina and grabbed her by the shoulders. "My brutal truth is that I don't give a damn about what happened to the *Eagle's Nest* unless it has something to do with what my brother is on about, but I won't lose another person." Finn's gaze briefly flashed to meet Zurah's. "Get in the rover."

Finn spun Angelina around and pushed her toward the vehicle at the same moment the sand entity lifted its arms. Great walls of sand flowed upward with the motion, blotting out the suns and plunging the landscape into a muted darkness. Pushing out from the wall of sand was another humanoid shape, but this time, the particles of sand shimmered, weaving a pattern of flesh.

"Gregori," Zurah said.

"No," Angelina corrected as she turned back around. "Captain Ujthout. Gregori was his younger brother."

The figure took a few steps forward, the wall of sand moving with it. "Still alive, Commander? I thought you would have died years ago. But you know, I think I can honestly say that I'm pleased to see you again," a gravelly voice said.

"I'm not sure I can say the same," Angelina replied, crossing her arms against her chest. "I need answers, Captain."

"Are you not even a little bit shocked to see me?"

"There was a time when I would've been, but not anymore. Answers, now."

Captain Ujthout shook his head. "Pity. I always liked a little bit of shock value." He moved forward, and in that heartbeat, Finn and Alex had their weapons drawn and trained on the man. "As for answers, I'm actually not allowed to give them. And what you learn about this place, about what happened after you defied my orders, will be determined at a later time." He took one more step forward.

"I wouldn't do that," Finn said. "Stay where you are."

Captain Ujthout threw Finn an amused smile. "So tiny and small thinking." He lifted a hand, and a second wall of sand erupted behind the rover.

Alex spun around, weapon held at the ready, while Finn stayed fixed on the captain.

Zurah crouched, peering out from between the seats. Her heart hammering, she watched in equal parts horror and fascination. Forcing herself to look down, she tapped the screen on her left arm and scrolled through the menu, running a comparison between the frequencies emitted from the cryrot and the captain. To her frustration, Zurah saw that the sands were producing a wide variety of frequencies, including those she had used against the cryrot.

"If you're not the one in charge, then take us to who is," Finn said. "I have a few questions of my own."

The captain's grin only seemed to widen. "I'm not sure you know the right questions to ask. Not yet, at least." He flicked his wrists inward, and the two walls of sand moved to form a perimeter around the team. "But if you survive, then you might be ready."

"Fire!" Finn ordered. She and Alex opened fire but did little to no damage.

"Switching ammo," Finn said as her empty clip was discharged. She grabbed the modified attachment the teams had developed to aid in the fight against the cryrot and clicked it into place. Within seconds, she was firing again.

The weapon didn't appear to cause any lasting harm to the captain but did at least temporarily disrupt the flow of sand. Zurah tasked a program to isolate the frequencies produced by the weapon and the effects on the sand.

"Fall back!" Finn ordered, expending another clip and reloading. "Options."

"Can we drive through it?" Alex called out as he moved back to the side of the rover.

"Captain, please. If there is any shred of humanity left within you, then help me understand what is going on," Angelina pleaded as she took a few steps back.

"What do you remember of your final day of training?" he asked.

Zurah glanced up and noted how pale Angelina's face had gone.

"I remember it all," she replied.

"Then you should already know." The grin abruptly fell and was replaced by a look of sheer rage.

The walls of sand screamed as they moved inward, threatening to crush the team.

"Get in!" Finn yelled, reaching for the door, but as her fingers made contact with the handle, there was a look of shock on her face. She clawed at the side of the door, trying to find something to hold on to.

"Finn!" Zurah screamed, and she leaped over the edge of the seat, slamming her hands against the side console to lower the window. Finn's legs were swallowed by the sand as her fingers wrapped around the door handle.

"Hold on!" Zurah shouted as the window rolled down. Twisting herself, she thrust her arm out, but the door handle snapped.

Then Finn disappeared into the fury of the sands. Zurah stared at the spot where Finn had been seconds before, disbelief coursing through her thoughts.

"We've got to get out of here," Alex's voice came through the comms, yanking Zurah back to reality.

She pushed herself back over the seat, out of the way, as Alex got one leg into the rover, ready to scoot over into the driver's seat. Zurah watched Angelina turn and race back to the rover. "Find Isla. Tell her I love—" Angelina's last words were stripped away as the sand pulled her down.

Zurah's gaze desperately sought out Alex, then she realized he had gripped the edge of the passenger's seat and the inside of the rover's doorframe. Frantically, she repositioned herself to try to pull him into the rover.

"Hold on," she grunted, grabbing his left wrist.

There was a flash of pain across his face as he looked up at her. "Don't. At least one of us needs to tell Objer what has happened. Destroy the gates. Destroy them all. Then get the hell away from—" He winced as his body was yanked out of the rover.

"I won't leave you," Zurah cried as she was pulled forward along with him.

"Let go." A look of peace fell over Alex's face. "I hear them, and they're—" He twisted his arm so Zurah's grip would falter, and he slipped out of her grasp.

"No, Alex!"

There was nothing she could do. Zurah looked through the front window of the rover and saw Captain Ujthout watching her. The sands that had come together to form his body were dissolving, leaving a horrific half-formed figure with small streams of sand pouring like blood from flesh wounds all over his body.

Desperate, Zurah scrambled into the driver's seat and threw the rover into reverse, slamming her boot down on the gas pedal. The rover's wheels spun into action for a split second, then the rear wheels sank into the sand, throwing Zurah back against the seat.

She switched into drive, her foot pressing the gas pedal to the floor. The rover swerved back and forth, unable to escape the sand. Scared and knowing if she got out of the rover, she would meet the same fate as the others, Zurah activated the rover's weapons systems and fired.

The engineers who had worked to modify the weapons had also modified the rover's systems. Along with the traditional weapons, the rover was equipped to produce high frequencies in an effort to fight the cryrot.

The weapons' effect wasn't strong enough and barely caused a ripple in the sand. Fear coursed through her as she fired again and again. The sand walls were steadily moving closer, cutting her off from any other course of action. An alert flashed across the dash of the weapons console, warning of overheating, but Zurah ignored it. Sweat rolled down her face, and Zurah was certain she was about to die. *Forgive me, Nissa.*

Steeling herself through the fear, she looked up at what was left of Captain Ujthout. There was barely anything left of the captain or a humanoid shape. The rover's rear end was sinking, and Zurah braced against the momentum threatening to pull her out of the seat. Resetting the target on the weapons panel to adjust for the rover's severe tilt, Zurah yelled, "If I go down, I'm taking you with me!"

She slammed her hand against the controls. Streaks of energy flew out from the rover and ripped through the sand again and again until Zurah realized the sand was slowing in its ability to reform. Not caring about any potential damage to the rover or its systems, Zurah switched from manual control to a continuous-firing pattern. The sand wall was beginning to show minute gaps, and each time a burst of high-frequency sound hit the sand, the particles shivered and shifted into peculiar patterns.

The rover sank again, and Zurah grabbed the bottom of the seat to hold on. She only had a few seconds to make a decision. *Better to be on my own two feet than trapped in this thing.* Pushing the door open, Zurah jumped out of the vehicle as it disappeared into the sand.

As soon as her boots touched the sand, she felt her body being pulled down. "I don't think so," she growled. She pulled out her weapon, changed clips, then rolled to the right. A dark abyss opened up where she had been standing, and Zurah scrambled to her feet, darting away from the gaping hole.

Another swirling vortex of sand opened up in front of her, and Zurah lurched to the side. The sand slipped away from her feet, though, and she fell. She felt the sand wrap around her lower legs and pull. Zurah twisted around and fired shot after shot at the sand, causing just enough disruption to kick herself free. Once more getting to her feet, she ran then stopped and turned, aiming her weapon for the small pillar of sand that had once been the captain. She fired until her weapon overheated, but in the end, it was enough. The sands shivered and erupted into a strange mandala-type pattern before letting loose one last terrifying scream.

Then, as abruptly as the sands had turned against them, they fell. Each grain settled to the surface, no longer screaming, no longer trying to swallow her whole. Cold sweat ran down Zurah's face as she sprinted, putting as much distance as possible between herself and the area where Captain Ujthout had appeared. When her lungs were on fire and her suit's emergency medical system forced the joints to lock and stop her, Zurah fell to her knees. The surge of adrenaline that had pushed her to safety had worn off. Her suit flashed warning after warning, telling her the emergency medical aid it was going to administer. A five-second countdown began, allowing for the choice of canceling the drugs. Zurah ignored it as she rolled over onto her back. *If the sands take me, then so be it.*

There was a slight pinch at the side of her left thigh where one of three potential injection sites could be chosen. Within seconds, her heart rate slowed, and the fog of an adrenaline crash lifted.

A recommendation to seek further medical advice was given, along with encouragement to rest for the next twenty-four hours. She stared at the alert, its gentle glow against the background of the sky.

Twenty-four hours. We were here less than six, and already, they're gone. Zurah felt the need to cry as overwhelming grief and anguish flooded her body. But the tears wouldn't come. Instead, a furious cry of rage and helplessness rose up within her, and she screamed and screamed until her voice was hoarse.

Angry, she got rid of the alert and stared up at the darkening sky. The teams had sent the probes through at varying times, and several had been tasked with mapping the stars, trying to determine exactly where the gates led to. She couldn't remember reading any conclusions, and she switched the clear overlay on her helmet's screen to a star map.

The suit tried to identify the stars, but in the end, everything came back as inconclusive. *Either the suit's systems aren't powerful enough, or we really are in uncharted space.* Zurah knew the second option was the most likely. Despite feeling as if humanity had spread across the galaxy, Zurah knew only a fraction of the galaxy had been explored. The gates could have taken her anywhere.

Even to another galaxy. The new thought abruptly sprang to mind. Even though she wasn't a scientist, Zurah dismissed the idea. The idea of traveling outside of their galaxy was science fiction, not fact.

Zurah lay there, watching the sky continue to darken.

As the reality of her situation began to truly sink in, Zurah shivered. If the sands didn't take her, then she would only survive as long as her suit held out. *And I'll be alone on an alien world.* Finn, Alex, and Angelina's faces flashed through her thoughts. Even Montgomery's. Then Dr. Ordotham and how he had quickly become someone Zurah knew she would trust. Then Mexa, who had worked numerous jobs with her. And lastly, Nissa.

Squeezing her eyes shut, she worked on remembering every detail of Nissa's face then tried to remember her mother's. She couldn't help but wonder what similarities she had missed. Perhaps, but she hadn't been looking for anything either. In all of the time she'd spent alone after her parents had left, she had never considered the idea that there might be family out there she could find or that would help her. Neither her mother nor father had ever talked about their families. They had, instead, always gone on about their work or doted on Zurah.

What happened to cut you off from your families? Why didn't Nissa tell me who she is?

As she considered these thoughts, Zurah realized that those questions didn't sting as they used to. More pressing concerns were weighing her down. In the short time she had been on Objer, something had shifted within her, and Zurah understood there were forces out there far more important than her family history. Perhaps she was becoming numb to the idea of loss, but Zurah was increasingly aware of how vital their mission was—and the assignments Finn had given her. The image of the emperor taking the cryrot or the sand and turning them into supersoldiers was horrifying.

Pushing herself up, Zurah scanned the area. Nothing appeared out of place. There was no hint of the horror of the last few minutes. No biosigns. No pingbacks from any HalfLife biochip system. Just like with Montgomery, every indication that the others had been there was gone.

A new alert popped up. Irritated, Zurah started to delete it, but she realized it wasn't coming from her suit. This alert was from the probes. All three probes had remained airborne during the confrontation and were confirming their assignments.

"Well, shit," she muttered, quickly tapping into their systems and tying the probes to her suit. "That's something, at least." As she reprogrammed their systems, Zurah knew she should still be in shock. She was all alone, with no supplies or backup equipment—everything had been packed into the rover. Not to mention watching Montgomery, Angelina, Finn, and Alex be taken by the sand. Tears threatened to overwhelm her, but Zurah bit down on the edge of her tongue. The sharp pain helped to stop the breakdown.

"I knew the risks," she told herself. "I knew that coming here meant one or all of us could die. I knew that there was a chance I was never going back. But I came here"—she pushed herself up to her feet—"for a reason. To make sure that no one else got hurt."

Of course, you didn't accomplish that, did you? A small voice inside tried to argue, but Zurah pushed it aside.

"As long as I'm here, there's still a way to understand what's going on and how to stop it… whatever that is." She forced herself to turn off her emotions, to ignore the pain of loss, and focus on her job.

The base for the blind had finished, and Zurah started in on the second phase, stacking the melting codes into a randomized delivery structure. Without knowing what was in store, Zurah uploaded what she had to the fourth probe Finn had programmed to stay behind. Then, she instructed her SeeClear tech to run automatic uploads every half hour until the blind with the melting codes was complete.

She glanced up at the night sky and decided to also program one of the probes to track her movements by the stars. *At least I have more intel than when we started. When they activate the gates, I can share what I witnessed and ensure the gates are permanently shut down.*

Zurah couldn't picture more personnel and rovers coming through the gates. Not after what had just happened. *If I don't succeed, how many more will try to come through and die when they do? Not to mention what might go through the gates back to Objer and spread to the known worlds.* She triggered a new countdown clock with her SeeClear tech. *Twenty-seven hours until the gates are activated.*

Glancing back into the darkness where Zurah had lost the others, she felt a strong sense of resolution. If nothing else, Zurah was going to survive and make sure she completed her part of the mission. *Whatever happened to the* Eagle's Nest *will remain a mystery, and the emperor won't get his supersoldiers. They'll be another footnote in the history of humanity.* Zurah would make sure of that.

6

Zurah shivered and checked her suit. The planet was well into its night cycle, and the temperature had fallen again. For now, the suit would be able to adjust, but if the temperature kept plunging and stayed there for too long, the suit would start to have trouble keeping up. *Too many nights of that without fresh power supplies, and I'll start having trouble.* She checked in with the probes and noted there hadn't been a change in their scans. The sand dunes were quiet. She opened a new map, tagged the location of where the gates had spit them out, then overlaid a standard search grid and the star maps. Tagging the probes, she set them at a radius of three hundred meters, continually moving clockwise around her position.

Walking for roughly another hour or two, Zurah continued to check in with the probes, trying to discover any unusual anomalies that would provide clues.

Yet all the scans and data came back negative. As far as the reports were concerned, Zurah was standing in the middle of a desert, with nothing unusual.

At last, Zurah finished stacking the melting codes and their rotating schedule. Double-checking her work, she started a back-trace program to look for any potential misplaced pieces of code or holes in her work. Then, she started a cross-reference program with the research on the gates, ensuring that despite her lack of solid understanding on how the gates functioned, her work would shut down the systems the teams had rigged up.

Her body and mind exhausted, Zurah slid down one of the taller dunes and sat down. She was tempted to have her suit administer a cocktail of drugs to keep her awake. The idea of staying in one spot for too long unnerved her. But depleting her suit's supplies too early wasn't wise; she had no idea what the future might bring. Her body desperately needed to rest, and Zurah reasoned a few hours of sleep wasn't going to hurt. After tightening up the radius of the probes and setting a timer on her suit, Zurah settled into the sand and let herself drift off to sleep.

Zurah's dreams were an odd mixture of childhood memories and nightmare scenarios. When she was jolted awake by her suit's alarm, she had a difficult time unwinding her thoughts from the horrific images of her parents' rented hab unit turning into sand and gobbling them up. She shook her head and stretched, double-checking with the probes and current temperature—minus two degrees Celsius. With the probes' reports not showing any unusual activity, Zurah decided she would chance another couple hours of sleep, which would leave her with twenty-one hours before the gates were activated. *After a bit more rest, I'll finish working on the blind and melting codes.*

Sleep washed over her once more, and as her eyelids drifted closed, one of the probes sent an alert. She was instantly awake. Pulling up the probe's data, Zurah froze then slowly looked up.

The sand in front of her was moving, as if a small subterranean spring were trying to bubble up to the surface. Getting to her feet, Zurah climbed up the side of the dune then turned and crouched down to watch. Every instinct inside her was telling her to run, to put as much distance between the anomaly and herself as possible. The rational part of her mind told her she needed more information, and confronting whatever was happening here was the only way that was going to happen. She pulled her weapon from its holster and made sure she had a fresh clip inserted. Adjusting her SeeClear tech to enhance her night vision, she waited and watched.

Another humanoid figure appeared, and Zurah decided to call them sand creatures. No matter what shape they took or what they might say, they weren't human any longer. The sand creature's eyeless head tilted to one side and looked up at Zurah.

She pushed herself back a few inches and took aim. Zurah wasn't sure how long they stayed in that position, each one watching the other, until at some point, the sand rearranged itself to form a gaping hole in its head in an imitation of a mouth.

There was a soft whisper of music, which reminded Zurah of the iridescent jio horns produced when played above water—a clever piece of engineering by the Neethos, developing an instrument that could be played both below and above water with distinctly different sounds. Zurah knew about the jio horns because of a night spent at a small rock hopper station, where a crew of Neethos were docked and celebrating some festival of theirs.

The sound came again, this time a bit louder. It started off with one note then cascaded into a handful of complementing tones. The sand creature lifted an arm and pointed at Zurah. When she didn't move or respond, the sand creature repeated the sound.

Zurah didn't need a degree to understand what the sand creature was attempting to do. Without thinking, she blurted out the first thing that came to mind. "What the hell are you?"

The grains of sand that formed the creature shifted as if briefly pulling away from each other then formed again. It made another sound, this one by far the loudest, and the tones it chose were jarring. *All right. I get it. You didn't like that. If I run out of ammo, then at least I can scream at them. For all the good that'll do me.*

Gritting her teeth, Zurah softened her approach. "What are you? And where are the people I came with? What did you do to them?"

The sand creature reformed its mouth and gave three short bursts of a single note, then without warning, it disintegrated. Zurah stared at the pile of sand and scanned the area. The results were the same—the sand was a mixture of organic and inorganic particles, with roughly half of the particles unidentifiable.

Zurah waited and watched to see if the sand creature would return. *This is a security puzzle. How do I crack not only the gates but the sands?* She ran through what she knew. The sand was no more than seventy-five meters thick, with bedrock and clay underneath. According to the geologists, that was a standard reading of a desert landscape. The sand did respond to varying frequencies, and continual bursts from the weapons appeared to distort the sand.

But how? She scooped up a handful of sand and let it run through her fingers. Understanding if the sand she saw was separate from the sand creatures was beyond her training. All she could speculate on was if some of the unidentified particles were what allowed the sand creatures to take form. *Do the sand creatures disappear to wherever they took the others? Are they the same as what we witnessed with the transformed members from the* Eagle's Nest?

When nothing happened, Zurah stood and brushed the sand from her suit. A new thought ran through her mind. *Didn't Montgomery say something about potential corrosive issues with the sand? What happens if some of it gets* inside *my suit?* Not happy with that new consideration, she double-checked her suit's seals and integrity. Everything was in the green, but gazing around the desolate landscape, she didn't feel reassured.

"All right, guys," she said, looking up at the probes. "We've got some decisions to make. Do I keep going, hoping to find some answers, and programming you all to return when it's time? Or should we all hike back to the fourth probe and wait there?"

The decision caused her chest to tighten. It was a tactical choice, one she still wasn't used to making. She preferred having a boss so she didn't have to think about the big picture and could zero in and focus on her tasks. "But that's not going to happen here, is it?"

Decision made, Zurah retasked one of the probes to return to where the gates should appear as a backup. Coding it with the same intel as the fourth probe Finn had left behind, she synced the automatic updates for the blind and melting codes between the probes. The more information she could gather, the better prepared the research teams would be in case something went wrong with the blind.

"Time to get cracking." She started walking.

The planet's rotation wasn't much different from Old Earth's, and by the time Zurah needed to stop and rest, the suns were beginning to peek up above the horizon. Her SeeClear tech automatically adjusted into standby mode, and Zurah checked in with the probes as she sat down on top of a sand dune. She pulled up the maps and noted how far she had walked northeast of the gate's activation zone.

Mentally rolling the dice, Zurah settled on moving east. Carefully rationing her suit's nutrient supplies, she activated the feeding straw and ingested a little of the bland paste. Once she felt rested and refreshed, she headed out.

"Okay, time to think this through," she said, needing to hear her own voice. "The sand creatures are shaped from the sand, which means they are either a part of it or have some type of technology that mimics the sand, like a camouflage. And I'm going to run on the assumption that the sand creatures are different from Gregori and the others. Or else why the stunted form of communication I just witnessed? Perhaps the sand creatures are a base form or a different kind of probe, sent to gather information, and Gregori and the others figured out how to integrate that tech with human biology. Either way, there has to be something that allows them to form a cohesive shape. And that means there has to be a way to hack it. And if I can do that, then I'll gain the upper hand."

Zurah paused for a moment to have her suit start running through a handful of programs with the data that had been collected while she checked on how the base of the blind was coming along. "At least it's a—"

"Hello."

Zurah froze then slowly looked up. Standing on the top of another dune to her right was a sand creature. The creature wasn't alone. There were three of them.

"Hello?" Zurah called out tentatively while slowly pulling out her weapon, careful not to make any sudden moves.

"No fear, please. Come. We'll show you what you need."

Yeah, right. Like I'm going to fall for that. "No thanks. I'm good right here. Just looking for my buddies. Can you help me with that?" Zurah zoomed in and was startled to see that the creature who was talking looked almost human. Its flesh was pale and smooth, with a bald head and crudely formed clothing. But where its eyes and mouth should have been were nothing but swirling maelstroms of sand.

The more human looking of the two turned to the sand creature, and they exchanged a series of musical notes. Eventually, their voices intertwined into a strange pattern of give and take.

"Name?" they called out.

"Winters." *That can't hurt anything… I hope.*

They repeated it as if tasting the word for the first time, eventually getting it correct.

"Winters. Come. We'll show you what you need."

Zurah's grip on her weapon tightened. *Using my name isn't scoring you any points.*

Keeping her eyes on the pair of creatures, she carefully moved backward, wanting to put some more distance between her and them. Her options weren't great. Making a run for it didn't have decent odds of making a difference, and she didn't want to expend her weapons until it was absolutely necessary. But the decision was made for her. The creatures disappeared in a blink of the eye, and Zurah immediately raised her weapon, turning around in a full circle.

As she completed the circle, the sand creatures returned. This time, several dotted the crests of the dunes all around her.

Great. Looks like they're not going to take no for an answer. But why not just pull me down like the others? What are they waiting for?

"Please, come. We'll show you what you need," the humanoid creature called out.

There was a hint of desperation in its voice, which made Zurah happy. But as the creatures all took a step forward in unison, that brief moment of happiness disappeared. Panic threatened to set in. There was no way her handheld weapon would protect her from all the sand creatures, and the probes weren't equipped with a weapons system.

"Don't come any closer," Zurah warned, trying to make her voice sound as rough and displeasing as possible, and for good measure, she fired off a few shots.

There was a chorus of discord, and the sand creatures appeared to shimmer as they lost cohesion. *Okay, maybe I can do this. Maybe I'll figure this out.*

The agitated discord continued and reached an almost deafening level. Zurah fired off another warning shot, then a shadow fell over her. She looked up just in time to see a wall of crystal explode out of the sand.

"Shit!" she yelled, startled, and skidded down the side of the dune. When she reached the bottom, her feet dug into the sand as she tried to run. A sand creature popped up next to her, its arms reaching out to grab her.

Zurah tried to spin out of its way and fell, her hands sinking deep into the sand. A crystal speared the sand creature, and its strange melody was twisted into an ear-splitting scream. Not wasting any time, Zurah got to her feet and crested the next dune. The sand creatures continued to appear all around her, and each time one did, another crystal appeared to pierce it, dissolving the creature.

As she worked to cross over to the next sand dune, the strange melodies of the sand were overshadowed by the hum of the crystals, which were now pushing through the dunes all around her. Zurah had to slow down in an effort to carefully wind her way through the crystal fields until there was no way to move. Zurah was trapped.

Fear coursed through her as she watched crystal after crystal erupt from the sand, forming a solid barrier around her. The crescendos of sand and crystal grew to such an intensity that Zurah was forced to seal the external comms. A pulsating light appeared in the center of each crystal surrounding her, and the sand beneath her boots trembled. Zurah tried to keep her balance but was forced to her knees as the sand rolled away from the crystals, gradually causing her to sink deeper and deeper within the crystals' embrace.

"Hell no." She charged her weapon, aiming for the crystal nearest her.

But in the heartbeat of moving her finger to the trigger, the crystals stretched and reached out to engulf her.

Zurah screamed, the cry of her panic echoing inside of her suit. Pinpricks of pain blossomed along her body as the crystals continued to push inward. An alert popped up on her helmet's screen, warning her of impending damage. Zurah tried to break free, but the more she moved, the faster the crystals pressed in on her. The crystals forced their way into her suit, their cold surfaces growing and moving in stops and starts across her skin. As the crystals crept up her neck, Zurah involuntarily sucked in a deep breath and held it as the crystal wound itself around her face.

Her lungs burned, screaming for oxygen. Zurah was

forced to open her mouth, trying to take a breath, but shards of the crystal broke and landed on her tongue. As if she were swallowing red-hot coals, pain snaked through her body. All Zurah could focus on was the pain coursing down her throat, into her belly, and creeping out along her limbs.

She lost track of time in the haze of pain until she heard a voice yell, "I need a med tech. Now, Henderson!"

The pain was still present, but the crushing press of the crystals was gone. Through the fog of pain, she felt a hand push on the back of her neck while another hand moved her head from side to side.

"No immediate signs of contamination," another voice said. "But I'd recommend a clean sweep. You know they're getting better and better at hiding from our scans."

Zurah's eyes fluttered open as she felt a weight settle on her chest. She mumbled and tried to move her hands in order to push the weight off, but someone held her down.

"Hold still," the first voice growled.

Despite the pain and confusion, Zurah fought against the restraints, but she wasn't able to break free. The hands holding her down only tightened as she struggled against them.

"Clear!" the first voice shouted.

For a brief moment, Zurah realized she had control of her body. She tried to lift her arms, ready to push the weight off her chest, but a jolt of electricity ran through her body.

"She's clean. Give her the serum," the second voice instructed.

The fog started to lift from her mind, and Zurah tried to say no, but the hands twisted her head to the side, and there was a sharp burst of pain as a needle was inserted. Warmth flooded her body, instantly relaxing her muscles. Then a wave of coughing hit. Zurah couldn't stop. Her chest heaved with cough after cough.

"That's it. You've got to cough it all out," the voice said. "Couple more, then you should be clear."

As the coughing eased, the strange weight was lifted from her chest, and Zurah rolled over. One of her hands was bracing against the floor, while the other held her chest as the coughs turned to a painful wheezing.

"Send for the Old Mother. She needs to know what's going on," the first voice said. "And find Clara. We need to double-check security protocols."

What the hell happened? Zurah's vision was starting to clear, and she realized she was staring at a pair of heavily patched boots. Her eyes slowly traveled up the pair of legs, noting the jumpsuit was also covered in mismatching patches of fabric. The individual who was wearing the jumpsuit stared down at Zurah, his expression holding a strange mixture of disgust and hope. His bright-green eyes continued to watch Zurah as she struggled to push herself into a sitting position. The pain in her chest was overwhelming, and for a brief moment, she closed her eyes and took a few slow breaths.

"Don't try and move. The seeds normally don't do much damage, but you're not one of us, so we can't be for sure."

Zurah opened one eye then the next and glared at the man. She was sure his words were meant to comfort, but he needed to work on his tone of voice. But she took his advice and stayed still as the pain in her chest eased. Seizing the moment of opportunity, she blinked, activating her SeeClear tech, and ran a few scans, trying to ascertain where she was. *Definitely not where I was a few minutes ago.*

Dark metallic paneling and dim overhead lights had replaced the sand dunes. Startled, Zurah saw there were other individuals moving around them. They were in some type of corridor or tunnel. There were no signs or marks along the walls to provide any clues as to where exactly she was. She glanced down and noted someone had removed her suit.

If that was for security, tough luck, guys. Zurah blinked and brought up the SeeClear menu, double-checking the programs she'd had running in the background. Both programs were nearing completion and hadn't thrown up any major red flags. Relieved to know her work had been worth it, she glanced at the countdown. *Nineteen hours. I only have to make it for nineteen hours to make sure the probes' transmission goes through and gather what intel I can.* Relieved to know her programs were almost done, she scrolled down to the control lines for the probes. The probes were still there and sending data, but when she tried to triangulate her signal against the probes' intel, an error message appeared.

Damn. Zurah glanced up at the man standing over her. He looked human. *Or at least outwardly, he looks human.*

Soft footfalls filled the corridor, and the man turned and bowed. "Old Mother."

Zurah leaned to the right to peer around the man and saw a wizened old woman. Her skin had an impossible assortment of wrinkles, and her face was framed by a few wisps of snow-white hair. Dark-brown eyes peered back at Zurah, and when the old woman spoke, Zurah caught a glimpse of one lonely tooth holding on for dear life.

With a raspy voice, the woman asked, "Who are you?"

"Winters."

"What are you?"

That made Zurah pause for a moment, then she decided to say, "Human."

"When are you?"

Zurah's eyes darted to the man then back to the woman. She was unsure how to answer the question. "I'm thirty-one."

The old woman frowned. "When were you birthed?"

"Twenty-five ninety-three."

The old woman's frown deepened, and with a hard glare in Zurah's direction, she lifted her cane and pointed it at her. Then she whistled a few notes and shook her head, turning to gaze at the man. "An impossible. Flesh?"

"Yes, Old Mother. Our scans show she is flesh and blood. She is one hundred percent human."

With a disappointed harrumph, the old woman turned then started to hobble back the way she'd come, followed by a pair of younger men.

Before Zurah had a chance to ask any questions, a woman dressed in a military-styled outfit stormed past the old woman with barely nod. "Jaks, we need to talk."

"Not here," he growled.

"Yes, here. Or else you'll blow me off again. What were you thinking? Bringing it here could alert those bastards to our location."

"I'm aware," Jaks replied. "But do you understand what she might mean?"

"And are you even sure it's flesh?"

Zurah pushed herself up and wobbled around a bit, but she stayed standing. "*She's* right here and would like to know what the hell is going on."

The woman jabbed her finger into Jaks's chest, ignoring Zurah. "You found it and brought it here, so it's your problem. If it threatens us in any way"—she turned and stared at Zurah—"then I'll liquefy it myself."

"Liquefy?" Zurah asked, desperately wishing she still had her weapon.

"Clara—" Jaks started, but Clara huffed and stormed off. "At least get the perimeter scans fixed!" he yelled after her.

Clara made a rude gesture but didn't stop.

Jaks turned to stare at Zurah.

"What? Something in my teeth?" she snapped. "Where is the rest of my team? What did you do with them?"

"Not until you tell me where your ship is," Jaks replied.

When Zurah didn't answer, Jaks tilted his head to the side as if weighing his options. The subtle change in posture unnerved her. He narrowed his eyes and let out a long, low whistle. The strange sound reverberated along the walls, and Zurah shivered and glanced around, half expecting to see sand creatures or crystals burst through the walls.

"I asked you a question."

"And why should I tell you anything? You've taken me and my team. That doesn't score you any points," Zurah said. *But I'm guessing you don't know much either. Or else you would know we didn't come here with a ship.*

Jaks let out another whistle, and this time, Zurah's nightmare came true. Where a part of the wall had been patched, a faint glow appeared, followed by the tiny bud of a crystal.

Zurah stepped back instantly, assessing her options. Jaks appeared to be physically fit, and Zurah wasn't confident she would be able to gain the upper hand, especially with the pain that lingered in her chest. If she managed to subdue him and escape, Zurah had no idea where to go. She had seen enough people to doubt being able to find a place to hide before being spotted.

Feigning a posture of defeat, Zurah let her shoulders slump forward, and she sighed. "Look. I'm just the back-up pilot. A low-level tech who got pulled into an assignment I had no business being a part of. When we crashed, I was disoriented, and I've been trying to find the other members of my team ever since then." She shivered for good measure and crossed her arms, hugging them tightly to her chest. "And I'd like my suit back."

"Weapons? Supplies?"

"Don't know. Like I said, low-level tech," Zurah said, surprised at not having any pushback about her lie. "What about my suit?"

"What department?"

Crap. What would a low-level tech work at? Who would also be a back-up pilot? What was it that Mexa had talked about when he was a kid? "Hoppers. Low scrubbers and the like," Zurah said hastily. She wasn't sure that was really what Mexa had talked about. He had shared a few stories from when he was young but mainly had kept to himself. And if Zurah were being honest, she had only half listened to them. A tendril of grief wound around her heart, and she berated herself for not taking the time to truly listen to him.

Zurah held her breath, waiting to see if Jaks would buy her story. When all he did was frown, Zurah prayed she was in the clear. *For now, at least.* She hated playing games, but she was way past what she liked or didn't like. All she needed to focus on was staying alive. She had to find her suit and finish working on the codes to shut down the gates. And if she had to play a few games along the way in order to see her goals through, then so be it.

"Come on." Jaks motioned for Zurah to walk with him.

"Not to sound repetitive or anything, but what about my suit?"

He didn't stop to answer her question. "Your suit has been confiscated, but you won't need it here. At least as long as you cooperate."

Damn. Despite the planet's resemblance to a desert from Old Earth, the atmosphere was only thirteen percent oxygen, too far below what the human body required. With a real shiver of concern this time, Zurah hoped that whatever was maintaining the atmosphere in the tunnels wasn't about to quit anytime soon.

She glanced down the corridor, noting Jaks hadn't stopped. She briefly considered staying put to see what he would do. But doing so meant Zurah wasn't going to be able to figure out what had happened, where she was, or who these people were. She hurried after him, staying just a step behind so she could continue to use her SeeClear tech to scan the area.

The walls, floor, and ceiling were composed of metal, with exposed pipes and wiring. She let her SeeClear tech run, turning the data into a map. If Zurah was betting credits, she would have gambled she was walking through the interior of a ship. And not just any ship, but the infamous *Eagle's Nest*. Despite years of degradation and being stripped for parts, the mess was old tech. Really old.

That led her to believe Jaks and the others weren't what the emperor's team was after. Not if Finn was correct and their goal was to find tech in order to create supersoldiers. Nothing Zurah was seeing would fit that narrative. *Besides, if I'd been captured by the Shadow and their team, I'm sure I'd be strapped into some kind of restraining device and undergoing a rather unpleasant interrogation at this point.*

The tunnel they moved through had several intersections, but most of those tunnels that branched off were dark. Even with her enhanced vision, she wasn't able to get a clear picture of what might have been in those tunnels. Zurah couldn't help but wonder if the lights were turned off to conserve power or if there were darker secrets tucked away in the bowels of the ship.

Before long, the metal walls gave way to rock. The corridor led to a large cavern with walls that were a bizarre hybrid of metal and rock. Its thick struts were exposed at random intervals among the rocky ceiling. The intel from the SeeClear programs took what Zurah could see of the metal and extrapolated from there, pulling the images of the artificial infrastructure and matching it with the schematics from the *Eagle's Nest*. Zurah wondered if this had once been a generously sized cargo hold. *But how could it have become fused with the rock?*

Zurah's shoulder jerked as she inadvertently bumped into someone. She jumped to the side, her first instinct to protect herself. But when no one came rushing at her, she realized she had been so intent on the composition of the cavern, she hadn't noticed the handful of people working and had stopped paying attention to where she was going. All of the individuals were dressed in well-worn, patched jumpsuits that matched Jaks's. Even the containers several of them were carrying appeared to be an odd assortment of patched materials.

"Clear the room," Jaks ordered.

Everyone stopped and turned to stare but quickly averted their eyes.

"Now."

Containers were hastily laid down, and everyone scampered out of sight. Jaks turned to face Zurah then tilted his head back. She followed his gaze but wasn't sure what he was looking at.

"Why are you here?" he asked at last.

Lies are best when wrapped up in the truth. "We were scouting."

"For?"

Zurah shrugged. "I wasn't cleared for that information. When the cap says jump, you jump."

He stopped gazing at the ceiling and stared at her. "And why don't I believe that?"

"Believe it or not. We were scouting. Everything went wrong, and here I am. Which is where exactly?"

Jaks's gaze was intense, and Zurah looked away, trying not to blush and to act casual. "The *Eagle's Nest.*"

"The what?" she asked, feigning ignorance.

His eyes narrowed, then a devilish grin spread across his face. "The *Eagle's Nest.* Don't tell me you haven't a clue as to what it is."

"And what if I do? So what? Some long-lost ship? Who cares?"

There was a faint look of uncertainty in his eyes before it vanished. "No glorious treasure hunt? No hoping for a bit of fame for finding it?"

A few different responses sprang to mind, but Zurah decided to settle on a part of the truth. She would do what it took to find the others, but in the meantime, she would gather some of the information they had been looking for.

"Look, I won't lie," Zurah said. "Maybe I overheard my cap talking about what it would mean if we found the ship. But what good is it? A museum piece? I hate to break it to you, but in three hundred years, we've come a long way. Your tech wouldn't even be compatible with what we've got, nor are we hurting for resources."

"No doubt," Jaks dryly commented. "But something tells me there's a lot more to your story." He whistled one long, low pitch.

Zurah heard a distinct crack from above. She glanced up then paled as another piece of crystal poked through the ceiling. This wasn't a small piece of crystal that might fit in the palm of a hand, though. The fractured tip of the crystal was roughly the size of the rover.

Without thinking, Zurah moved. Intel or not, she wasn't going to wait around for the crystal to entrap her again. Racing toward the corridor they had come through—the only exit she had seen—she was almost there when a hand closed around her arm and dragged her back into the middle of the chamber.

"Who are you?" Jaks growled. "You are clearly flesh, but running is what *they* do." He glanced up at the crystals, which continued to emerge. "We know their abilities have grown, and if they're mimicking flesh good enough to fool our sensors…" His grip tightened on her arm, making Zurah wince. "Who are you?"

"I'm nobody," Zurah said, trying to get out of his grasp. "Just a low-level tech." She reached around with her free arm and tried to pry his fingers away. "Let me go!"

His eyes darkened as he regarded her. "I don't think so. I want the truth. Why did you just try and run?" He grabbed her jaw and forced her to look up at the crystal. "What is that to you?"

The memory of being trapped by the cryrot in the medical bay reared up with such clarity, for a moment, Zurah wasn't sure if she was back there, and everything else had been some type of fever dream. Either way,

Zurah wasn't going to be taken by the cryrot or any of its allies again.

Zurah tried to twist her lower body to the side, to kick at Jaks's knee, hoping to strike hard enough to make him let go. But he held on while stepping to the side. Without hesitation, Zurah changed tactics and reached up to grab his ear, pulling as hard as she could. The maneuver did the trick. Jaks's grip loosened, and with a well-placed kick to the groin, Zurah was able to get free. Not wasting a moment, she ran into the corridor. Her only thought was to make it far enough to find one of the darkened corridors and hide.

The moment of freedom didn't last long. Jaks was right behind her, and he tackled her, wrestling her down to the ground. Zurah slapped her hands against his ears, and when that didn't help, she tried to push her thumbs into his eyes. But Jaks grabbed her wrists and pinned them to the ground above her head, the rest of his body a heavy weight on top of hers.

"Who are you? You've got remarkable restraint if you're one of them. Those spineless cowards would have tried to shift by now. Yet you remain flesh."

Clara stepped out of the shadows. "Now, we try it my way." She aimed her gun at Zurah's head as Jaks moved off to the side. "Who are you?"

"Winters, Zurah Winters," Zurah gasped. "That's the truth."

"And what are you doing here?" Clara asked. "What are you looking for?"

Zurah's eyes went wide with fear, and she wasn't sure how to answer. *I have to stay alive, so truth or no truth?* She made a split-second decision. "I'm here with my team. We were looking for the ship. But we were attacked by the sand. I don't know how that was possible, and I don't know what happened to my team."

"And what do you want with the ship?" Clara pressed.

Sometimes, you have to bet the lot. "We were helping Commander Angelina Adeyemi, second-in-command of the *Eagle's Nest*, figure out what happened to her ship and crew."

Clara's eyes widened, then her expression shifted into one of frustration. "That's a lie. That bitch is dead," Clara snapped. She crouched down next to Zurah and pressed the gun to her temple. "Tell me the truth. Who sent you here? What are you really looking for?"

"No, it's not a lie," Zurah said, focusing on Clara. "I swear. Angelina is alive. She survived in the escape pod. She gave me a message to pass on to an Isla." Zurah prayed they would believe her. Her instinct told her to keep quiet about Finn's true reason for coming here and trying to find an in through Angelina's information was the smart route to take.

Clara glanced at Jaks. "She's got to be dead. There's no way..."

"How do you know the name Isla?" Jaks asked.

"Only from a message Angelina asked me to pass on," Zurah replied.

"There's no way you could have that intel," Jaks said.

"It's a trick," Clara growled. "We should kill her and be done with this. They could have sent her as a decoy. Trick us into trusting her."

"I don't believe so. Those records were purged on the Eleventh Eve, after the Great Assault."

"It's a distraction. They must know we're close to breaking through their defenses and finding their central nodes."

"No," Jaks said. "Stand down, Clara. Even if she is a distraction, we can use it to our advantage."

For a split second, Zurah didn't think Clara was going to follow orders. The gun's muzzle dug into her skin as Clara glared at her. "Damn the sand," Clara said and holstered her weapon.

"If what she says is true, then she needs to know," Jaks said.

"Well, I'm not going to be the one to tell her. You can," Clara said. "Like I said before"—she looked at Zurah—"*it's* your problem. My advice? Wring all the information you can from its flesh then throw what's left in the stock tank. The next cycle is approaching. You know my unit will stand behind you when the time comes."

Jaks stood and dusted himself off. "I'll consider the advice. For now, you'd better head back." He glanced at Zurah. "Get up."

Zurah didn't hesitate. *I need to become valuable and fast.* She played the one trump card she had. "Do you want off this planet? Do you want to see Old Earth? I can give that to you."

Jaks and Clara froze in their tracks.

"What did you just say?" Clara asked slowly.

"I can help you get back to Old Earth." Zurah swallowed hard, hoping her gamble would pay off.

7

Without saying a word, Jaks grabbed Zurah and pulled her with him down the corridor, Clara hot on their heels. They didn't have far to go before he turned off to the right at one of the intersections, and they plunged into darkness. Zurah's SeeClear tech adjusted instantly, revealing nothing new. The corridor was the same as the other, a strange patchwork of metal and rock.

"Don't ever say that again," Jaks said. "Got it?"

Despite the confusion and fear, Zurah was angry. "Don't touch me. Again," she growled.

"Then keep your mouth shut," Jaks replied.

"I'm telling you. Just throw her in the tanks. If the Elder Sons hear of this, we're all doomed. This can't get out," Clara said as she stood guard just behind the edge of darkness.

"And it might just be the leverage we need." Jaks's eyes had taken on a strange, unearthly glow as he regarded

Zurah. Her SeeClear tech threw up an alert, and as she absorbed the information, Zurah felt her chances of making it through this strange encounter shrink. Jaks's body had thrown off an unusual energy reading as they crossed into the darkness. Zurah's tech had recognized that energy signature. Inside of Jaks were pieces of the cryrot.

"I need the truth," he said softly. "Can you really take us to Earth?"

Zurah bit the inside of her cheek. Now that she had solid evidence of the cryrot or a similar entity, the decision to stay on this side of the gates was clear. No one could return. The energy readings Jaks was giving off were different enough that Zurah wasn't sure if the weapons or inoculations would work. The risk was simply too high. What she needed was a believable lie. From the questions they'd already asked, lying about where she'd come from would be a dead giveaway.

"We were slated to return, yes," Zurah said, nicely sidestepping a solid yes or no.

"And Earth, it's still there. Humanity is still… alive?"

The question wasn't quite what she expected, but she nodded again.

"In the flesh? Not… anything else?" he pressed.

"Old Earth is there. And humanity has spread throughout the known worlds." Zurah wasn't sure how to take his questions concerning the flesh. *Could there be a chance they don't want to see the cryrot advance? Or are they asking so they can help it spread?*

"Thompson," a voice cut through the exchange.

Clara grabbed a handheld receiver attached to her shoulder and replied. "Here, sir."

"You're wanted at the Watch Tower."

"Understood. I'm currently finishing up—"

Jaks hissed and shook his head.

"Never mind. I'm headed your way. Thompson out." She whirled around, her eyes carrying the same unnatural glow as Jaks's.

Zurah ran a quick scan and captured the subtle differences in energy signatures between the two.

"You shouldn't do this on your own. We don't know what she's capable of. Let me call in and find a—"

"No. You go. We don't need to raise any suspicions. There's enough unrest and rumors flying around as it is. And you'll be able to hear if the Elder Sons start anything. Let me know before we get caught with our pants down."

Clara's expression clearly stated she wasn't happy. But she didn't argue. "Do whatever you need to do, but make it quick. Word of the flesh will spread. The Old Mother might dote on her two Hands, but we know how they spy for the Elder Sons." She stepped up to Jaks and squeezed his arm. "But if you need us, just signal. You know we're ready."

"Thank you," Jaks replied softly. "Hopefully, it won't come to that. Not yet, at least. Go. They'll be wondering where you are."

Clara nodded, spun around, and left.

"Now, what do I do with you?" Jaks mused.

"Give me my suit and let me go?" Zurah asked.

Jaks wasn't amused. So Zurah tried again. "What do *you* want?"

For a brief moment, the soft glow of his eyes disappeared as he looked away. But when he looked back, his eyes were ablaze. "I want to survive. I want to see humanity survive."

His response wasn't the clarification Zurah was hoping for. There were too many different ways she could interpret his answer.

"In the flesh? Or as the cryrot?" she asked. Whatever happened next was intel. She opened a line to the probes and started recording. If she didn't survive, at least Objer would receive the information. Then it would be up to wiser individuals to decide what to do.

"The cryrot?" Jaks asked. "What is that?"

A feint or true ignorance? "What's inside you," Zurah replied.

The more subtle facial features were lost in the dark, even with her enhanced vision, and Zurah couldn't decipher the strange look he gave her.

"Come with me," he said then turned.

Zurah glanced over her shoulder toward the softly lit corridor. *I could still make a run for it. Find someone else to bargain with.* Her instinct told her that option was foolish. She'd already found someone to negotiate with, and judging from Jaks's conversation with Clara, whatever was left of the *Eagle's Nest* was already in a precarious political state. Clenching her teeth until her jaws ached, Zurah made her choice.

Jaks hadn't waited for her, and Zurah had to jog a few steps to catch up. "Where are we going?"

"Just follow, quietly."

"Fine," she muttered. Zurah double-checked her connection to the probes. The signal had weakened but not enough to cut off communication. She tried to triangulate her position again and was perplexed when another error message appeared. If the connection with one or more of the probes had been severely hampered, Zurah could have understood the error message. But there was enough of a signal that the updates from her SeeClear tech were still transmitting and being received, and with those still operating, the probes should've been able to locate her position. It was as if the programs were being selective about what they were doing.

Not possible. Something else has to be at play here. Logic dictated a type of security barrier. Considering Zurah's ability to breathe without the aid of her suit, the underground complex had to be protected. And not only environmentally but on matters of security. Clearly, Jaks and the others were afraid of the sand creatures. *If that's the case, then there are computer systems. And systems I can hack.*

The corridor gradually grew smaller and consisted of only rock. The edges were jagged, and in a few places, Zurah had to turn sideways to pass safely. Her unease grew as she spotted small glowing pockets of crystals scattered throughout the passageway. In a few places, she even stepped over the clusters. The colors the crystal emitted were varied, with blues, greens, and purples. Each crystal emitted a slightly different energy signature, which made Zurah question all of the work the scientists and medical teams had done. *If there are endless variations of cryrot, how are we supposed to protect ourselves?*

Jaks came to an abrupt stop, and Zurah narrowly missed running into him. Stepping to the side, she watched as he pressed his hand against the rock wall. She was intrigued and alarmed as Jaks's hand appeared to actually *sink* into the rock. The rock rippled outward, revealing a solid sheet of gleaming crystal underneath its surface. When he pulled his hand back, a door appeared, and without hesitation, he pulled it open and slipped inside.

Zurah peeked through the doorway, and the wall opposite the door had numerous nooks and crannies crammed full of various objects. To the right, she saw the edge of a bed, and to her left was a small table.

"Come in before someone sees you," Jaks said.

Zurah stepped inside, and Jaks quickly shut the door. Alarmed, she glanced behind her and was dismayed to discover that the door—whatever it truly was—melted into the wall. The crystal faded, and the illusion of the rock wall appeared.

"We'll be safe here for now. The bunks are supposed to be private."

"Bunks?" Zurah asked. "Like a hab-unit?"

Jaks threw her a quizzical look. "Bunks. As in where you live," he replied as if talking to a child.

She rolled her eyes and ignored him, turning her attention to the various objects tucked throughout the room. Several of the objects were metal, and judging from their appearance, scrap metal had been twisted and turned into something new. Zurah spied a few pieces of broken crystal—she stayed away from those—and took interest in one of the larger crannies. Three books were stacked on top of each other, and she was tempted to pick one up. But judging from the covers, the books were in critical condition, and she was afraid the paper might crumble into dust if she did. Instead, she continued her inspection and saw something she'd only seen in museums: an old still photograph.

That's got to be worth a lifetime of credits. She leaned in and studied the picture. The color had been leached out over time, and the edges were rough. The upper-left corner had what she thought looked like mold, and the background was hard to discern. Zurah thought she saw a stand of trees in the back, and in the center stood three young men. Their arms were draped over each other, and wide grins of pure excitement lit up the picture.

"My great-great-great… well, a lot of them, was one of the bridge scientists on the *Eagle's Nest*."

Zurah refused to react, waiting for the punch line. She had no doubt this information was going to come at a price. Until she knew otherwise, she had to act as if she were in hostile territory. And no one allowed their enemies a glimpse into their life without doing so with a specific purpose in mind.

"Dr. Aaron Robert Reed. The one in the middle. He was fifty-seven when the *Eagle's Nest* started their mission."

"Why the old photograph?" Zurah couldn't help but ask. "Even back then, this was ancient tech."

Jaks shrugged. "Don't know. The man to the left was Dr. James Paters. The story is he was a historian. Maybe the photo was his idea."

Without missing a beat, Zurah asked, "And the crystals? What do they represent?"

There was a sharp inhale of breath. "Reminders of why we fight."

"Fight what?" Zurah turned to face him.

Despite the brightly lit room, Jaks's eyes glowed with the unnatural light of the crystals. "To survive."

Putting space between them, she moved over to the table. "Against what?"

"You tell me." Jaks leaned up against the wall as he stared at her.

I need to channel my inner Finn, Zurah half joked with herself. *If I was Finn and he was me. What would she tell me? The truth?* Zurah snorted at the thought then quickly composed herself.

"How do I find the rest of my team?" she asked. *Completely sidestepping is totally a Finn move.*

"By providing the information I need to know," Jaks replied. "You help me, and I'll help you."

Heard that before, Zurah thought sourly. *But I'll bite.* "And how can I help you?"

Jaks pushed off the wall and sat down on the edge of the bed. "By telling me exactly what you're doing here and what has happened to Earth. To humanity."

Zurah took a deep breath and considered tiptoeing around her answers again. But she was running out of time. She needed to finish setting up the codes to shut down the gates. Yet having confirmation about the cryrot meant she also needed to make sure no one learned about the rendezvous time frame, especially after listening to Jaks and Clara's conversation. She had to understand their intentions and what was at play, or else she might inadvertently trigger a full-on attack—the very thing she had hoped to stop.

"I'm a part of a team which was assigned to come through the gates. Angelina wanted to know what happened to the *Eagle's Nest*, and the others were tasked with evaluating the threat from the cryrot," Zurah said. "When we encountered… and dealt with the cryrot, we realized what it truly is—that the cryrot was out to wreak destruction and death across the known worlds. Something we won't allow to happen. *I* won't let that happen."

Jaks tensed but didn't make a move. "And this cryrot? What do you think it is exactly?"

"It killed several of our people," Zurah replied. "And it's threatened the known worlds. What more do you need to know?"

Jaks pursed his lips and stared at her. "Killed."

"Yes. The cryrot attempted to take over several individuals and manipulate…" She paused, unsure how to phrase it. "Take over the bodies of others. Making them do what the cryrot wanted."

Jaks stood and started pacing. "By force?"

"Yes."

"What else?"

"No, now, it's your turn. Are you or are you not a part of the cryrot? You certainly seem to have a cozy relationship with these crystals."

"All I can tell you is that our relationship with what you consider a crystal has been nothing but beneficial. I know of no instances of individuals saying they've been controlled or killed due to our relationship."

"And the sand? Why did it take the rest of my team?"

Jaks signed in frustration. "That damned sand."

"Excuse me?"

"Nothing," he said. "The sand… It's complicated. There are a handful of theories, but no one has settled on one singular idea. We know it's dangerous, which is why after the Great Assault, the survivors broke into the bedrock underneath the sand and crafted a series of different places they could hide and protect. We periodically move from one location to the other, trying to keep the sands from finding us."

"I think you're going to have to start from the beginning," Zurah said. "What is the Great Assault? Or the Old Mother, for that matter?"

"It would appear that the two of us need what the other knows. But I'm already taking a big risk by bringing you here. I need assurances that you'll do as I tell you," Jaks said.

"And I need assurances that the cryrot won't become a threat to the known worlds," Zurah replied. "Look, this isn't going to get us anywhere. I don't trust you, and you don't trust me. But *if* you're the enemy of my enemy, then we have something in common. So what are you? Are you working for or with the cryrot?"

"I'm not exactly sure what you're referring to but—"

"Lieutenant Reed, you're wanted in command."

Zurah glanced up to figure out where the voice had come from and noted a small box positioned above the door. *Damn. Should've seen that before.* Running a quick scan, she didn't detect any other energy signatures or fluctuations.

"I'm in the middle of working on—"

"This isn't a request. The Elder Sons have pulled your name."

Jaks paled. "Understood." He moved to the bed, reached underneath, and pulled out a small crate. He pried off the top and pulled out a pristine-looking uniform. With care, he laid it out on the bed then started to pull off his jumpsuit. Immediately embarrassed, Zurah averted her gaze, but she couldn't help but glance over as the jumpsuit fell from his shoulders. His back was covered in scars of various sizes. Some of the tissue appeared to be red and angry, while other areas looked puckered and hardened with age. She looked away while he finished getting dressed, her mind moving through several gruesome scenarios to explain the scars.

When Jaks finished, he sat down on the edge of the bed and pulled out a pair of knee-high boots. Zurah instantly recognized what he was wearing.

"Really?" she asked. "You still have one of the original uniforms?"

Jaks jerked his jaw in the direction of the photograph. "It was his. All direct descendants have one. It's the one thing no one has tried to turn into scrap."

"Then why are you putting it on?" Zurah asked, an ominous feeling creeping through her.

"When you're summoned by the Elder Sons, you are required to present not only yourself but your family. I'm the only direct descendant left in the Reed line, so I wear the uniform."

There was no hint of emotion as Jaks confessed this intimate detail. The words were spoken as simply another fact. Zurah felt an immediate connection with him, even though she didn't want to. The more personal he became, the harder it would be for her to manipulate him. *No wonder Finn keeps everyone at arms' length.*

Once he had pulled on his boots and tucked the pant legs inside, he stood. Zurah had to admit, the uniform looked good on him. *Stop.*

He appeared to hesitate, as if conflicting ideas were weighing heavily upon him. "I don't know why I've been summoned. It happens from time to time, and we've had a lot of activity along the southern rim. The Elder Sons could simply want an update in person. Or they could already know about you and want to catch me in a lie about why I didn't immediately contact them."

"But it's complicated," Zurah said. "I get it."

"Do you?" Jaks asked, his eyes searching her face. "Because right now, I've got two options. And I don't like either one. First, I could take you with me. Present you to the Elder Sons, gain some good grace with them, and maybe avoid execution. But then I'll have given them the upper hand, and everything I've sacrificed would be for nothing. Or I could—"

"Leave me here and hope I don't make a peep," Zurah finished. "Like I said, I get it. But—" She stepped forward and crossed her arms across her chest. "Tell me why I should put my faith in you. It sounds like these Elder Sons are the ones in charge. That they're the ones I should be talking to."

Jaks bent down and pulled out one last crate from beneath the bed. Setting it on the table, he opened the lid and pulled out an officer's hat. Once he had it settled on his head, he reached into the crate one last time. This time, he pulled out a small crystal. A faint glow of purple illuminated it from within, and Jaks cradled it in his hands like it was the most precious object in the world. Turning, he said softly, "Because if the Elder Sons figure out who you are and what you represent, then I can guarantee you all hell will break loose. Not only here but back on Earth and wherever else humanity has spread to." Jaks looked up and held the crystal out for Zurah.

She took a step back and shook her head. "I've already dealt with the cryrot once. I don't care to do it again."

"This isn't the cryrot," Jaks said. "At least, if I'm understanding you correctly, it isn't. Listen to it. Learn from it, and perhaps then, you'll understand. But if you can't, then run. Get away from here as fast as you can and go back to wherever you came from." He laid the crystal down on the bed, then he pulled out a very old handheld data pad and set it next to the crystal. "This holds a map of the area. We're currently within the eastern rim. Use it to get out. But at least promise me you won't tell anyone." He moved to the door. "Come here."

"Why?"

He huffed. "I don't have time to explain. Just come here."

Zurah couldn't explain why she complied, but she did.

Instead of grabbing her arm again, he held out his hand. "Let me have your hand. I'll give you access to this bunk."

"Will it—"

"Just trust me, please," Jaks said.

Something in his voice lowered Zurah's internal shields, and she placed her hand in his. He placed her hand against the wall then put his hand next to hers. The wall shimmered, revealing the disguised crystal, and a tremor of shared awareness ran through her. "If you need to return here for whatever reason, you have access."

Zurah was taken aback by what Jaks said, and she didn't get a chance to ask further questions as he simply opened the door and left.

8

"What the hell just happened?" Zurah muttered, glancing down at the crystal. She had no intention of touching the thing. And she did not want to stay there. Picking up the tablet, she found the power switch. The device took over a minute to boot up, and when it did, there was a chime and the logo of a company Zurah didn't recognize. *No doubt from some long-ago human company which was probably gobbled up by the Goldsmith Consortium.*

The menu was basic and easy to navigate, and it didn't take her long to find the map Jaks had talked about. She zoomed out until the tablet's screen held the entire schematic, then she blinked to take a picture with her SeeClear tech. Adding the map to what her tech had started putting together created a clear picture of the eastern rim. The area was a honeycomb of corridors, and for a split second, Zurah's vision swam until the SeeClear tech oriented the map to her location. She pinned Jaks's room for reference and added another for where she had woken up. As Zurah studied the map, she had serious doubts about being able to find an exit, until she realized there were symbols embedded in the map. Understanding the symbols wasn't a hard code to crack, and once she did, Zurah highlighted each little triangle indicating an exit.

There were three possibilities. Each one was roughly the same distance from her current location. Zurah settled on one of them then mapped backup routes to the other two just in case. Decision made, she reached for the door. Then she hesitated. Turning back around, she took another look at the discarded jumpsuit. In a closed system, Zurah was sure everyone would know everyone, and dressed as she was, Zurah would stand out like a sore thumb. She grabbed the jumpsuit, briefly wrinkling her nose at the smell, but pulled it on. She undid her braid, used her fingers to comb through her hair, then pulled it back into a ponytail at the base of her neck, letting a few strands hang in front of her face. As disguises went, it was one of her worst. As long as she stayed quiet, kept her head down, and moved like she belonged, Zurah might be able to buy enough time to make it to one of the exits. Plus, she had her SeeClear tech. Turning on the thermal overlays helped calm her nerves. *At least I'll have a heads-up if someone is approaching.*

Feeling as prepared as she could be, Zurah touched the wall and slipped out of the room. But she hesitated, spun around, and hurried back. She grabbed the first thing she spotted, the blanket off the bed, and ripped off a strip, which she wrapped around the crystal.

Thankfully, it was small enough to fit in one of her pockets. Even if she had no interest in using it as Jaks had suggested, perhaps it would provide information down the line.

Satisfied, Zurah slipped out of the room and headed to the left. There was a significant amount of walking to do in order to reach the nearest exit, and she quickened her pace but tried not to appear too much in a hurry. The pain in her chest hadn't eased up, and each breath she took hurt. *If I had my suit, I could dose myself.* But not having that option, she forced herself to push the small bursts of pain to the back of her mind, focusing on her goal of getting out.

Crystals appeared at random, in various sizes and shapes. With each cluster she passed, her anxiety grew, as did the questions. *Has the crew of the* Eagle's Nest *found a way to coexist with the cryrot?* Zurah found that hard to believe after witnessing what had happened on Objer and the cryrot's threats. Even without knowing Jaks, she was confident he hadn't been under the influence of the cryrot. *Perhaps they've found a way to subdue it, make it bend to their will?* She remembered how the crystals had responded to Jaks's whistling.

Briefly, she considered figuring out how he had done that and if there could be potential applications in helping fight against the cryrot. But as soon as she entertained the idea, she dismissed it. Her experience told her that the cryrot wasn't something she wanted to mess with. If it tried to attack again, it needed to be destroyed. Period. *I wish I still had my weapon, but if I have to, I'll just start screaming.* It was a grim thought, but she chuckled to herself.

A red dot appeared on the map, indicating Zurah was about to pass someone. She kept her eyes down and her footfalls steady as she walked right past. The other individual didn't even glance her way or slow down. Once the red dot disappeared, Zurah let out a sigh of relief. The next two encounters passed the same way. *Maybe I'll make it through this.* She did note one difference between herself and the others—they were carrying crates.

Tucked back in one of the darkened offshoots was a small stack of crates. After double-checking to make sure no one was around, she took the one on top—it was surprisingly light—and continued on. Within seconds, a cluster of red dots appeared as she turned the next corner. Zurah slowed down, trying to assess the situation without drawing suspicion.

A line of people stretched out from a metal grid that had been placed in the corridor. As she looked past the gridwork, she spotted another line of individuals, and on the other side of the grid were two men who carried themselves like IGJ goons. *Great. Not what I needed. Of course they'd have their own form of the IGJ or policing system down here.* She double-checked the map and decided her best option was to head for one of the other exits.

Trying to stay within the shadows, Zurah turned around and slipped back around the corner. After a few more turns, she found herself walking through another series of the darkened passageways. Taking advantage of the moment, she set the crate down and studied the map again. Dropping a new pin where the checkpoint was located, she evaluated her options and decided to stick with the plan of heading toward a different exit.

Trying to work around the security would take too much time. And too much time wandering around dramatically increased the odds of being discovered.

Zurah rolled her shoulders and stretched, trying to ascertain if the pain in her chest was more muscle than internal. When the movement forced a cough, she knew without a doubt the problem was internal. *If I pass anything that looks like a med kit or medical center, I'll see if I can figure something out. If not…* Her thought tapered off, as she didn't want to consider the worst-case scenario. Picking up the crate once more, she got back on task.

"Hey," a voice called out.

Zurah was fairly certain the voice had to be speaking to her as there wasn't anyone else around. But she didn't stop walking.

"Hey, you, with the mec box," the voice said. The individual had definitely gained on her, and while Zurah didn't want to stop and engage, she felt there was no choice.

Zurah stopped and turned, a tired smile on her face. "Sorry, been on my feet a while."

"Where are you headed?" a middle-aged man half walked, half jogged up to her. His suit was the same as everyone else's she'd seen, a mismatched patchwork of repairs. He gave her and the crate the once over. "Mec route's north, not east."

Inwardly, Zurah winced. She shrugged. "Just had a reroute order."

The man leaned forward, and Zurah's heart raced. "Don't recognize you. What crew you on?"

"Jaks," Zurah said without thinking.

"That bastard," the man muttered. "Always thinking he can take whatever goods he needs without clearing it. You listen to me, and you listen good," the man continued as he grabbed for Zurah's crate.

She pulled back and shook her head.

He huffed in frustration. "Don't get messed up in his claptrap. There ain't no way none of us are going to win this war. The Sons have got the idea. We make a deal, and we survive."

When Zurah didn't reply either way, the man stalked off, muttering to himself.

War? War with who? The sand or the cryrot? Or the emperor's team or… There were too many possibilities. Too many variables at this point. When the man turned a corner, Zurah whispered to herself, "What's my objective?"

She used the simple yet effective question when a job went south or she found herself presented with too many options. "Find a way out. Get the coding delivered to the probes to shut down the gates." Then, without thinking, she added, "Rescue the others."

The need to save the others weighed on her, wanting to be her main objective. Yet in the short time she had been stuck in the corridors, in her heart, Zurah knew that saving the others wasn't something she should waste precious time on. Once the codes were delivered, and *if* she survived, then she would try to find the others. But something was brewing with the descendants of the *Eagle's Nest*, something that her instinct told her spelled disaster if the issue was transferred to the known worlds, let alone the other threats of the cryrot and the emperor's crazed plans. "I need to ensure the gates are destroyed." Completing that part of her mission was the one thing she could do to protect everyone.

This had been Finn's assignment for Zurah all along—the one thing she needed to stay focused on. Zurah had seen enough to know that something of the cryrot was here on this world, interacting with these people. Not only that, but the sand creatures were now another threat. And so far, Zurah hadn't spotted any type of advanced tech the emperor would be interested in, unless that tech *was* the cryrot and the sand creatures. That idea was very unsettling.

Nothing of this world could get through the gates. She couldn't gamble on the idea that the teams on Objer would be able to stop an assault. Her thoughts only reaffirmed her early choices. The only thing she had to do was destroy the gates and prevent anything from spreading to the known worlds.

As she considered her best options to accomplish her objective, Zurah realized she had a major flaw in her plan. *You fool, you don't have a suit. Do you really think there's going to be extra ones just waiting for you at the exit?* When she slipped out of Jaks's room, she hadn't even considered this.

Zurah had grown up in a time when extra suits were always readily available. The extras might not be the best make and model, but suits were considered emergency gear. Ships, space stations, hubs, and the like all carried extra suits. The security codes and insurance companies mandated that extra suits be available for the maximum capacity of each. Of course, there wasn't a law against charging a fee for the use of these suits—governments and corporations always found the loopholes they could exploit—but the suits were always there.

But judging from the heavily patched jumpsuits she had seen, Zurah doubted there was going to be extra equipment lying around the *Eagle's Nest*. Especially not something as valuable as a suit.

"Dammit," she muttered. Darting into another unused tunnel, she looked for a place to hunker down and rethink the plan.

Without a suit, heading for the exits was a moot point. And if she was able to find a console or workstation, Zurah highly doubted she would be able to blend in like she had on Objer. Not to mention the systems would be old tech. Zurah knew she was good, but without a frame of reference for how the tech's systems operated, she would waste too much time trying to understand the operating system and be spotted before she was able to get started on a hack.

A second wave of foolishness washed over her. She brought up the SeeClear menu and pinged her suit. Using the information, she extrapolated its location and added a new pin in the map. Taking a deep breath, she reminded herself this was like any other job. Objectives changed when the situation called for it. There had been more than one job where Zurah had needed to quickly change tactics in order to meet the new parameters. She had a location to head toward, and if she looked like she belonged, the chances of being noticed went down.

It wasn't long before there were red dots all around her, and the corridors branching off the main one were lit and full of activity. Most individuals were moving supplies, a handful were standing and talking with each other, and a few had to be some type of security. Those individuals were standing next to various doors or corridors, and Zurah hoped the suit's location wasn't going to be in one of those locations.

The pin identifying the suit crept closer, and when she was a few meters away from its location, her heart sank. She needed to turn to the left, but there was a security guard standing in the way. Slowing down, she considered her options. In any other job, Zurah would play the new-employee card and feign ignorance. Or if she knew the name of a target, she would've tried to bluff her way through. With neither of those options, Zurah wasn't sure which angle to take to get past the guard. She wondered if the suit was worth it. *I have to have something I can work with, though. I need to make sure no one can get to the gates.*

A plan came to mind, and Zurah walked up to the guard, at first trying to move past him like she belonged.

The guard, a tall, broad-shouldered woman with a square jaw and a look of no nonsense, stepped in her way. "This area is restricted."

"Sorry, I was recently transferred to this crew and route."

"Declare yourself, then."

Zurah was ready to give one of her normal excuses about misplacing a form of identification when a wave of calm washed through her. A burst of warmth blossomed in her hip pocket where she had tucked the crystal. The sensation spread through her body and raced up her spine. Her head tingled, and the warmth wrapped around her skull, until the unusual feeling settled in both eyes.

"Remind the pit boss to check the schedules," the guard said as she stepped to the side.

Zurah ducked her head in a sign of deference and hurried past the guard, not questioning her stroke of luck. *I can worry about it when I'm out of here and safe. Then I'll freak out.* The room wasn't completely cleared, with a handful of rock pillars scattered through the space. Workstations dotted the area, and as far as Zurah could see, someone was hunkered down over a table toward the back of the room.

She scanned the room and saw her suit lying across one of the tables. She walked over and laid the crate down on the table, next to her suit. She balled it up, tucking it under her arm. Because she didn't see any other crates, Zurah didn't think leaving with the crate would look right. But she couldn't just walk out of there with the suit. Taking another look around the room, Zurah decided she needed a distraction.

The workstation was metal with an old screen embedded on the left side. The casing of the screen angled up from the table, and an old keyboard was below it. Zurah tapped one of the keys, and the screen came to life. Scanning the menu, she chose settings and started changing anything and everything she could. Before long, an error message appeared. Not quite what she was going for. Zurah tried again, searching for something that she could hack and set off an alarm.

Feeling the edge of panic creep in, she glanced up.

She'd been stationary for too long. Even though the worker was still hunched over their station, the chances of them looking up and seeing her were increasing with every second she lingered there. As she was about to move to another workstation, one she felt was better hidden from the worker's view, the odd sensation of warmth flooded her body again.

There weren't any words, no discernible vocalizations that could be translated, but Zurah knew what she was being guided to do. She touched her hand to the screen and watched as her fingertips glowed with an unearthly purple. The light seeped into the screen, moving through it like a worm, wiggling across the monitor. Error messages and coding text started to pop up, building on top of each other until Zurah couldn't see anything but the messages.

Then the clear image of Zurah exiting the room popped into her head, and she heeded the warning. As she passed the guard, a warning klaxon sounded, and the guard turned and rushed into the room. A handful of individuals in the area went to investigate as well, while the others all started rushing to and fro. Taking advantage of the chaos, Zurah hurried back the way she'd come.

"There she is," a familiar voice called out. "She's one of his."

Zurah glanced over her shoulder to see the man who'd tried to take the crate. He was pointing right at her, and standing next to him was the tallest individual she had ever seen. The person was bone thin, with elongated features. Their skin was pale, almost to the point of being translucent. Even at the distance they were at, Zurah could see their eyes were pure white, as if they had been blinded. Their appearance chilled Zurah to the bone. She turned and ran.

A shrill whistle filled the corridor, and crystals exploded through the walls. One of the crystals caught her foot, tripping her. The suit tumbled from her hands, and as she tried to reach for it, a cluster of crystals ripped through it.

"Dammit!" she yelled and scrambled back. Bracing through the pain, Zurah pulled herself back to her feet. Deciding to take the chance, she bent down and grabbed the edge of the suit, wincing as the sharpened edge of the crystals tore through what was supposed to have been indestructible. With the remains of the suit clutched to her chest, Zurah ran. Taking a hard right, she ducked into the darkness, and the whistling stopped for a moment. Then three sharp bursts of a piercing note filled the air all around her.

With no weapons or tech, Zurah felt helpless. All she could do was try to put as much distance as possible between herself and her pursuers. Racing through the dark, she abandoned the map, simply trying to find a place she might hide. The pain in her leg and chest finally grew unbearable, and Zurah collapsed in a heap of pain and fear. Shaking, she rolled over, trying to be as quiet as she could, and pushed herself into a small recessed part of the wall. Zurah attempted to calm her breathing, but each breath rattled and seemed to reverberate through the corridor.

Unable to face what was coming, she squeezed her

eyes shut, listening to the shouts ringing through the corridors. She braced for the hands to grab at her, to drag her out from her hiding spot. Instead, there was another shout of rage then a round of weapons fire. Zurah sucked in a breath, held it, and listened. The weapons fire didn't continue. Exhaling slowly, Zurah knew she needed to move. Forcing herself to crawl, she dug her fingers into the small bumps of the rocky floor, pulling herself forward millimeter by millimeter.

"I told you to not talk to anyone," a voice hissed.

Zurah glanced back, and to her relief, Jaks was jogging toward her. Even in the darkness, his eyes were bright and fierce.

"Come on." Without breaking his stride, he swooped down and picked her up.

Zurah whimpered as a fresh wave of pain rolled through her body, and she almost collapsed again, except Jaks held her steady. Without a second thought, he adjusted his grip and carried her. Despite her additional weight in his arms, Jaks moved quickly through the darkened tunnels. "We've got three minutes before Clara will be forced to close the doors. I don't know if we're going to make it in time."

In too much pain to respond, Zurah wrapped her arms around his neck to hold on. Each step he took was another jolt of pain through her body.

"Almost there. Hold on," he whispered and abruptly came to a stop. He backed up against the wall and awkwardly looked around the corner while continuing to hold on to Zurah. "I've got to set you down," he whispered. "I know you're hurt, but when I call out, you've got to come to me as fast as you can. Can you do that?"

Zurah didn't have any alternatives. She gritted her teeth and nodded.

As Jaks lowered her, he helped her find her balance by leaning up against the wall. Then, without any other direction, he rounded the corner.

"We've got a perimeter alert," Zurah heard Jaks announce. "I need access to the shields."

"Orders are to seal the tubes. No one in or out until we get clearance," a woman's voice answered.

"Check again. I've got clearance to do a sweep," Jaks replied.

"And as she said, our orders are to seal the tubes, until we hear from command—" There was the heavy sound of a body hitting the floor then the sounds of a scuffle. Zurah held her breath, waiting and hoping for Jaks to call out.

"Clara!" he hollered. "I need the tubes opened."

There was a burst of static, a garbled response, then a string of curses from Jaks before he bellowed, "Now!"

Zurah did her best. She turned the corner, hobbling as fast as she could. She barely missed tripping over the man and woman knocked out cold on the floor and started to move toward Jaks.

But he waved her past. "Go!" He was furiously working at pulling the metal casing off a keypad.

Zurah hobbled over to Jaks and helped yank off the cover. As it clattered to the floor, Zurah headed toward the other end of the room, and in seconds,

Jaks was once more at her side, all but scooping her up in his arms again. With his free hand, he grabbed his handheld receiver.

"We're clear. See you on the other side." He ripped the receiver off and tossed it to the side. The noise of something grinding came from behind them, and after Jaks had moved them forward a dozen or more steps, he stopped and turned around.

Pushing down from the ceiling was a thick bulkhead door slowly making its way to the floor, sealing off the corridor. As it hit the floor, the impact reverberated throughout the corridor, and the silence that followed was deafening. Without a word, Jaks turned them back around. The floor had started to angle upward, and it wasn't long until the air temperature started to warm.

"Hang on. Just a bit further. We've got a stash not too far up ahead, and I can treat those wounds," Jaks said.

Only through her sheer determination was Zurah able to stay conscious. Working to ignore the pain, she focused on the details around her. The rocky walls shifted from the darker undertones to lighter shades of browns and reds. More than once, grains of sand drifted down from the ceiling. The artificial lighting ended as a trickle of sunlight appeared ahead. Free of the tunnels, Zurah squinted against the glare until her SeeClear tech adjusted. The sand dunes stretched out all around them.

"It's not safe," Jaks said, "but right now, it's better than staying down there. We'll try and make it to the north second rim before sundown, but it'll be dicey. Hold on."

He gently let her slide down to the ground, and Zurah took a deep breath despite the pain. *If this is going to be the last thing I see, then so be it.* She glanced over at Jaks and couldn't help but wonder about the man. *Why did he help me escape? Does it even matter?* There were so many questions she wanted to ask, but she simply said, "Thank you."

Jaks glanced back at her, frowned, then started to dig in the sand. "It's here. I know it is." After a moment, he knelt beside her, an old emergency kit in his hands.

"It doesn't matter," she said, gently pushing it away. The pain with every breath was intensifying, and Zurah's vision was fading. "There's not enough oxygen in the atmosphere without a suit. Without suits, we're as good as dead."

"We aren't going to die," Jaks said. "I'll be fine, and so will you if you trust me."

Zurah gave him a quizzical look as he opened up the kit. Instead of the usual med supplies, he drew out a solitary container. The clear plastic let Zurah see what was inside—small pieces of crystal.

"Here. I know this is going to be unpleasant, but you need to breathe these in." He took off the lid and held the container under her nose.

Zurah pushed it away, the pain in her chest blossoming across her shoulders and her back. "No. I won't become one of them." As she tried to turn away from him, the crystal she had pocketed dug into her flesh. Confused, Zurah desperately hoped she hadn't done the wrong thing by taking the crystal Jaks had shown her in his bunk. She wanted to deny what had happened when she was able to get past the guard or create the distraction. And if taking the crystal had caused another corruption of her body like that of the cryrot, she wasn't going to compound the issue by taking more crystals. Even if it meant she was going to die. Her only hope was that Finn had left strict instructions for the team on Objer to destroy what they could if no one returned. She lay down, her vision coming and going as she struggled to breathe.

Jaks slid his hand under her neck and lifted her head. "They won't hurt you. You need another dose of the seeds."

Zurah turned her head away. "No. Just go. Let me die as a human. I won't become a mindless drone for the cryrot."

"Just take the damned things," Jaks growled. He shifted his body so Zurah's head was in his lap, and he grabbed the back of her head so she couldn't turn away. He shoved the container underneath her nose, tilting it so the crystals fell on her upper lip, tickling her skin.

The instant she felt their cool touch, Zurah tried to struggle, twist, and turn to get them off her. She held her breath for as long as she could, but in the end, the need for air was too overwhelming. The crystals tickled her nose and made her cough.

"See? Not too bad. They'll feel strange as they work their way into your lungs, but after that, you'll be good to go. You just need to breathe in a few more, then give it a few minutes and—"

Zurah tried to resist again, but no matter how hard she tried, she had to take the next breath of air. The crystals were cooling her airway, and she couldn't help but cry, waiting to hear the voices, to feel the effects of the crystals spreading through her body. She pictured Nissa waking up and listening to the message Zurah had recorded. *Did I tell Nissa I didn't care that she was my aunt? Did I tell her I was simply grateful for all she'd done for me?*

The cool sensation of the crystals spread through her chest, soothing the pain, but Zurah didn't want to feel relief. She braced for the voices, for the hum of the cryrot, trying to infect her mind and take over.

She saw Nissa standing next to the *HighTail Flyer*, a sly grin on her face as she waited for Zurah after offering her a job. When Zurah had climbed on board, Nissa had gently slapped Zurah's back in welcome. The physical touch had been jarring yet welcome at the same time.

Zurah's last wish was that Nissa would never see her as one of the cryrot's evil minions, that something would happen and she would die on this world instead of carrying out the cryrot's vision of death and destruction.

With one last breath, Zurah's vision went dark, and she stopped fighting. But the voices never came, nor did the hum of the cryrot. Instead, she took a deep, painless breath. She opened one eye then the other.

"Good grief, you're dramatic," Jaks muttered.

"How?" Zurah croaked.

Jaks sighed and looked up at the twin suns, squinting against their glare. "I don't know. Maybe one of the docs might know, but I doubt it. No one talks about it, how we've lost so much knowledge through the generations. All I know is that they work."

As the fog from her mind cleared, Zurah sat up and scooted away from Jaks. "This can't be possible."

He shrugged. "But it is."

She shook her head. "No, you don't understand. Whatever the crystals did, it shouldn't have worked. My immune system should have kicked in and resisted. At the very least, my breathing might have improved a little, but not a miraculous recovery like this."

"What do you mean?"

"It's complicated," she said and got to her feet. "How am I able to breathe? This is… incredible. But there's not enough oxygen in the atmosphere. I should be feeling the effects of hypoxia." She took a deep breath, cool air filling her nostrils and trailing down her trachea to fill her lungs. There was a decidedly sweet scent to the air now, none of the acrid heat and dust of the desert. A twinge of sorrow pierced her heart as she couldn't help but picture Dr. Ordotham and how if anyone would be able to understand what was happening, he would.

"All I know is that these seeds provide a type of air filtration system once they settle in your lungs. For most, the seeds won't need to be replenished for two to three weeks."

"Seeds?" Zurah questioned.

"I'll explain what I can, but we need to get moving. It'll take most of the day to reach the north second rim before sundown. And once the temperature drops, we'll freeze."

"And what about the sand creatures? What if they find us?" Zurah asked, eyeing the dunes.

Jaks reached into the pocket of his uniform and pulled out an oval object. The ring was metal, and in the center was another crystal. This one had a faint bluish hue. "With this, they shouldn't bother us. Too much interference." He bent down and picked up the tattered remains of her suit. "What was so important about this?"

Zurah took it, staring at the reminder of what her life had been only a handful of days ago. "I need some of the tech from my suit. Give me a few minutes." Stripping the suit of one of its screens and internal interfaces wasn't difficult. The parts had been designed for easy access and replacement in the case of emergencies.

She couldn't help but feel some disappointment at how easily the suit had ripped on the crystals, and she made a mental note to figure out where Finn had gotten them and make an official complaint if she ever returned to the known worlds.

"Can I use the container?" she asked.

Jaks shrugged and handed it over. With a few modifications—finding the container's material easy to manipulate—she created a rudimentary case for the screen and interface. Even though the suit hadn't held up, the battery and operating system of the screen had. Relieved to see there was still a little over eighty percent of the system's power, Zurah refreshed the link between it and her SeeClear tech.

"Are you good?" Jaks asked.

"Yup."

Zurah thought he was going to ask her a few more questions, but he turned and started walking. She wasn't going to complain about the silence. Zurah noted she was down to eleven hours before the gates were activated. Back-feeding her programs through the suit's processor exponentially sped up the process, and before long, everything was green. No red flags had been thrown up, and the blind with the melting codes was ready to go. She uploaded the finished version, tightened up her security protocols between the probes and her SeeClear tech, then wiped the program from the suit's screen. *If anything happens now, they'll have to kill me in order to get to my programs. And if that happens, then game over.*

The moment she'd finished installing the SeeClear tech, Zurah had made sure to activate the kill switch. If she died, or if someone tried to extract the tech, everything would be wiped.

Satisfied she had done all she could, Zurah knew it was now a waiting game. Even though the probes would send the data dump if she was dead, Zurah felt the need to stay alive and make sure it really went through. Curious, she brought up her connection with the probes. Now that she was above ground, Zurah was able to triangulate her position.

She was over eight kilometers from where the probes had last pinged her. Slowing down to put a little bit of distance between her and Jaks, she blinked to open a line of communication with all the probes. Then, on second thought, she tied one of the probes to her ID, having decided keeping one of the probes tied to her system would at least provide alerts if the sands started to shift.

A new thought struck her, and she decided to add one last safeguard to ensure the gates were destroyed. To all four probes, she uploaded simple message: *Destroy the gates. Do not come through.* With a little bit of hacking, she coded the message with Finn's ID. If, for some reason—although Zurah felt quite confident in her hacking abilities—one of the researchers was able to isolate and stop the blind, a direct order from Finn would hopefully ensure the teams went through with destroying the gates. Satisfied, Zurah ordered the last two probes to return to where the other two probes waited.

Mission complete, Zurah hurried to catch up with Jaks. "Do the crystals control you, or do you control the crystals?"

"And if they did? What would you do to them? Or to me?"

"I'd make sure you or whoever couldn't hurt anyone else," Zurah replied.

"Then no."

"That's not an answer," Zurah said. "I need to know what to expect. Am I going to start losing control? Will I hear the voices?"

"First, I know it isn't an answer, at least not one good enough for you," Jaks said, giving her a peculiar look. "But when we get to the—"

Zurah stopped. "I've heard the same line from two other people in the last couple of weeks. Either you tell me now, or I'm heading out on my own." The irony of traipsing around with another mysterious man searching for answers wasn't lost on her.

Jaks gave her an appraising look. "All right. First of all, they aren't crystals. I know they appear that way, but they're not crystals in the sense of what you might find on Earth. Their composition has similar qualities, but collectively, they're known as the Io."

9

"The what now? Are you trying to tell me they're… What?" Zurah asked.

"Tell me what you know about the *Eagle's Nest*," Jaks replied.

Zurah gritted her teeth, hating the whole answer-with-a-question routine. "Not much. Other than the ship disappeared, and it's one of the great unsolved mysteries for humanity."

Jaks was silent for a moment. "That man? In the photograph, Dr. Reed? My great-great-great… Well, it was his request to investigate this rogue planet that wasn't behaving as it should."

"Which led you to the gates, and ultimately here," Zurah added.

"The gates?"

"That's what we call them, how we were able to get here from Objer."

"Hmmm," Jaks mused. "So you really don't know what they are, then? I would have assumed humanity would have the tools to figure it out by now."

The dig would've stung more if Zurah was a scientist. "Do you know the original mission of the *Eagle's Nest*?"

That question made Jaks pause. Zurah couldn't help but wonder if he was scrambling for an answer or concocting a story to tell her.

"Asking that kind of question has severe consequences around here."

"Why?"

"Why do you want to know?" he countered.

Zurah shrugged, trying to downplay her curiosity. "Just curious, I guess. Everyone has their theories."

"And everyone has their secrets," Jaks commented dryly. "There are scattered pieces of information among several families. We've each held on to the truth as best we could, but we stay quiet on the matter. The Elder Sons have ensured people are too afraid to talk and put the pieces together."

"And…" Zurah prodded.

Jaks let out another sigh, more annoyed this time. "The Elder Sons maintain the story that Captain Ujthout was tasked by the Central Alliance of World Leaders to investigate a series of unusual energy readings that had been detected by a scout ship. My family, on the other hand, has maintained that the captain was given a completely different assignment. One that was classified. How much history do you know?"

"I'm a little rusty on ancient history. Fill me in."

"Ancient history?" Jaks commented as he turned to

give her a sour look. Then he snorted and continued walking. "When the *Eagle's Nest* was commissioned, there was a lot of unrest on Earth. The Central Alliance of World Leaders had steadily been losing control to the Emperor's Seat. The public opinion of the CAWL was declining and fast. There was a lot of talk about different projects to boost morale and the like, but the big talk was trying to beat the Emperor's Seat at the Great Expansion Race."

"Now, that sounds familiar," Zurah interrupted. "Wasn't there something about big colony grabs going on at the time? Different corporations and businesses trying to snatch up new colony opportunities?"

Zurah had a few fuzzy memories of studying that moment in history before she'd been abandoned. The Great Expansion Race had been a boon to humanity's influence and presence among the known worlds. Scientists and corporations all pushed each other in their competitive attitudes to revamp and develop new technology and new ways for humans to flourish on a wide variety of planets, ships, and stations.

"Yes. And the Emperor's Seat held several of those contracts. The CAWL was desperate and believed they had an ace up their sleeves. Whatever it was, that became the mission they tasked to Captain Ujthout. We know that his discovery was supposed to put the Emperor's Seat to shame and open up new areas of space. The rumors at the time were that it was some type of alien technology from a lost civilization. All of those original reports and documentation were lost after the revolt, but through memorization, my family has remembered and passed down the information of some of the original reports.

"Captain Ujthout had a definite set of coordinates he directed the *Eagle's Nest* to investigate. When they reached those coordinates, they came across what appeared to be an abandoned space station. Or that's what they first believed. But upon closer inspection, the research team concluded it was an unknown alien structure."

"The platforms," Zurah murmured softly enough that Jaks didn't notice. *That must be why there was a record of the ship and the crew.* "What happened?"

"There's a gap in our knowledge at that point. Dr. Reed had a few journals the family tried to preserve, but they've been lost. And what was remembered from the journals has become garbled information. What we do know is that it was the crew's first encounter with the Io. The *Eagle's Nest* spent three months researching the station, and from the information they gleaned, they found something unexpected. A rogue planet.

"Dr. Reed was the lead scientist on the bridge, and after a lot of debate between the command crew, he felt that investigating the planet would help provide answers. My grandfather told me that he remembered Dr. Reed writing in his journal that he hoped they would find the alien race on the planet. To be able to make first contact and unravel their technology. Anyway, the captain agreed and sent a party to the planet. But as far as we know, Commander Adeyemi was very vocal in her disagreement."

"And was that the argument which landed her in an escape pod?" Zurah asked.

"No. If my understanding of what happened is correct, that came later. The team went to the planet to investigate, but to their great disappointment, there were no living aliens, only strange rock formations. No signs of life at all—not even bacteria. The captain was not happy, and he recalled the team. And that's where our understanding goes blank. We don't know exactly what happened after that, only there were more teams eventually sent to the planet, and at some point, the *Eagle's Nest* moved from there to this world. Where the crew realized there were two different life-forms. The Io and the Kin."

"I can fill in a small piece of information, then," Zurah said. "That planet, it had to be Objer. And the ship must have gone through the gates."

"Seeing as that is where you've said you've come from, it would make sense," Jaks commented.

"What I can't wrap my head around are the crystals"—she gestured at the dunes—"and the sand creatures."

"The Io and the Kin are two completely different alien species, but both are sentient," Jaks said.

"Sentient. Like humanity? And other species in the known worlds?" Zurah suddenly felt uncomfortable with the crystal tucked away in her hip pocket. *Is it aware of me? Watching me?*

"Yes, and why not?" Jaks replied. "Space is infinite, and humanity—even now, I'm guessing—has only explored a minuscule portion of the universe. Who is to say what's out there? What's tucked away in the hidden corners, life and existences which bear absolutely no resemblance to humans or other bipedal life-forms."

"I get that. It's just—" Jaks's story was a lot of

information to process, and Zurah needed a moment to sort through it all. They continued walking in silence for some time, and she mulled over what Jaks had said and the concepts of the Io and the Kin. She wished Dr. Ordotham were with her to help puzzle it all out. His research and medical knowledge would undoubtedly be helpful.

Zurah realized why she was uncomfortable with the idea of the Io being sentient. Her experiences on Objer and dealing with the cryrot had been black and white. The cryrot was an enemy she needed to stop. Thinking of the cryrot as nothing more than an invasive disease or a bit of malware made it easy for her to condone the idea of destroying it all. But having to entertain the idea that the Io were a fully fledged alien entity complete with the trappings of a civilization—even if wildly different from humanity—shifted the picture.

It did make sense, though, given what she and Alex had encountered on the platforms. The words of the crystalline figure on the platform were about disturbing the sacred field of dead. *Isn't there something about behavior with understanding all this stuff?*

"Tell me about what you call the cryrot," Jaks said, interrupting her thoughts.

Zurah decided to share what had happened. By providing him with information, she hoped it would help keep him talking and perhaps offer a way to untangle the mess. When she finished, Jaks was thoughtful for a moment. Unfortunately, when he did speak again, it didn't shed any more light on Zurah's concerns.

"When we reach the north second rim, you need to talk with the Old Mother."

"The Old Mother? Wasn't that who I saw when I woke up?" *The sands aren't safe, not even for the Old Mother.* The warning flashed through her head. *Does that mean the Old Mother is aligned with the sand creatures?* But Zurah wasn't sure how that could be true. She'd already met with the Old Mother, and Jaks and Clara had made it clear they were fighting against the Kin.

"Yes. But it's important for you to tell her what you've told me. I will request a visitation, asking her to join us at the north second rim. You'll understand when you hear what she has to share."

"And why should I talk to her?"

"Because she'll help you understand."

"I don't like cryptic," Zurah warned.

Jaks gave her a half smile. "I'm picking up on that. But the information the Old Mother has isn't mine to tell. I'd be breaking trust with her if I did. And right now, we can't afford that. What I can tell you is that what you call the cryrot is a part of the Io. Just like humanity has hundreds of different cultures, there are different factions within the Io."

So was the platform crystal different from the cryrot? All a part of the Io, just a different faction? "And what about the war you mentioned? What war are you fighting?"

There was a sharp intake of breath then a long, slow exhalation from Jaks. "There are so many gaps in under-standing our history here, what really happened. After the *Eagle's Nest* was brought here, the crew fractured, and somehow, we found ourselves caught up in the middle of a war between the Io and the Kin. And their fight has continued that division within the descendants of the original crew members. Some of us fight with the Io, and some fight for the Kin."

Zurah stopped and reached out to grab Jaks's arm. "Those that are with the Kin… Are they the ones responsible for taking the rest of my team?"

"Yes. I would believe so."

An unwelcome revelation occurred, and Zurah's stomach sank. "Those who have gone to fight with the Kin. What happens to them? Physically, I mean?"

"In order to fight, both sides have had to sacrifice many things. For some, that sacrifice has been—"

"Enough with the riddles. Tell me. What happens to them?"

"They are transformed to resemble the Kin. We're not entirely sure why, but we believe there is benefit to both the human and the Kin. Those who have undergone the transformation are tight-lipped about it."

"Shit," Zurah muttered. She and the others had been manipulated from the start without even knowing it. Johnston and Harrison had destroyed Tuner's research on the gates, but Gregori had given them everything they needed in order to go through. Yet Gregori had talked to her as if he needed her help in *saving* individuals, not unleashing death and destruction. *Had it been a lie? Meant to manipulate me into getting us to come through the gates?*

During times of war or struggle, it was well known that individuals could switch sides. Some had a change of heart or realized they had chosen the wrong side for a variety of reasons. It stood to reason that Gregori and the others may have originally been fighting for the Kin but changed their minds over the years. Yet if

Zurah followed that reasoning, she couldn't understand why he had wanted her to go through the gates. If she had been in his place, the smarter play would've been to prevent anyone from traveling through the gates or even the smaller portals.

Not to mention the pesky fact that Gregori was actually the captain's brother. *That's something Angelina could have mentioned from the start.* Zurah wasn't seeing a solid answer, and all she could settle on was that nothing was what she had believed it to be.

"On Objer, we encountered three original members from the *Eagle's Nest*. If none of you use the gates, how did they end up there? Why are they there?"

Jaks frowned. "You didn't mention that before."

Zurah shrugged. "Now, I am." And she told Jaks the rest of the story.

"Then it's settled. You have to talk with the Old Mother," Jaks said. "She would know more about the motivations of the original crew members than I would."

"So what do the Kin want? Or the Io, for that matter?" Zurah asked. "Why are they fighting?"

"The Io do not share their history with us. The Io reached out for our help, and the majority of the original crew decided to aid the Io instead of the Kin. What we do understand is that the Kin need certain nutrients in order to survive—silicates, metallic particles, carbon-rich molecules, hydrogen, and helium. The ship's arrival provided several of those things, which helped the Kin to momentarily flourish, and the Io needed to make sure the Kin couldn't become too strong. We're assuming the Kin must move from world to world and strip them bare."

"Meaning the Kin must have tried to do that with the Io, and that started the war?" Zurah asked.

"The Io won't confirm it. But it's what most people believe, yes."

Zurah chewed on that information for a moment. "But that can't be all of it. What about the platforms? The alien structures? Surely, the Io or the Kin have no need for buildings or ships like that. There's got to be more to this. Why else would some of the original crew have helped the Kin if they're a threat?"

Jaks stopped abruptly and pulled Zurah down with him. "Hush." He pointed toward the east, and Zurah blinked and zoomed in. Three sand creatures—*no, the Kin*—stood on one of the far dunes. Each looked humanoid. Jaks started wiggling his body backward, down the side of the dune, and Zurah quickly followed suit.

"I thought that crystal thing helped keep us safe," she whispered.

"It is. The Kin can't sense us, but it doesn't mean they can't *see* us."

"How much further, then?" Zurah asked, careful to keep her voice as quiet as possible. "We're kind of walking around on the enemy here."

Jaks looked up at the sky. "About two more hours. If we're lucky, we'll hit a patrol before then and can have backup." He motioned for her to stop talking.

Zurah frowned but did as he asked.

Quietly, they wound through the valleys sculptured

by the dunes until Jaks pulled Zurah back down into a crouch. "Wait here."

He started to climb the dune, but Zurah grabbed his arm and shook her head. "Let me." Without waiting for an answer, she belly-crawled up the side of the dune and scanned the area. The Kin were gone, and she didn't see anything in a five-hundred-kilometer radius. Sliding back down, she said, "All clear."

"How are you so sure?"

Zurah tapped her temple and grinned. "Nifty little upgrades."

Jaks stared at her for a minute before he understood what she was telling him. "There are stories of cybernetic research being done when the *Eagle's Nest* left on their mission, but that's just a part of the fairy tales for the children."

"Hate to break it to you, but it's not a myth. There's a whole wide range of bioupgrades available now. Most are pretty helpful. Some are pure vanity."

Jaks was a deep well of questions for the rest of their journey, and Zurah filled him in as best she could. There was a lot of history she had no clue about, but Jaks seemed amazed by what she could tell him. Before long, Jaks stopped them again. This time, he crawled to the top of the nearest dune then motioned for Zurah to follow.

"What the hell? When we took our scans of the area, there wasn't anything like this." The view was breathtaking. Red-rock formations pushed up through the dunes toward the sky. Their stripes of varying hues of reds, oranges, and creams created a pleasing pattern to the rocks.

"The seeds provide a few other gifts besides helping with the atmosphere," Jaks said. "Come on."

Well, damn. Zurah wasn't so sure about the crystal being able to manipulate her brain.

Jaks picked up the pace and jogged toward the rocks. He angled to the east a few degrees, and Zurah realized he was headed for a cleverly disguised opening. The rocks jutting forward created an optical illusion, but the striping made it appear to be one solid wall.

When Jaks was a handful of meters away, a whistle, long and low, followed by two short bursts shattered the silence. Zurah slowed her pace and ran a scan of the area. Jaks answered with a nearly identical pattern of whistles, and a figure appeared on the top of the rocks and waved. Zurah checked her scans and frowned when they didn't pick up on any other life-forms.

Without hesitation, Jaks pushed on toward the entrance, while Zurah slowed down to a walk. Their little jaunt across the dunes had produced a lot of information the researchers on Objer needed to know. Despite working to make sure the gates were destroyed, Zurah felt the researchers needed to know that the cryrot was far more than what they'd realized, that it was a part of a sentient alien civilization. And even though she felt confident destroying the gates would also trap the Kin on this world, giving the known worlds a heads-up about another possible threat wasn't going to hurt.

She checked the time—nine hours left. Then she

signaled to one of the probes and quickly updated her message.

"Pick up a stray?" a voice asked as Zurah caught up with Jaks.

The figure had slid down the rock face and landed neatly in front of them. A man with snow-white hair, pale skin, and blue eyes watched Zurah like a hawk as she approached.

"You could say that," Jaks replied. "Maybe just what we need."

"Didn't think I'd see you out here for another cycle or two. Last noise on the wire was that you were summoned by an Elder. Any truth to that?"

"I spoke with them, yes."

The man raised his weapon and pushed the muzzle into Jaks's chest. Zurah immediately stepped back and felt another muzzle press into her back.

"I wouldn't," a female voice said.

"You go and get cozy with an Elder then show up here?" the man asked. "Don't seem the usual order of things."

"If I may?" Jaks carefully moved one of his hands to his pocket and pulled out the strange crystalline object. "If I'd been compromised, do you think I'd be able to carry this?"

"No, s'pose not. But that doesn't mean things can't change. Both sides always looking for new ways to get behind enemy lines."

"Mayfield, you and I both know what I'd do if it came down to it," Jaks said. "No life is more important than the lives of others."

The two men stared at each other for a tense moment before Mayfield lowered his weapon. "All right," Mayfield said. "You too, Daisy."

"Don't recognize her," the woman said.

"No, you wouldn't," Jaks answered. "She's not one of us. But still flesh. She's come through from the other side."

Mayfield let out a hearty laugh. "Right, and I'm the Old Mother." When Jaks didn't join in on laughing at the joke, Mayfield's smile fell. "No, you're shitting me."

"I can assure you I'm not," Jaks said.

"Damn, all right. We always knew it was a possibility. Come on, get in here." Mayfield slung his gun across his back and turned to head toward the rock.

Before long, the small group was inside another set of tunnels. Artificial lights were strung above them, and small clusters of crystals sporadically gathered along the base of the walls. Mayfield led them to a decent-sized cavern with several tables and chairs scattered about. With a jolt, Zurah realized it was some type of commissary.

"Heya, can we get three cuppas?" Mayfield called out.

Zurah looked around and realized Daisy hadn't followed. A gray-haired woman hollered back, and in a few minutes, three steaming mugs were placed in front of each of them.

Jaks cupped his hands around his mug and visibly relaxed. "We don't have much time. I lied to the Elders—which we both know they'll figure out soon enough—and assaulted two of the guards. Clara did damage control, but she can only do so much without showing her hand. And we need to summon the Old Mother."

"That's all? Sounds like your typical day," Mayfield said with a rueful shake of the head. "Is it time? Are we going to go full assault on them?" Mayfield asked, then took a sip of his drink.

Zurah sniffed at the steam wafting up from the cup and wrinkled her nose. The smell wasn't inviting. Instead, it reminded her of engine grease and worn-out oil.

"You know I'd rather avoid bloodshed if need be, but if we have to, we'll fight. But first, the Old Mother."

Mayfield's gaze flickered in Zurah's direction then back to Jaks's. "If you're sure. That just might be the tipping point if she doesn't like what she hears."

"I understand, and we're prepared for that," Jaks said. "This is important. Trust me."

"Brother, you know I do." With a sigh, Mayfield stood. "I'll alert Tomas, and he'll send in the request." Mayfield left the commissary.

As Zurah and Jaks sat in the silence, she tried a sip of the drink then instantly regretted it.

"Not to your liking?" Jaks asked with a sly smile.

"What in the worlds is this stuff?" Zurah wiped her mouth, desperately wishing for something to cut the flavor lingering on her tongue.

"Fiona's special." Jaks nodded toward the woman working behind a counter. "You get used to the taste over time. But it's packed full of nutrients and all the good stuff."

"Yeah, no offense, but no thanks," Zurah replied, pushing her mug away. "I'll just take some good old water."

Jaks's smile dropped for a moment. "Afraid you'll have to brave Fiona's special brew. Water is a scarce commodity around here. We take what we can get."

Zurah wasn't sure how to respond to that, but she definitely didn't want to have to drink any more of the noxious brew. Before she could try to smooth talk her way into a glass of water, Mayfield returned. When he sat down, he took another long swig of his drink. Zurah gagged inwardly.

"You're set," Mayfield said then turned to Fiona. "How about some food to soak up your special?"

Fiona nodded, and within minutes, she had several bowls of various types of food and plates on the table.

Zurah eyed the lumpy white food, but when her stomach rumbled, she said a quick prayer that whatever it was wouldn't be as bad as what the suit had been equipped with.

"Thanks. While we wait, we have a rescue mission to plan." It took a few seconds for Jaks's words to fully sink in, and when they did, she glanced over at him.

"We don't know what the Kin may have learned since taking the other members of your team. Nor do we know what might have been done to them. But either way, we'll help you find out, and in exchange, you'll talk with the Old Mother."

"Whoa, hold on there. I thought *you* needed to talk with the Old Mother?" Mayfield looked at Zurah. "But her? Do you really think that's a good idea? I know she's got a soft spot for you, but they're her *sons* we're talking about. They're not going to like this."

Jaks replied to Mayfield but stared at Zurah. "Do you remember what the Old Mother was originally called?"

"I do, same as you. We all know the stories. She was Isla Kincaid, chief medical officer of the *Eagle's Nest*."

10

Zurah shook her head in disbelief. "You're kidding. How many of the original crew are still alive? How is that even possible? Did she transform like the others?" She took a spoonful of the mash and ate it. There wasn't much flavor, but the taste wasn't bad.

Mayfield frowned, and Jaks shook his head. "Not in the way you're thinking. But again, that part of the story isn't mine to tell. When we summon her, she'll be able to answer your questions. For now, we focus on how we get the rest of your team back."

"But why? Why would you do that? It sounds as if you've got plenty of problems to deal with instead of adding another."

"She's got a point," Mayfield said. "Jaks, everyone's dancing around the issues here. No one wants to pull the trigger, but we know if we don't what's going to happen. You've got to stay focused on the bigger picture, brother."

The bigger picture. What is my *bigger picture now?* Zurah couldn't help but turn the question around in her mind. Once the gates were destroyed, Zurah would be cut off—alone on an alien planet. Nissa would listen to the message she'd left, and Dr. Ordotham... Zurah set down the spoon. She would never know if the doc had lived or died.

Jaks dismissed Mayfield's concerns with a shake of his head. "We have time to save her. You and I both know what the Kin do with their prisoners."

Zurah threw Jaks a sharp look. *Perhaps my bigger picture is ensuring the gates are destroyed and trying to save who I can. Dr. Ordotham sacrificed himself in order to save me. The least I can do is try to pass on the favor. But what if I'm too late? What if the Kin have already hurt—or done worse to—the others?*

Jaks's offer to help rescue the team offered a tiny sliver of hope. An emotion Zurah wasn't sure she could handle. Not now, not after there had been too many losses. She didn't want to raise her spirits only to have them destroyed. She pushed the bowl away. *Better to stay realistic than optimistic. Right?*

Mayfield spit out his drink. "The Kin? You're talking a rescue mission from the Kin? Have you done lost your mind?"

"No. What do you think the Kin will do when they realize they've captured humans from the other side? Along with the Io, we've been able to keep them here"—Jaks threw Zurah a peculiar look—"at least the majority of them. How do you think they're going to react once they find out the lies they've been told? That there are fresh worlds out there, ripe for the picking."

"Brother, if they decided to attack, there isn't anything we can do to stop them. The balance between the Kin and Io is tenuous at best, and we both sure as hell know that the Elder Sons have no interest in carrying on the duties of the Old Mother. They're greedy sons of bitches is what they are, and they'll sell us out the first chance they get," Mayfield said. "I know you've pledged your life to the cause, trying to minimize casualties, but the time will come when we're going to have to fight. No matter the cost."

Zurah tried to follow the threads of the conversation, but her heart and her mind were at war. "Do you really think there's a chance my team could be saved?" She had tried to distance herself from the others because thinking about them was painful. All she wanted was to stay focused on ensuring nothing that would harm the known worlds went back through the gates. But now that the chance had been presented, that the others could be rescued, she knew she couldn't turn away.

She didn't want to dwell on the emotions and tried to resist the tension that tightened her chest and the nervous flutters in her gut. And as much as she resisted, it was impossible to deny the hope Jaks offered. But the fear of what a rescue team might discover contaminated that hope with horrendous images and the unbearable grief which would ultimately follow.

Zurah squeezed her eyes shut, trying to stop the tears, then bit down on the edge of her tongue to shift her focus. But when the sharp burst of pain did nothing, Zurah opened her eyes and stood. "Excuse me."

Quickly walking out of the room, she blindly took turn after turn, not caring where she was headed. She just needed to get away, to find a place to quiet her thoughts and regain her focus. Eventually, she stopped and sagged against one of the walls. She'd been working outside her comfort zone since joining the team to go through the gates, watching the others be swallowed by the sands, and being thrown in the middle of a situation she didn't understand. The mental strain was beginning to take its toll.

Zurah prided herself on her tough exterior, putting on a brave face in the face of adversity. But now, she needed a minute to break down, to let the flood of emotions wash through her. Taking the moment to catch her breath, she released her hold on everything she had buried.

She slid down the wall and hugged her knees close to her chest. *I'm not trained for this sort of thing. I'm just a security hack. Why did I ever think I could do this? I should have just waited for the gates to be activated, gone back to Objer, and let someone else make the decisions.* As the tears flowed, Zurah realized she could identify one of the aches in her heart. She was waiting for Alex to show up, sit down beside her, and tell her everything was going to be okay.

In the handful of weeks she'd gotten to know him, she had come to rely on his presence. As she longed to have him miraculously appear, she couldn't stop herself from picturing the horrors he must be facing. *If he's still alive*, she reminded herself. Zurah let her head fall back against the wall. *He has to be. They all have to be.*

After listening to Jaks and Mayfield, Zurah feared what a rescue might find. *Even if Alex and the others are still alive, will they still be completely human? Or will they end up as something like Gregori? And if that was the case, can they ever go home?*

No. I've made sure of that. There wasn't going to be a way for them to return home now. At least not the way they'd come. So even if they rescued the team, they would be doomed to spend the rest of their lives in this hellish place. Zurah couldn't picture what sort of life that might be. She doubted Finn would blame her, having ordered Zurah to destroy the gates in the worst-case scenario. But Zurah wasn't so sure about Alex or Montgomery. And if Angelina survived, Zurah considered the possibility Angelina would be happy to be reunited with her crew.

At least I completed part of my mission, she thought. *At least the known worlds will be safe. That's what matters. That we've kept the rest of the known worlds safe. They have to understand that.*

As her tears dried, Zurah gazed up at the rocky ceiling and a tiny cluster of crystals that appeared to be hanging on for dear life. Even if they weren't able to save the others, Zurah felt the weight of her new reality trying to overwhelm her. She was stuck here, with no chance of seeing Nissa or visiting a Rockerton's again. She was doomed to live among the ghosts of the *Eagle's Nest* and be caught in the middle of a war she had no interest in fighting. *But that's why I came here in the first place, isn't it? To fight for others? To make sure that no one else got hurt?*

She reached into her pocket and pulled out the tiny bundle. Unwrapping the cloth, she was careful how she held the crystal, ensuring her skin didn't make contact. "What are you?" she whispered, half expecting to hear something in return. As she stared at the crystal—both familiar and strangely alien—she felt a surge of anger. Anger at everything. At her situation, her lack of direction, and the unknown alien entities that had dragged her into this mess. "Why can't you just sort out your own problems?"

Zurah raised her arm as if to throw the crystal, and the warmth she had felt when retrieving her suit moved throughout her hand and down her arm. A faint glow emanated from within the crystal. Zurah hastily set it down and scooted away from it, the warmth quickly fading from her body. She sat there and stared at it for quite some time, wondering how the crystal could be a life-form.

"I wish you could talk to me," she whispered. "It would make this a lot easier, you know."

The crystal didn't do anything. She pulled out the screen she'd scavenged from her suit and ran a quick scan of the crystal. The anomalous energy readings were there, faint but detectable. Taking a deep breath, she reached out and touched the crystal. "Is there anything you can show me that will help me find some answers?"

Just as she was about to give up and let go, her fingers tingled, and the crystal began to glow. The energy readings spiked.

"Is that a yes?"

She watched the screen and the real-time readout as

the energy readings continued to fluctuate. "If that's an answer, I'm sorry, but I don't understand yet."

There was one more sharp spike of energy from the crystal, then it faded. Zurah tried to hold the crystal in a few different ways and asked a variety of questions, but nothing happened. With a heavy sigh, she carefully wrapped it back up and tucked it back into her pocket. She tagged the data then let the screen cycle into a sleep mode. Without batteries or an energy source to charge the screen, she knew she had to be careful how much she used it.

Sitting there in the dark, Zurah considered a new question. *What am I now?* As Zurah turned that thought over and over, she came to the conclusion that if it was time for a career change, then helping others stay safe wasn't a bad one. *And sitting here feeling sorry for myself isn't going to change a damn thing.*

Wiping her tears, Zurah stood. After a few wrong turns, she found her way back to the commissary. Jaks and Mayfield were still there, and they'd been joined by three other individuals who appeared to be ravenous judging by how fast they were shoveling food into their mouths. The newcomers were two women and another man. They were all dressed in the same style of jumpsuit, heavily patched and stained. None of them regarded Zurah with anything but suspicion.

Jaks glanced up as Zurah approached but didn't say anything. She sat down quietly and played catch-up with the conversation.

"I'm telling you, if we go in through the eastern route, we'll have a better chance of taking them by surprise.

We know for a fact the research labs are in that area. It'll cause maximum damage," one of the women argued as she loaded her spoon with another heap of the mash.

Jaks shook his head. "This isn't a strike. This is a rescue."

"And why shouldn't we take the chance to try and knock some of their resources out?" Mayfield asked. "If we're going to risk a run, then why not just go for the whole deal? Because you know we're not going to get out of there without causing a little bit of fuss. And the Kin won't take kindly to it."

"And risk igniting a conflict we can't win?" Jaks countered.

"If we do this, we're going to ignite the conflict," Mayfield argued.

"But what if it isn't? What if we can devise a plan to minimize the impact?" Jaks pressed.

"You're not getting it," the other woman said. "You've been gone too long from here. Things are already worse. It's either now or never. If we keep putting off a full-scale assault, the Elders are going to have succumbed to the Kin's offers. And when that happens, you know as well as the rest of us that we'll never have a chance."

"Look at it this way," Mayfield said as he shifted his weight. "If we go in hot, we might be able to do a fair bit of damage. Enough to knock 'em back for a while, and that'll set the Elder Sons back too. Maybe even squelch some of those deals they've been considering. This could be a game changer for us, Jaks."

Jaks let out a long sigh and ran his hand through his hair. "Look, I hear you. I do, but—"

Everyone grew still as the temperature in the room rose a considerable number of degrees. A stream of sand fell from the ceiling in the middle of the room. As the sand accumulated, it rose in the air, swirling around as if it were a miniature version of a tornado. And from the sandstorm, the figure of a woman slowly took shape.

Zurah jumped up and backed away, afraid the Kin had found them and was attacking. But when Jaks and the others merely stood without taking up defensive postures, Zurah tried to calm down. When the sand took its shape and formed into its humanoid figure, Zurah understood. Standing before them was the Old Mother. Isla Kincaid.

"The Old Mother is the Kin? You didn't exactly make that little detail apparent."

Jaks growled and stepped in front of Zurah. He turned and bowed toward the Old Mother. "I beg your forgiveness for the interruption, and I appreciate your journey to see us. Especially at this critical hour."

The Old Mother turned and stared at Zurah. "You told me she was flesh."

"And she is, Old Mother. I did not lie."

"And yet the Io are within her."

"A necessary step in order to save her life," Jaks said. "I used only what was needed of the seeds to help. This I swear on the crest."

"Then why have you summoned me?" The Old Mother's tone was sharp and accusatory.

"I would ask you to share with her. To listen to her stories, to consider her questions, and to provide the wisdom you carry within you," Jaks said.

There was a long, drawn-out silence as the Old Mother's gaze never left Jaks's bowed head. Zurah wasn't sure what the Old Mother might do if she decided not to cooperate. The tension in the room was palpable, and Zurah's gut tightened. Even without a solid understanding of what was happening, one thing was certain. The Old Mother was their leader, and if she decided to alert the Elder Sons, Zurah's presence would be the cause.

"And what about you?" Zurah asked. "You're so concerned about me being flesh. What are you? Kin or Io? Friend or foe?"

"You're talking to the Old Mother, girl," Mayfield groaned. "Show some respect."

"Respect is earned," Zurah said.

"That may be so," the Old Mother said. "But common decency is easy to give in its place."

Zurah crossed her arms and tilted her head to the side. "You haven't answered my question."

"And nor shall I. It is not your place to question what I may be or the choices I've made," the Old Mother replied. "But it seems as if Jaks believes I should make time for you. Tell me why."

"I have a message for you" was the first thing Zurah could think of without revealing anything important. Her words earned a sharp hiss of disapproval from Jaks, but she ignored it. "From Angelina." Zurah kept her voice as steady as possible, when in truth, there really wasn't much of a message. If the Old Mother was going to be angry, then so be it.

The edges of the Old Mother blurred, as if she were

about to disintegrate in a maelstrom of sand, but she retained her shape, her sharp eyes studying Zurah.

"Walk with me," the Old Mother commanded.

Zurah stepped forward to follow, but Jaks reached out to grab her arm.

"Be careful with your words," he whispered. "We are living on a knife's edge."

When they were well past the commissary and ears that might overhear, the Old Mother slowed down. "Tell me this message."

"I must beg for your forgiveness," Zurah said, trying her best to be polite and make up for her rude behavior. "I was startled by your... connection with the Kin." Zurah knew she shouldn't have allowed her shock to let her lose control of her mouth. Tact hadn't been one of her strongest skills, but Zurah knew if she was going to survive, it would have to move up her list of strengths.

The Old Mother inclined her head in acknowledgment, and Zurah took a few deep breaths to calm her beating heart.

"Angelina wasn't able to completely tell me what it was she wanted you to know. But I believe she wanted me to tell you that she loved you."

The Old Mother's eyes flared with an unnatural light. "Do not lie to me."

"I swear to you I'm not. Angelina came with us, through the gates, in order to understand what happened to the ship and its crew. We were"—Zurah was about to say *attacked*, but at the last minute, she decided to change tactics—"overwhelmed by the Kin, and Angelina and the others who came with me were taken."

The muscles along the Old Mother's jaw rippled, and she stalked forward. Zurah hesitated, unsure what she had done or if she should follow. But she decided to follow, careful to stay at a respectful distance. At the first junction, the Old Mother turned and pulled open a door. The room was large enough to accommodate three workstations and a handful of individuals. As soon as they saw who stood on the threshold, everyone froze.

"Out" was all the Old Mother had to say, and their work was forgotten as everyone left the room, giving respectful bows as they passed. The Old Mother strode into the middle of the room, surveyed the area, then sat in a chair. "Close the door."

Zurah did as she was told, and once the door was secure, she stood there, not knowing what the protocol was.

"For heaven's sakes, don't just stand there like a lout. Find a chair."

Relieved and feeling scolded like a little kid at the same time, Zurah pulled one of the chairs out from the workstation and set it down facing the Old Mother.

"Now, start from the beginning."

She opened her mouth to start telling the Old Mother everything, but something inside of her urged her to remain quiet. Leaning back, she decided to risk listening to her intuition. "How are you still alive?"

A flash of annoyance passed through the Old Mother's eyes, and her winkles deepened as she frowned. "You will tell me your story."

"Not until you answer a few of my questions," Zurah said. *I hope this works.* But Zurah's gut was telling her that the Old Mother respected individuals who didn't cower and immediately jump without questioning.

"Why should I?"

Zurah considered the question, not fully sure how to respond. *Because I'm tired of being pulled in multiple directions, given only half-truths, and expected to do the impossible?* But those responses seemed a bit too much as she pushed back against the Old Mother's authority. "Because I'm tired of not understanding what's going on and afraid that if I make the wrong choice, people will die."

Those words represented a deeper truth Zurah was trying to come to grips with. As a security hack, her part of a crew was essential, and the decisions she made could mean life or death. But the responsibility lay with the boss of the crew. If they didn't spend enough time prepping for a job or making sure their crew had considered all the angles, then when things went sideways, it was up to the boss to try to get everyone back on track. And if they were a halfway ethical boss, they worked hard to make sure their crew survived.

I've been thinking of myself as another member of a crew. Still just the security hack following Nissa's orders or Finn's and now even Jaks's. But that's not true anymore. I'm my own boss. And now, these decisions rest on my shoulders and no one else's.

Zurah braced for the Old Mother's ire. Instead, the Old Mother smiled. "Angelina and I frequently had the same conversation. Though we had uniquely different positions on the *Eagle's Nest*, we both held the lives of the crews in our decision-making. A sentiment which has been lost, I fear." She pushed herself up and made her way to one of the workstations.

Intuitively, Zurah followed. The computer was ancient, and as she watched the Old Mother work, Zurah grew impatient at the clunky interface and slow processing times.

A series of file folders appeared on the screen, and the Old Mother selected one titled "Isla Kincaid, Chief Medical Officer." When the file opened, an image of Isla appeared, albeit quite a bit younger, along with a readout of her personal and professional history.

"I was selected from a long list of applicants. I never fully understood why she chose me as the chief medical officer. There were far more qualified doctors and research medical personnel who had applied. Maybe it was more of a personal reason than professional. Angelina might have felt that spark between us when we went through the interview process, I don't know. I never really questioned her about it, simply accepted the win and did my best to live up to the standards she placed upon herself and everyone else."

The Old Mother paused then gently traced the outline of her picture with a gnarled finger. "Being selected for the position was a big honor at the time. And of course, none of us could imagine what was going to happen. We believed we would return to Earth at the completion of our contracts and be hailed as heroes.

"At first, everything was filled with hope and possibility. We were explorers searching the edges of the known worlds for the mysteries of the universe. Gradually, that hope started to wane as it was clear the captain had other priorities. Requests were denied, and exciting research opportunities were ignored.

"Angelina was concerned about the well-being of the crew, as was her job as second-in-command, and she had me run multiple tests to ensure there had been no psychological or physical damage after the exploration teams returned to the ship. Every test I ran came back the same. Except for one. The captain's. He wasn't supposed to have gone with the exploration crew to the rogue planet. But he was the captain and overrode Angelina's concerns." The Old Mother sighed and moved back to her chair. "How did Angelina survive?"

Zurah was startled by the question interrupting the Old Mother's narrative, but she answered as she sat down. "Her escape pod was discovered, sold at an auction, and the buyer helped revive Angelina."

"After all that time? I would not have thought the pod could have maintained its integrity. Let alone the energy required to survive."

The question was one Zurah hadn't considered. She'd taken Alex's story at face value, but now, she wondered what he *hadn't* told her. *Was there more to the story about Angelina's miraculous survival?*

"What happened between Angelina and the captain? Why was she in an escape pod in the first place?" Zurah asked.

"I don't know," the Old Mother replied. "Not for sure, anyway. I know the stories that have grown into myth, and most if not all have turned Angelina into something she wasn't. I can hazard a guess, from my interactions with both Angelina and the captain, but to know for sure, you'd have to ask her. Or the captain. But I can guarantee you that his thoughts are so twisted and corrupted that it would hardly be the truth. Just a fanciful version of the reality he wanted."

"Then tell me, how are *you* still alive?"

The Old Mother smiled. "A far easier and more difficult question to answer." She leaned forward and extended her arm, holding her hand palm up for Zurah to inspect. The particles of sand that worked together to create the illusion of flesh dispersed, swirling around the stump of the arm for a moment, before once more taking on the appearance of a hand. "The gift of the Kin. Or if you talk with Jaks, he would consider it a curse. I believe it is a little of both."

"Why?" Zurah couldn't help but ask.

"Because at the time, I believed I was doing the right thing."

"And now? Will you go to war?"

The Old Mother's expression abruptly became guarded, and she pulled back. "Is that what they're considering? They would betray us?"

Though tempted to respond, Zurah stayed silent.

The Old Mother's expression softened, and a faint blue glow appeared around her irises. "Conflict has always been inevitable. This war between the Io and Kin was one being fought long before the *Eagle's Nest* was tangled up in the middle. But the fact does remain, the captain betrayed us, ultimately, in the end. A victim of greed undoubtedly. But he wasn't without his reasons. Not completely."

Zurah frowned at the seemingly disconnected thoughts and wondered if the Old Mother was being purposefully cryptic or if there was a touch of senility to her words.

"My sons… my poor boys. Born of regret and futility.

I'm afraid the Kin have whispered for too long in their ears." There was a look of loneliness etched in the Old Mother's features, and she gazed upon Zurah with a desperation that broke Zurah's heart.

What would it be like to have lived for so long? Even with the bioupgrades which are available, there aren't many who choose this long of a life. How many friends did she watch die? A shiver ran through Zurah, and she pushed the troublesome thoughts aside.

"Isla… Old Mother. Angelina and the others have been taken by the Kin. Is there any chance that they are still alive? That they're okay?" Zurah asked.

The Old Mother's eyes fluttered closed, and her mouth moved as if consulting with herself. When her eyes opened again, they shone brightly with that inner blue light. "For now. There is a flurry of activity among the Kin, which has not been known for quite some time. There is—" She stopped as if listening to some faraway voice, then her entire demeanor changed. Her face contorted in rage, and she lunged for Zurah. Despite the Old Mother's age and seeming physical condition, Zurah wasn't able to move fast enough. They toppled together, crashing in a chaotic tangle of limbs and pieces of the chair.

"What are… you doing?" Zurah gasped, unable to gain the upper hand despite the Old Mother's frail appearance. But when Zurah reached for her arm to try and push it away, the flesh crumbled into sand then reformed, with a firm grip around Zurah's arm. The Old Mother's other hand found Zurah's throat and squeezed.

"Lies. All lies," the Old Mother hissed. "You've come to destroy us."

"What? No!" Zurah tried to say, but the pressure on her throat made it difficult to speak. "We needed… to make sure we were safe… There was the cryrot and a threat…"

"You came here in order to desecrate the dead. To enslave us. We will not be at the mercy of others ever again," the Old Mother snapped. She leaned forward, her weathered face distorted as she lost control over the sand. At the same instant, there was a flash of surprise in her eyes, and the pale-blue light ignited behind her irises until that was all that appeared in her eyes.

"We were not the cause of your enslavement, nor is the flesh." The Old Mother's mouth moved as if the words came from her body, but the voice was delicate, and the words had a sing-song quality about them. "Release her."

The Old Mother's hands flew from Zurah, and taking advantage of the moment, Zurah pushed out from underneath the woman and scooted out of the way. She sprang to her feet, ready to defend herself, but the Old Mother crumpled to the floor, her body twisting and turning.

"Old Mother?" Zurah cautiously asked. "Can you hear me?"

The Old Mother's eyes opened wide, the light blazing from within. "I'm sorry, child. I thought I had more time, but—" A scream tore from her body, and blood pooled along her lower eyelids then ran down her face. "Tell her to forgive me. Tell them all to forgive me."

The door burst open. "We just received word—" Jaks stopped, and a look of pure horror struck his face when he saw the Old Mother on the floor and Zurah crouched over her body. He rushed to the Old Mother's side and tried to hold her body still. "I need a medic!" he shouted. "Medic, now!"

Mayfield skidded to a stop in the doorway, assessed the situation, then took off.

"It's going to be okay," Jaks murmured, trying his best to help the Old Mother.

Within minutes Mayfield returned with a woman and a handful of medical kits. Jaks moved out of the woman's way, while Mayfield stalked over to Zurah, pushing her out of the way.

"What did you do?" he growled.

"Nothing, I swear," Zurah replied.

Mayfield shook his head and grabbed her arm. Zurah twisted free and tried to move out of his reach. But Mayfield lunged for her, and this time, he held on tightly. They stood there, watching the medic work. From one of her bags, she took out a crystal encased of some type of polymer coating. With reverent movements, she held the crystal over the Old Mother then gently placed it on her chest. Zurah had a flash of a memory of the unidentified weight on her chest when she had woken up in the corridor.

"She's seizing," the woman said. "Worse than I've seen before."

"Can't you do anything for her?" Jaks asked.

The woman shook her head. "The Io are not immortal, and neither are we. Our bodies weren't designed to live as long as she has."

The crystal on the Old Mother's chest flared blue then shifted to red.

"I'm sorry, there's nothing I can do. The Elder Sons have to be notified," the medic said.

"I know," Jaks said, rubbing his forehead. "Just allow me a few minutes, please."

The woman didn't look particularly happy, but she nodded.

Jaks stood and turned. His expression was stony and resolute. "Mayfield, take our guest and find an appropriate accommodation for her, then send out the alerts. In five minutes, I will send an alert and notify the Elder Sons."

"Understood," Mayfield said, his jovial manner all gone. He pulled at Zurah, forcing her to move with him.

"I didn't do this. I swear," Zurah said as they moved past Jaks.

He turned to stare at her, his eyes glowing with a cold green light, which spread like web-like veins across his face and down his neck. "Get her out of here."

Zurah threw one last look at the Old Mother's quiet body. Blood had begun to pool around the old woman's head, turning the edges of her jumpsuit along her shoulders dark and slick.

The woman who had come to help gently picked up the crystal and placed it back in her bag. "The Old Mother is dead. Long shall the Elder Sons watch the divide."

11

Mayfield marched Zurah out of the room and down the corridor then yanked open a door. Even through the haze of shock, Zurah could identify the outline of the door. Having a handle placed in the center helped too. Without any grace or consideration, Mayfield flung Zurah into the room and slammed the door. She caught the sound of tumblers falling into place and rushed to the door. She twisted and pulled on the handle. But the handle and the door morphed into the rock wall. Losing her grip on the handle, Zurah stumbled but quickly regained her balance and rushed forward to where the door had been mere seconds ago. Desperate, she pressed her palm against the rock, waiting to feel the warmth flood her body and give her the ability to unlock the door.

When nothing changed, she pounded on the wall. "I didn't kill her! Please, you have to believe me!" She pounded and pleaded her case until her fists were bloodied and bruised. Exhausted and scared, she turned and sank to the floor. Her mind replayed her last minutes with the Old Mother over and over again. *What in the worlds happened?*

Zurah shivered and rocked back and forth, trying to quell the rising tide of panic threatening to overwhelm her. She had felt confident and in control while talking with the Old Mother, trying to find the answers hidden under layers of cryptic information. Yet everything had spiraled into chaos. Zurah couldn't understand why the Old Mother had attacked her and what in the worlds she could have said or done to trigger the woman.

I told her about Angelina being taken by the Kin, and she… She went nuts. Accusing me of stealing her secrets. Had the years and love twisted into something horrible within the Old Mother? Triggering some kind of reaction?

As the worst of the shock wore off, Zurah took several deep breaths, forcing herself to calm down. Anger slowly and steadily replaced the shock and fear, and she stood and started to pace the room. With each step, a fresh surge of irritation rushed through her, focused on herself and gradually expanding to include everyone else. She had been a fool to not take any precautions when Jaks brought her here. Instead of giving in to her emotions, Zurah wished she'd taken the opportunity to do some scouting or tried to find someplace she could tap into their systems and do some digging. Despite not seeing a lot of tech scattered around, Zurah was confident somewhere, there were workstations and a command station of sorts. *Something has to be maintaining a breathable atmosphere and decent temperature.*

Moving around the room helped to focus her body and mind, and Zurah worked through what had happened, methodically replaying each scene and taking it apart. She needed to make sense of what was happening. But each time she replayed the events, Zurah found nothing but gibberish and chaos. Frustrated, she shook her head. "Forget this. I'm not just waiting around for them to decide what happens to me."

Zurah paced off the dimensions of the room then visually inspected the rock walls. She ran her hands over the uneven surface, looking for any compartments or panels that might have been disguised. Not finding anything on a physical inspection, she worked through a variety of visual overlays. As she scanned for energy fluctuations, she hit the jackpot.

The SeeClear tech picked up on two anomalous energy readings. The first was from where the door had been, and the second emanated from a smaller location on the opposite wall. Something was embedded in the rock, and Zurah's best guess was some type of conduit or control circuits. Working slowly and methodically, she enhanced her vision as she ran her fingers over the rock in the area of question, double-checking for some type of access panel.

"Bingo." Her fingernail snagged on a small line running vertically, and as she followed the minute line, she traced the outline of a small rectangular panel.

"Clever but not clever enough." Running another analysis of the rock, her tech pinged with results stating the rock in that particular area was a type of sedimentary rock—meaning it was soft enough that she had a chance.

Taking a quick inventory, she settled on the two hip pockets of her undersuit. Both used zippers. After carefully prying off the pull tab from the unused pocket, she used the edge to chip away at the rock, cursing each time she dropped the tab and sucking on her bloodied fingers. Zurah was finally able to wear away enough of the rock to pry off the control panel.

To her surprise, the conduit wasn't what she had expected. Zurah had assumed she would discover an old conduit scavenged from the ship. Instead, three pieces of crystal had been spun into perfect cylindrical tubes and nestled into the rock. "Well, that's not really helpful." She chewed at her lower lip as she stared at the crystals, not sure how to use them to her advantage. Reaching into the opening, she felt along the edges in the slim hope of finding some type of control panel or node, anything she could hack into.

"I wouldn't advise that," a flat voice cautioned.

Zurah spun around as Mayfield stepped into the room. She picked up the panel and brandished it like a weapon, threatening the crystals. "If you come any closer, I'll smash them."

"Go ahead," he said, leaning against the wall. "But I can assure you, it won't do you any good."

Zurah was tempted to follow through on her threat just out of spite. But the echoes of her conversation with Jaks about the Io being a sentient race stopped her. She had no idea if all or only some of the crystals she was encountering were a part of the Io.

"Look, I know we don't really know each other, but you've got to believe me that I didn't do anything to the Old Mother."

"Oh, I do. But I'll make sure the others don't," Mayfield said as he took a step toward her.

"What the hell?" Zurah jerked back in surprise at his abrupt candor. Her whole world turned upside down as Mayfield's face melted then rearranged into someone decidedly not Mayfield.

"Finn?" Zurah gasped then immediately knew her guess was wrong.

A devilish grin spread across the woman's face. "I'm surprised my daughter would choose someone so ill equipped to accompany her on such a mission. I had hoped my lessons would have had more weight."

Shit, shit, and shit. This was exactly what Zurah had hoped wouldn't happen. If they were going to have to deal with the emperor's team, Zurah had hoped Finn or Alex would be present—someone who understood how to play the game or who could deal with their family drama. Instead, Zurah was face-to-face with Finn's mother. Suen Kailani.

"So, my daughter and others have been taken by the Kin? Perhaps they'll be able to do what I haven't," Kailani mused.

"Which would be what?" Zurah crossed her fingers, hoping it would be as simple as asking a question and getting a straight answer.

Kailani laughed. "Silly girl. Who do you think I am?"

Of course it's not that easy. "I know exactly who you were and are. You're a Shadow."

Kailani raised an eyebrow. "At least you're not totally inept."

"Was there ever a Mayfield?" Zurah asked.

Kailani glanced down at her body. A jumpsuit as white as snow now covered her lithe, athletic frame. "Of course there was. Building a form from scratch is rather challenging, expends far too much energy, and raises too many questions."

"What do you want?" Zurah asked.

"I have a proposition for you," Kailani replied. "This life, this meager existence on this forsaken world, isn't for anyone. The items that you and I have become accustomed to aren't available. Adjusting is difficult, and I would much rather be back among the known worlds than on this damnable planet. While my databases may be slightly out of date, it appears your skill set is as a security hack. A rather good one. I am assuming this information is still correct?"

Zurah didn't move or respond. At least she thought she didn't, but something in her expression must have told Kailani her intel was still correct.

"Then how do you think you would be useful here? You have no skills to offer. Neither the Kin or the Io have interfaces or technology that you would be used to. Would you be able to spend your days mindlessly carrying supplies from one place to the next?"

No. But she wasn't going to admit that aloud.

Kailani didn't appear bothered by Zurah's silence. She stretched, lazily moved a few steps, then leaned against the wall, staring up toward the ceiling.

"I can tell you that I certainly don't intend to spend the rest of my life here. But before I can go back, I have to finish my assignment. And I could use a bit of help."

"What about the rest of your team?" Zurah asked. "I know you didn't come here alone."

Kailani shrugged. "Perhaps I should've chosen my team a bit more carefully."

"The Kin?"

"No. The Io. Don't let them fool you into thinking the Kin are the problem. The Io are clever, manipulative, and know exactly how to prey on the deepest desires of an individual."

Just like you. Zurah had encountered her fair share of unsavory individuals—from working with them on various crews or stealing from them on the different jobs she'd participated in. She understood what Kailani was doing. And she admitted, a part of it was working, playing on her insecurities and making her continuously second-guess whether she was valuable to the crew she was working with. She'd struggled with that desire and fear since her parents had left.

"Then what happened to them?" Zurah asked, adding a touch of fear into her words. She wasn't a master manipulator or skilled at playing the games Finn and Alex had grown up with, but she would try.

Kailani glanced up at Zurah, shadows hiding a part of her body and expression. "We were attacked. A patrol party. They attacked without asking questions then left us for dead. To rot under the suns. Lucky or ill-fated, I survived, and after some time of wandering the sands, I found a way in."

Zurah highly doubted any of that was true, except for Kailani being the only member to survive—that, Zurah could believe. She even entertained the notion Kailani had killed or sacrificed her other team members in order to complete her mission. If she was the mother of Finn and Miles High, the notorious leader of the Little Asteroid Gang and would-be Emperor of Old Earth, then anything was possible.

"Help me finish what I came here to do, and together, we'll make sure we get back to the known worlds," Kailani said.

"You must think I'm fresh off the docks," Zurah finally said. "I would no more trust you than a Neetho selling real estate."

Instead of becoming upset, Kailani grinned. "Good. But my offer stands. Just let me know what you decide." She straightened, and this time, Zurah caught the sequence of blinks that activated Kailani's tech. *Clever. Very clever.* Once more disguised as Mayfield, Kailani threw Zurah one last grin and slipped out of the room.

Staring at the door as it slid shut, Zurah sighed. Part of her questions were answered, but she wished somehow, she could have wrangled the truth from Kailani, to understand how Kailani or the emperor believed they were going to be able to create a supersoldier.

What if Finn's intel had been wrong? What if it's not about a supersoldier? She mulled over the possibility the emperor's objective had something to do with how the gates worked—being able to instantaneously jump from one location to another. But as she considered that idea, Zurah couldn't quite get behind it.

Zap 'N' Roll tech, while deadly and not widely used, had already been developed. And she assumed at some point in the future, it would be perfected. There had been whispers of a new version of the tech due to hit the markets soon. But if the whispers were true, Zurah didn't understand why someone would risk so much in order to reinvent the wheel. In all of her years of understanding what the client wanted—the ultimate prize—she knew there had to be a lot more to it than that.

No, Finn's intel is more than likely correct. They're after tech to make supersoldiers. And my assumption means either the Io or the Kin has to be correct. But how in the worlds are they going to accomplish that?

Deep in thought, Zurah almost missed the door starting to open again. When she realized what was happening, she braced for the worst.

Jaks slipped into the room and closed the door quickly. Zurah hesitated. Kailani was well equipped, and the other members of her team would've been as well. The masking tech Kailani was using wasn't new to Zurah. While she'd never personally used it before, she had read about it and worked through schematics for the tech in the off chance she would be asked to hack that kind of system. The downside was that type of hack required an external control node with specs designed for that particular type of hack. If SeeClear tech or other innocuous and popular bioupgrades were capable of hacking masking tech, then there wouldn't be much point in using the disguises.

Kailani could have multiple faces programmed into the masking tech. By first posing as Mayfield, she could be trying to throw Zurah off course then double back as Jaks and try to gain more information by posing as a sympathetic ear. Except there was one part of the tech Zurah had no doubts about. While tech masked the appearance of the individual, the tech was not equipped with an uplink to a neural network. None of the specs she had read hinted at any type of interface. Of course, someone like Kailani who had an infinite amount of resources would have the credits to pay for those types of heavy modifications. But that would only work if the person she was disguised as had a compatible neural interface. The chances of Kailani implanting the necessary tech in her marks—because that type of tech was too advanced for the descendants of the *Eagle's Nest*—were slim enough that Zurah decided it was a weakness in the tech she would have to rely on.

Jaks took a step forward. "What happened between you and the—"

Zurah held up her hand to stop him. "I'm curious. When we were in your bunk, why did you waste so much time asking about… What bioupgrade was it again?" Inwardly, she cringed. As subtle questions went, it wasn't her best work.

Jaks pursed his lips and stared at her for a moment. "We didn't discuss any bioupgrades in my bunk. We talked about a wide variety of interesting tech on our way here, though. I believed the one I was most interested in was the tech which enhanced your vision."

Zurah let out a sigh of relief. "Just checking."

"Why? What happened?" Jaks asked, his posture tensing as he did a quick scan of the room.

Zurah knew she couldn't jump at shadows for the rest of her life—however long that might be. And if she was going to make sure Kailani didn't succeed in her mission and hope for the slim chance of rescuing the others, then she needed to trust someone. Not too much, but enough to try to make sense of the messy situation.

But first, she needed to make sure something was absolutely clear between them. "I didn't kill the Old Mother. She attacked me."

"I know."

"You believe me? But you were furious with me. You told Mayfield to throw me in here."

His eyes flashed green. "I was furious. But not at you. At this whole mess. I know you didn't kill the Old Mother. She was"—his shoulders slumped forward—"having trouble long before you came. Like the medic said, our bodies aren't designed to live as long as she had. Her death… It's not good. While tenuous, her presence helped maintain what was left of the semblance of balance between the Io and Kin."

Zurah wasn't sure how to respond to his candor, but she appreciated it. With a heavy sigh, Zurah filled Jaks in on her encounter with the Shadow. Jaks didn't get angry or seem surprised. Instead, Zurah decided he looked worn down and exhausted.

"Damn. I'll be right back," Jaks said.

"Don't do anything rash—" Zurah started to say, but he was gone.

The temptation to let her mind run in a thousand different directions and spiral into darkness loomed on the horizon. *How can I hope to fight against someone like*

Kailani? Another Finn, only older and definitely on the evil side of things. Finn was a source of irritation, and Zurah didn't completely trust her, but intuition told her Finn was nothing like her mother. *Or perhaps she's even worse, where you don't expect it—stop! Speculation won't help.*

Realizing she was still holding the panel, she set it down and turned around to take another look at the crystals. There weren't any identifying marks, and as far as Zurah could see, each one simply rested in a small indentation in the rock on either side. She ran a few more scans, noting the energy fluctuations emanating from the crystals, but found nothing she could hack. Zurah considered why the crystals were hidden behind a panel.

Are they a part of the controls for the door? The door for the room didn't appear to function like the one for Jaks's bunk. *But how in the worlds is the door being operated?* Given that the only two energy readings in the room came from the door and the crystals, Zurah was certain they operated together. Understanding how the tech worked was the mystery.

"But that's just the thing, isn't it?" she said, staring at the crystals. "If you're a part of the Io, then you're not just another piece of tech. You're a sentient life-form. Or rather a part of one." She pulled the small piece of crystal from her pocket. As she lifted the crystal toward the others, the faint purplish glow appeared in its center. The closer she moved it, the stronger the glow grew.

A sickening feeling crawled through her belly. *If the Io are sentient, a completely new and different type of alien life than what the known worlds was used to, then what are they doing here, with the descendants of the* Eagle's Nest? *Are they here of their own accord? Or have they been brought here and used for...* Zurah didn't want to even consider the idea. Slavery was a taboo topic on several worlds, and yet she was fully aware of the dark currents beneath the shining and glittery lights of the known worlds.

Humanity, despite its history, hadn't learned its lesson, and there were human traffickers on the IGJ's watch list. The Glipglows also had a complicated history with using their own kind as slave labor, and there were ethical debates over whether the Weplie culture was a form of slavery.

Zurah knew she had been fortunate to escape a life bound to types of work that churned her stomach. The memory of the encounter with the crystal on the platform sprang to mind, along with the strange ship and the images of the *Eagle's Nest* and its crew.

There were a few details Zurah wasn't clear on—such as *when* or *how* the emperor had sent his team through the gates. Zurah wondered where the research or tech used to activate the gates had gone. *Why did Finn and Alex appear to have to start over from scratch?* It was possible Finn and Alex's research teams setting up camp on Objer had somehow interrupted Kailani's team, perhaps displacing anyone left on Objer, making it impossible for Kailani to return without raising suspicion. The logic was hazy, but it was there somewhere, floating between all of Zurah's hypotheses. *And now, the thing Kailani needs most is a way to return to the known worlds.* Zurah chuckled to herself. *Well, if that's true, tough luck, lady, 'cause I done burned that bridge.* Her mirth died quickly. *But if that's true, does it mean she's accomplished her mission? And if so, then what does she have that's going to create these supersoldiers?*

An alert popped up, and Zurah realized the countdown had ended. The probes should have sent the data, and the gates on Objer should've been destroyed. A weight lifted from her shoulders, and Zurah let out a long sigh of relief. *At least that part is over. Kailani, the Kin… all of them. They're trapped here, just like I am.* The reality was sobering but oddly exhilarating for Zurah. She had helped protect the known worlds. She had helped to make sure Nissa, the doc, and everyone left on Objer was safe.

Satisfied, Zurah turned her attention back to the crystals. She wondered what, if anything, the Io experienced. *Do they have senses? Can they feel me holding them? Do they experience sounds or smell? How can they communicate with each other? What about nutrients or reproduction?* She whispered to it, "Are you aware that I'm holding you right now? Do you sense the change when I wrap you up and place you in my pocket?"

She waited in the silence for some type of answer. Nothing changed except for the faint noise of something grinding against itself. Zurah glanced over her shoulder in time to catch Jaks slipping back into the room. Hastily wrapping the crystal and tucking it back into her pocket—silently hoping the crystal wasn't screaming at her for that—she asked Jaks, "Who made the painting of your great-great-whatever in your bunk?"

"It wasn't a painting. It's an old photograph," Jaks said. "Pineapple. Chocolate. Palm Trees."

"Excuse me?"

"Those are three things I've read about and would like to experience or see some day," Jaks said. "Next time, I'll say one of those things, or you can ask me."

"An all-day pass. Gambler's Rift, and…" Zurah bit her lip, trying to think of a third item. "Julcrest cream."

Jaks nodded. "Understood. I checked the tickets. Mayfield has been stationed here for the last three weeks. Before that, he was bumped around a bit. When do you think… this Shadow and her team would have infiltrated my people?"

"I don't know," Zurah replied. "I wasn't given any specific information. But I would definitely say far longer than three weeks."

"Which means this Shadow could have been posing as Mayfield or someone else for quite some time. And it is reasonable to conclude that he's dead."

Jaks glanced away as he said those words, and Zurah caught the hint of sorrow in his voice. She wished she could tell him otherwise. But Zurah agreed with his assessment of the situation. When he turned his focus back to her, his jaw was clenched, and there was fury in his eyes.

"Mayfield was a good friend. One of the few individuals I trusted. Now, I have reason to believe everything has been compromised. Everything." Jaks balled up his fists and pressed them into his thighs.

"Has Mayfield—or rather Kailani—been asking about anything in particular? Trying to get information from you or someone else on a specific topic?" Zurah asked.

"Yes," Jaks replied without hesitating.

"And?"

Jaks shook his head. "They won't get it. Not without—" He stopped. "If we rescue your team, we'll have to do it ourselves. Just the two of us."

"From the little I overheard you discuss, it doesn't sound like that's possible."

"It is. Just… the chances of success are small. But—" He ran a hand through his hair. "Damn. I don't know if there's another way."

"I can't help if you don't tell me—in complete sentences—what you're thinking," Zurah said.

Jaks scowled. "This war, between the Io and Kin, had a tenuous agreement to stop the fighting. It's held for a little over three hundred years. And now, without the Old Mother speaking for both sides, it's going to get ugly fast. I was hoping with the rescue…" He stopped again, and Zurah huffed. "It was foolish. The others were right—whoever they really might be—we can't avoid bloodshed much longer."

"How do we rescue my team?" Zurah asked.

"We need to go to the Elder Sons. That's the first step."

"But I thought they—"

Jaks stopped her. "They're not to be trusted. No one is. But they have what we need."

"Which is…?"

"The Io's heart."

12

Zurah tried to ask a few more questions for clarification—all she could picture was a beating heart sequestered away behind glass walls—but Jaks wouldn't answer.

"Right now, you and I are under a lot of suspicion. The Elder Sons are putting on a great act of the bereaved. I've no doubt that in a short while, they'll issue orders for our arrest."

"What's the play, then?" Zurah asked. "Do we get arrested and taken to them?"

Jaks shook his head. "No. You don't understand what they're capable of. We need to get to their complex, but under our terms, not theirs. Fortunately, as the original members of the crew splintered off into different factions and family groups, no one really trusted each other."

"Why is that helpful?" Zurah asked with a frown.

"Because it means I've got a few tricks up my sleeve,"

he replied with a grim look. "We need to be quick and quiet. Understood?"

Zurah nodded, and Jaks led her out of the room. They moved through the tunnels, Jaks pulling her back into the shadows whenever someone was headed their way. He took them through a maze of corridors, and when they couldn't hide, Jaks kept his voice relaxed as he greeted individuals.

After another series of convoluted turns, Jaks slipped behind a portion of rock that jutted out into the passageway and crouched down to crawl through a narrow opening.

"I'll be able to see without the need for the artificial lighting system," Jaks said. "Will your upgrade adjust?"

"Yeah, not a problem there." Zurah eyed the small opening with suspicion, but she told herself it wasn't any different than crawling around in the framework of a ship or station for a job. They didn't have to move too far on their hands and knees before the tunnel widened and they could stand.

"Did the original crew create this tunnel system? Or was it already here?" Zurah asked. "Because if they did, they could've made it a tad bit more comfortable."

Jaks chuckled. "A little bit of both. Whatever this planet was, there was a preexisting underground cavern and tunnel system. There is speculation that they were created rather than naturally formed. Neither the Io nor the Kin have ever confirmed anything for us. We know both were using the tunnels before the *Eagle's Nest* landed here. But the original crew did work on expanding some areas, reinforcing others, and created the different regions we could periodically rotate to."

"I can't imagine the work it must have taken," Zurah commented. She remembered Nissa's story, that her father—*my grandfather*—had been a scratcher. She didn't think she could live her life knowing there were tons of rock overhead that could come crashing down at any moment. She shivered at the thought of being trapped underground. *Give me the wide-open expanse of space any day. I'd rather die free-floating than be stuck in someplace like this.*

Jaks took one last turn and came to a stop in a small alcove with three passageways branching off in different directions. He pointed to the tunnel. "See the symbol?"

Zurah looked but had to enhance her vision to figure out what he was referring to. Above the tunnel leading off to the right was a triangle with a crudely carved *r* in the center. The middle tunnel had a square with the same letter, and the tunnel to the left had a single circle with an *r* carved above its darkened interior.

"These are some of the oldest tunnels. The original runs carved by the survivors. The symbols are crude representations of the different departments on the *Eagle's Nest*. The triangle is for security, the square is medical, and the circle is for engineering. As things grew desperate, the family groups started hoarding supplies and tucking them away in hidden locations," Jaks explained. "When a kid is old enough to remember, they're brought to a location similar to this. But only one time. From then on out, it's up to each individual to remember where the hidden stashes are at."

"Seems a little harsh," Zurah said.

"And repeatedly visiting the same place over and over again isn't suspicious at all," Jaks commented dryly. "We don't have the fancy tech you're used to. We have to rely on our own skills in order to survive."

Zurah bristled at the remark. "Hey, just because I have bioupgrades doesn't mean I haven't gotten where I am without hard work."

Jaks appeared as if he wanted to argue then snapped his mouth shut. Instead, he turned to his right and ducked into the tunnel marked with the security symbol. "We need gear, and our best chances of finding anything useful are through here. Most everything…" He paused as he had to kneel and scoot forward until the ceiling rose high enough for him to walk. "Has been picked over countless times."

"How many different places did your family hide stuff?" Zurah asked.

"A few. Unfortunately, this is the only place left for my family. The rest were either discovered or emptied out."

"And you're sure no one else knows about this place."

"For the most part. We all know each family has their own stash hidden somewhere, and for the most part, it's respected. Not because of what might be left in those stashes but more out of a sense…"

Zurah sensed he was struggling to find the right words.

"Our dead aren't buried. We don't have graves or anything like what the stories describe, where families can go and remember their loved ones, so these tunnels have turned into a type of a gravesite or tombs. A sacred place, I suppose."

The idea was a touch morbid, but Zurah understood. It was no different than the stigma around looting or reclaiming crashed ships or shuttles. Companies or scrap dealers made the news from time to time when they tried to harvest tech or parts from the downed ships. Invariably, a family would come forward, lodge a complaint, or file a lawsuit to stop anyone from desecrating the spot where their loved one died.

"Look." Jaks pointed to the floor. "See the marker?" There was another triangle and R carved into the floor at the junction of where a new tunnel branched off to the right.

"I see it," Zurah said and started to move in that direction.

Jaks reached out and stopped her. "Take a closer look. What's the difference between this one and the one we saw before?"

Zurah frowned and crouched down. As she studied the symbol, she realized the first *r*'s she had been shown were lowercase, while this R was uppercase. "The cases are different."

"Good. This is a false marker. Meant to confuse anyone who might not care about the unwritten rule of not taking from another family. Take the lead. Look for the next turn."

Zurah hesitated but slipped past Jaks and slowly started walking. She automatically flipped over to a visual filter to sort out the natural indentations and scratches on the rock, but remembering Jaks's comment, she shut down the filter. Zurah looked for the next marker without any help. She almost missed it. The marker was to her left, almost level with her line of sight. She stopped, took a step back, and pointed it out. Jaks nodded and urged her forward. There were three more markers before they stopped in front of a metal grate.

"I'm told it was taken from engineering, a part of the floor," Jaks said as he placed his hand on an ID panel.

"How is there still power down here?" Zurah was surprised to see Jaks wince at the question.

"They did what they had to, in order to survive," he answered.

The panel blinked green, and Zurah heard a series of locks disengaging. Then the grate swung open. Lights blinked on overhead, their sickly yellow light casting an unearthly tinge to the crudely carved-out room. Most of the crates were in various states of disrepair, with their lids either missing or discarded.

"Here. These are old, but still effective." Jaks pulled down a crate that had been tucked behind a stack of older ones. He reached in then handed Zurah a gun.

"You've got to be kidding me. There's no way these things still work," she said.

Jaks grinned. He took one for himself, reached back into the crate, and pulled out a power cell and a clip. Once he had them loaded, an indicator light on the side of the gun glowed green. "Might be old tech, but it was built to last."

Impressed, Zurah took two power cells and a handful of clips for herself. Before she could ask how she was supposed to carry the extra gear, Jaks had dug through another crate and pulled out an old jumpsuit and weapons belt.

"No," she said, eyeing the disgusting-looking piece of clothing. "I'm not wearing that."

"You're disrespecting my ancestors," Jaks said with a frown.

"The moment I start to put that thing on, it's going to disintegrate. There's no way that I'll—"

Jaks burst out laughing and tossed the jumpsuit to the side. "I'm kidding. Just take the belt."

Momentarily confused, Zurah stared at him then laughed with him, appreciating the moment of levity. As she adjusted the belt and secured the gun, backup power cell, and clips, she turned to inspect a few of the other crates. Most were empty, and the few that did have items still inside appeared fragile. She didn't want to break something, so she turned her attention to a piece of cloth hanging on the wall. The abstract design was pleasing to the eye, and despite the faded colors, there was still a bright and cheerful feel to the piece.

"Dr. Reed brought that with him. The story is the quilt was made by his mother in some history crafting class. Wasn't supposed to be anything special, but he liked it and brought it with him as a reminder of home. Fabrics like this were fought over at one point, and so my family hid it. There's been a few times when I've been tempted to use it to help patch up my clothing, but I've never been quite able to make myself rip it up into scrap."

He stepped forward and gently pulled the quilt to one side.

Zurah gasped. "Is that what I think it is?"

"One of the original mainframe units from the ship," Jaks confirmed.

Zurah couldn't help but run her hands over the metal casing. "I've read about these units. Never thought I'd ever get this close to one. There's a few museums that have them displayed, but they're behind layers of shields and protection." She bent over to get a closer look. "Are the quantum cards still intact? What about the internal processors? Is there any way to—"

"Slow down there," Jaks said with a half smile. "My understanding is that this is just a piece of a larger whole. They weren't designed to run on their own, were they?"

Zurah couldn't help but grin. "No, I don't think so, but that doesn't mean they can't be rigged." She turned to Jaks. "Why did your family keep this?" An alert popped up in the lower left of her field of vision, and Zurah blinked it away, eager to learn more about the mainframe unit.

He shrugged. "Not sure. My grandpa only mentioned it a few times in passing. Truth be told, I think most of them forgot about it. Just another relic from the past. A reminder of everything that had been lost. For some, that is pretty painful."

"Everything you've shown me has been tucked away for a reason, though. People don't hide their junk. They hide what they know is valuable." She stood. "Trust me, I know." She threw a quick glance at Jaks. "But still not a thief, if that's what you're thinking."

He let the quilt fall, hiding the mainframe unit.

"I know. We should get going. We've wasted enough time as it is."

She glanced back at the quilt and what it hid. She was itching to get her hands on the unit and try to figure out how to power it up. But Jaks was already heading out of the room. With one last longing look, she hastily followed him out. "It would be really helpful if you filled me in on your plan."

"You're not going to like it," he said.

"Try me."

"We know the Kin took the other members of your team. Which means they've been trying to interrogate them, convert them, or kill them. Those are the only things the Kin know how to do."

"And if any of my team breaks, you're concerned the Kin are going to discover exactly where we came from. You mentioned something about how the Kin have been kept here, on this world. What is that all about?"

"It's complicated, and don't get ahead of yourself," Jaks said as he swung the grate shut and locked it. "But yes, I was concerned about that. But that's before I knew about the Shadow and her team. There's a strong chance the Kin are already aware that others have come to the planet. Which could explain why the Elder Sons were putting so much pressure on the Old Mother. There are many who want off this world, and if there's a way, they're going to do whatever it takes to figure it out."

"What kind of pressure?" Zurah asked.

Jaks led them back through the tunnels. She wanted to make a snide remark on how her *memory* was doing just fine and point out she knew he wasn't taking her the way they had come. A small part of her wondered what he was up to, but she squelched the thought. Zurah needed a partner or ally, and right now, Jaks was it. So she kept her comments to herself.

"The Old Mother, she was the bridge between the Kin and Io. There's a couple of different versions of the story, of what happened in the early days. But I believe—"

There was the deep rumble of thunder, then a few seconds later, a sharp crack like the sound of lightning. A fissure opened on the left wall of the tunnel, rapidly expanding toward the ceiling. Everything happened so fast, there wasn't much time to respond. A large portion of the ceiling fell in front of them, followed by a horrific cave-in.

Zurah screamed and flung up her hands to protect her face, then she felt the impact of something heavy tackle her. Pain blossomed along her right side as the ceiling and wall collapsed, the dust choking her throat. A round of heavy coughing racked her body, and a hand covered her mouth, forcing her to stay silent. Her first instinct was to resist or try to bite, but Jaks hissed in her ear, "Keep quiet."

Sand poured down from the cracks in the ceiling, pooling all around them. Zurah's heart pounded as the sand shifted and rearranged itself to take on three distinctly humanoid shapes. Two, she didn't recognize, but when her eyes landed on the third, Zurah's heart dropped. *Alex.* She wanted to call out… to say something to him, but Jaks kept a firm grip on her mouth. Panic and despair flooded her body as she watched him move about the area, searching for something. *What have they done to you?*

"I thought you said they were here," one of the other two individuals snapped.

"They were. I traced her signal to this location. They were right here," Alex replied.

The taller of the two men marched over to Alex and shoved him up against the wall. "Either you're lying to us, or they knew we were coming. Run your trace again." The man released Alex, who glared at him but nodded.

As Zurah watched in horror, the alert she'd earlier dismissed appeared again. *How is he not seeing us? We're right here. They're practically standing on top of us.* She opened the alert and recognized the code. Someone had been able to ping her HalfLife chip and was running it through her SeeClear identity tags. Zurah was shocked and dismayed. *No one should've been able to hack my systems.* Then she groaned inwardly. *The damn chameleon I let him set up with me so we could privately talk.*

"The results are the same. She should be right here." Alex shook his head in frustration.

"Damned Io," the man who'd threatened Alex said. "Blast it. The lot of it. We're better off with them dead than alive anyway."

The other individual exploded into a maelstrom of sand, moving through the cracks and crevices of the damaged wall and ceiling.

"You and I are heading back. We have a meeting to prep for," the man said. He and Alex dissolved into sand and pushed up through the ceiling. As new fissures ripped through the rock, a deep rumble filled the tunnel. Rock crashed to the floor and exploded into debris.

Zurah squeezed her eyes shut, waiting for the

inevitable sensation of being crushed to death. *Please, let it be quick.* She listened as more of the ceiling gave way and the walls caved in, until everything eventually settled into silence. She reluctantly opened her eyes to ink-black darkness. Jaks's hand was still pressed tightly against her mouth, and his other hand had snaked over her torso and pulled her close to him, holding her in place. Zurah couldn't help but wonder how she'd cheated death again.

As her eyes adjusted to the dark, Zurah realized her original assessment was wrong. They hadn't been plunged into complete darkness. They were surrounded by faintly growing green lines spread out around them like a giant spiderweb. As she watched, the lines seem to drift around each other, and she realized what they reminded her of. *The gates. The strange lines when the gates activated.*

Excited and terrified, she enhanced her vision, magnifying as much as she could. This time, her heart raced not out of fear but excitement. Just as she'd seen before, there were strange things moving inside the lines. Zurah started to record and watched in awe and fascination. As before, there were repeated images or symbols. She still didn't know if she was seeing some type of communication or coding interface, but it didn't matter—she had one solid piece of information about the gates. The gates and the Io were connected.

Could the gates even be a type of crystal? Or embedded with crystals? Zurah's mind started to race with a slew of theories and ideas, and she wished she had her suit or another piece of tech to start running comparisons and datasets.

Jaks's grip began to ease, and his hand slowly slid away from her mouth, but his other still held tight to her waist. "We're safe for now. But we'll have to wait it out."

"Okay," Zurah whispered, not fully paying attention; her mind was too busy focusing on the revelation about the gates.

"Who was he?" Jaks asked quietly.

"What?" Zurah asked, then everything shut down. The horrible image of watching Alex appear returned, along with the realization of what witnessing that meant. "Maybe one of the Kin was imitating him. Like a disguise. Or it was one of Kailani's team members disguised as him. Gregori took on different appearances."

"I'm sorry," Jaks said, then he paused before adding, "He was someone… special?"

His question was hard to answer. Alex had become important to her over the past few weeks, and she had grown accustomed to his cheerful nature and ability to make her feel better. He'd helped her believe that everything was going to turn out all right. As hard as the truth was to admit, Alex had become something more than a friend. She had let her guard down with him and had sought him out more than once while they were waiting to go through the gates. Alex had been there, comforting her and assuring her everything was going to turn out all right.

And now, seeing him like that broke her heart, knowing what he had been through with the cryrot and now the Kin. She wanted to believe that another of the Kin had taken his form in an attempt to fool her, but in her heart, she knew it wasn't true. The way he had moved and talked—she had known it was Alex.

"How much longer do we have to wait?" Zurah asked, suddenly uncomfortable with her proximity to Jaks.

"I would estimate only a few more minutes. The Io are cautious and will want to make sure the Kin have fully left."

"*How* are the Io doing this?" Zurah asked, needing to distract herself.

She could feel Jaks taking a breath, thinking he was preparing to answer her question, but he didn't. Instead, silence settled over them until he quietly spoke. "If I tell you, I need you to trust me."

"You don't think this is trust?" she snapped. "Trapped in a cave-in, surrounded by energy readings I don't understand, from an alien entity I definitely don't get, and ready to follow you to the heart of the enemy? And *now* you're asking me to trust you?"

"I would say it's been a matter of convenient trust, wouldn't you? You needed me, and I needed you. Everything is different now."

Zurah grumbled. "Fine. Sure. But you shouldn't have asked it. Anyone who phrases stuff that way isn't trustworthy."

A tremor ran through Jaks's body, and for an instant, Zurah thought something was wrong. Then, she realized he was laughing. "True, I probably could have phrased it a tad bit different. But I'm not lying. I'm asking you to trust me. Please."

"I'm not sure who or what to trust anymore," Zurah

answered. "I've been dealing with half-truths for this whole damn mission."

Jaks's arm around her waist pressed in a bit tighter. "I promise I won't lie to you, but I can't promise I'll share everything. There are some things that I know, which could spell disaster for us all if they fell into the wrong hands."

Zurah briefly closed her eyes and considered her options. They were few and far between, especially if Alex had been compromised. The odds that the others had also been converted or killed were not in her favor. *I am my own boss now. There is no one else but me.* The temptation to give in and give up was there, like a predator stalking its prey, just waiting for her to make the wrong move and attack. *Why did I think I could come here and make a difference? I'm a fool. I'm nobody. If people like Finn and Alex, Angelina or Montgomery couldn't make a difference, why on earth did I think I could?*

Kailani's voice whispered in her ear. *"Then how do you think you would be useful here? You have no skills to offer. Neither the Kin nor the Io have interfaces or technology that you would be used to."* Zurah wasn't a scientist, a researcher, or an engineer. She was a security hack—she studied systems by reading manuals and blueprints or schematics. There were none of those things here. Even if, by some miracle, she was able to understand how the crystals were able to create the gates, she didn't have the first idea how to stop them. *Why in the worlds did Finn believe I could do this?*

Unless she didn't. And she only brought you along to keep you quiet. What would have really happened if you hadn't taken her up on her offer? If you'd decided to go with Nissa? Do you really think you would have stayed alive? Or would Finn have found a way to keep you quiet? Finn had told Zurah about the emperor and her great-grandmother. That was information Finn would not have wanted leaked. And she wasn't the trusting type.

Nissa's face appeared, her gaze soft and full of empathy. Instead of lying dormant in the stasis pod, Nissa was telling Zurah how much she loved her and how she would protect her at all costs. Zurah couldn't help but cry, desperately wishing she'd truly heard those words from Nissa. But Nissa had never had the decency to confess the truth of their relationship. *What did that make us? Did Nissa truly love me as her niece? Or was I just another member of her crew, a useful tool for a job?*

The feelings of being lost and unwanted welled up within her. Each crew she had worked for had been a temporary replacement for the family she had lost, a way to pretend she was wanted and useful.

"What's wrong?" Jaks asked, and Zurah sniffed, realizing she had started to cry. "We'll find a way to help him. I promise. Even though the Kin may have changed him, he is still him. Maybe he was forced to in order to save the rest of your team or to prevent the Kin from doing something even worse. We'll find him, I promise."

Zurah tried to shake her head, to tell Jaks that wasn't the reason for her panic attack. But the words were lodged in her throat. After a few deep breaths, Zurah tried to explain. "As a security hack, the types of jobs I do... Well, they're not always honest or up-front. And I'm used to living in half-truths and compartmentalized information. I understand that not everything is meant for anybody to know. It's just that… in the last few weeks, I've been a part of something… more. And it gave me purpose, greater than anything I've ever experienced. And yet, because of the world I live in, the type of job I've chosen, I don't know if I can fully trust anyone. Not because I don't want to. It's just… not how these things work."

As she confessed her innermost feelings to a man she barely knew, a warmth spread through her body. The soft-green lines of webbing surrounding them shifted, and lines of deep purple joined the intricate design.

"I think the one thing I've been searching for above all else is a place to belong. Where I don't have to worry about hidden motivations or betrayals."

The glow intensified, and the warmth turned into a heat of longing—a desire to belong. Zurah's next words died on her lips as the lines burst into a dizzying array of colors, twisting and turning through the air.

"The Io have chosen you," Jaks whispered, a twinge of awe in his voice. "They haven't chosen a new host for several years."

"Host?" Zurah asked. A small part of her knew the word should have alarmed her, but she was too enthralled by the joy, which began to replace the sensation of warmth. As time appeared to slow, Zurah let herself sink into the sensation of absolute bliss.

"The Io, or rather the Io we work with, are nothing like what you described. They do not seek to take over a body or control it. There's a lot we don't understand, but they seem fascinated with experiencing life from the perspective of other life-forms. You will have access to some of the integrations between the Io and this world, and in time, you may nurture a deeper bond with your particular piece of the Io, being able to call upon it in times of conflict."

Zurah's hand moved to her pocket and felt the warmth of the crystal radiating through the fabric. A small tendril of fear encircled her heart, but as her hand rested on the crystal, the fear dissipated. The lights were gradually dimming, and within a few more moments, they were gone, leaving them alone in the dark. She felt a shell of herself, as if something import- ant were missing. A whine of discomfort escaped, and she clutched the crystal through her pocket.

"You'll get used to the sensation of both feeling the Io and existing without it," Jaks said as he pushed himself up into a sitting position. "Just take a few deep breaths and focus your mind on something that is important to you. Then listen to the world around you, what you can smell, and what you can feel— through your fingers and your feet. Ground yourself in this world."

Zurah took a deep breath and focused on the stale, dusty taste to the air. Her fingers scraped against the hard floor, pinpricks of pain igniting where she had dug into the wall to pull off the panel. There were smaller rocks falling from time to time, cascading down the destruction all around them. As she focused on these sensations, her mind returned to itself, no longer feeling the loss of the Io.

"When I offered you the chance to learn from the

Io, I didn't expect this to happen," Jaks commented. "If I'd known, I would have given you a choice."

The panic she'd once felt when worrying about the cryrot taking over her body was gone. Instead, she felt everything she had been searching for. She *belonged*—she was needed and wanted and accepted.

As she got to her feet, she looked around at the cave-in. "The Io, they protected us?"

"Yes. I try not to call upon them unless absolutely necessary, and sometimes, it naturally exerts itself in moments of extreme danger. I've only had that happen two other times," he answered. "You never did answer my question."

Zurah dusted herself off then looked up at Jaks. His gaze was intense but not threatening, mostly earnestly wanting to hear what she was going to say.

"I'll try." That was as honest as she could be.

Jaks nodded, accepting her answer. "Good. We need to move. We're running out of time."

"Time for what?" Zurah pressed. "I came here afraid of the cryrot expanding and taking control of the known worlds. Of the death and destruction it promised. Now, you've talked about the Kin but not the threat they pose. Is it just the war between Kin and Io you're concerned about?"

"Partly. Remember what I told you about the Kin? From what we understand, how they used to move from world to world, stripping it of life?"

Zurah barely remembered him saying that. So much information had been dumped on her, and she was struggling with keeping it all straight.

"We don't understand, but somehow, in their conflict, the Io trapped the Kin on this world—or at least the majority of them, from what you've told me. We know that this is important, to keep the Kin here and not allow them access to the gates. What we do know and fear is that there is something unique about human biology the Kin find appealing. The Io have never explicitly told us this, but the Old Mother has hinted at their concern several times. We believe that if the Kin were to leave this world, to travel through the gates, they would seek out any outpost—no matter the size—that has human life and consume it."

13

Thanks to the Io's protection, Jaks and Zurah were relatively unscathed, and more than that, the tunnel wasn't completely blocked. They carefully picked their way through the debris and headed back the way they'd come. Jaks backtracked all the way to the metal grate protecting part of his family's items, then they headed off in a different direction. Zurah tried to ask a few more questions, to understand what they were going to be facing, but Jaks was mostly silent. What he did say didn't help much. If she were working on a coding project, she would dump the lot and start over.

"I thought you wanted me to trust you," she muttered.

Jaks slowed down and rubbed his forehead. "I do. Look, we're going to head to the eastern rim. That's where the Elder Sons and the Old Mother usually stayed. We need to get you into the Old Mother's chambers."

When he glanced at her, Zurah thought he looked tired and worn down.

"I'm really sorry, but the rescue mission will have to wait. I promise we'll do everything we can, but now that the Io have chosen you, there's something you need to see."

"I'm going to hold you to that," Zurah said. "And see, this is me trying to trust you."

Her comment won her a small smile, and he nodded. "Thanks. First, we need supplies. Without being able to tag and track your Shadow, we need to be quick and quiet. Follow my lead."

"I know the routine—act like I belong," Zurah said.

Jaks threw her an appraising look, then he straightened and exited the tunnel. Zurah followed, keeping her body posture as relaxed as possible. But it was hard when she expected Kailani to jump out at them at any moment.

Sending up gratitude and thanks to any religious deity or name Zurah could think of, she and Jaks made it to the supply hall without incident. There were two other individuals in the room, and Jaks greeted them both then walked them off to the side for a quick word.

He shook their hands, and one of the individuals slapped Jaks on the back. Zurah heard a "Good luck." When they were gone, Jaks started calling out orders. The crates and supply lockers were well organized and easily accessible, and in no time, they had stuffed two packs to the breaking point.

"Now comes the hard part," Jaks said. "I'm allowed to move between the rims as needed. But I didn't secure any travel orders to bring you here—that was where Clara came in and helped. Now, normally"—he hefted his pack on his shoulders—"I wouldn't be concerned. This rim is fairly lax, one of the reasons we usually met here when discussing… alternative plans. But knowing about Mayfield… and having been called to meet with the Elder Sons, then helping you get out of there… well…"

"We're compromised is what you're trying to say," Zurah added.

"Yeah. That's one way to put it. We need to—"

The lights flickered on and off, followed by a deafening alarm.

"We're definitely compromised," Jaks said with a grim look. "When you shoot, don't aim to kill. Just slow them down a bit. If we get through this, we'll sort out who is who later. Stay tucked up behind me. Clear?"

"Clear." Zurah pulled out the gun and stared at its dull exterior. Then, shutting down any other thought beside getting out alive, she powered it on.

Jaks moved to the door and peered around the doorway. He took a step out and looked both directions, gun held at the ready. When the coast was clear, he turned to the right. Zurah stayed as close to him as possible, angling her body so she could keep an eye out for anyone coming up behind them. The lights continued to flicker, casting eerie shadows in the rocky corridors, and the alarm grated on Zurah's nerves.

"Down," Jaks ordered, and Zurah crouched down behind him. "They're sending out patrols. Dammit." He glanced over his shoulder. "The first thing we do in the case of a breach is seal the exits. Then they'll start sweeping the rim for the intruders. We don't know if Kailani has specifically named us or is simply using the emergency protocols to try and keep us here. I don't know how far she's embedded herself as Mayfield. I have a lot of supporters, and it would become my word against hers. Either way, we can't wait it out. We've got to get you to the eastern rim."

"Why? Why not just find a spot to hide and ride it out? Let the alerts drop then sneak out?" Zurah asked.

Jaks stared at her. "I didn't want to add another burden on top of everything else, but you don't have a choice. Now that the Io have chosen you, I've got to get you to the Old Mother's chambers. This all would have been done under the supervision of the Old Mother and a few others."

"Just tell me," Zurah hissed.

"If we don't finish the process that the Io have started with you, then you'll die."

Zurah's grip tightened around the gun. "Then we'd better hurry up, because that isn't on my to-do list."

"Good." Jaks stood.

The corridor opened up into a larger space. A few crates were piled in the corners, and in the center of the room were rows of benches, all lined up facing some type of podium. Zurah glanced up and noted hundreds of clusters of crystals of all colors had pushed through the rock. Despite the beauty of the room, Zurah didn't like it. There were too many entrances and not enough places to take cover.

As Zurah was lamenting these facts, a young woman

stepped out into the room, saw the two of them, and paled. Her hand whipped to her side as Jaks held up a hand to stop her from doing anything rash.

"Enid, this doesn't have to end poorly," he said. "I can hazard a guess as to what the alert is about, but I assure you I'm not the intruder. Nor is she. Please let us—"

Enid pulled out her weapon and tried to take aim, but Jaks fired. One clean and efficient shot. Enid let out a cry of pain as she crumpled to the floor. Jaks jogged toward her and assessed the damage. He had struck her hip, and her jumpsuit was rapidly absorbing the blood. He crouched and grabbed her handheld comm.

"Enid Malowe has been shot. Requesting immediate medical attention." He let the comm fall then glanced down at the woman, whose eyes were wide with fear and confusion. "Tell them I'm still on their side and it's not the Kin we should be concerned about right now. We have a new enemy."

Zurah felt a tug of empathy as she gazed at the injured woman, wondering how old she had to be. The image of another woman lying in a pool of blood tried to force its way into her head, but Zurah shut it down. "We need to move," she told Jaks.

"Yes." He stood and gave Enid one last sympathetic look, then he took the lead. Both of them were jogging now. "We'll have to take the long way."

He entered another corridor and took off at a run. Zurah was concerned about being able to keep up with him but found herself running alongside him with ease. *Huh, I'm in better shape than I thought.*

A warning shot was fired from up ahead, followed

by a voice ordering them to stop and lay down their weapons. Jaks returned fire and shoved Zurah to the side as one of the rounds clipped his shoulder.

"Ten paces up ahead, go to your left. Move!" Jaks laid down cover fire as Zurah sprang into action.

She made the turn and slowed down, waiting for Jaks.

He burst into the new tunnel then spun around, firing a few more shots. "Twenty-three paces, then another left! Fifty-three paces and a right!" he shouted. "I'm right behind you!"

Zurah had made it halfway through the second set of instructions when she collided with a burly-looking man. He was momentarily startled then snarled. He didn't have a weapon, but he lunged for Zurah. Without hesitating, she fired. The first two shots went wild as they ricocheted off the walls. The third shot hit her target. The man's eyes widened, and he looked down at his chest. A splash of red was seeping through his clothing, and he staggered to the side and fell.

Without taking the time to dwell on what she'd done, Zurah took off, making it through the next set of turns. But then she was forced to stop and wait for Jaks. She squeezed her eyes shut and bit her lower lip until she tasted blood, focusing on the physical pain to keep from thinking about how she had just killed a man.

"You okay?" Jaks asked as he made his way toward her.

Zurah nodded. "You?"

"I'll live," he said. "Come on. We're almost there."

They ran through the tunnels, making turn after turn until Jaks once again slowed down. "This is the main entrance. I'm taking a gamble on security moving out to the other, lesser-used entrances. That's where I'd try and sneak you out."

His logic was sound—trying to outsmart what the security personnel would anticipate he would do—but when they entered the narrow corridor leading to the exit, Zurah's hopes sank. Mayfield, or rather Kailani, stood in front of a large door taken from one of the ship's bulkheads. She and the two men flanking her were equipped with weapons far more powerful than what Zurah or Jaks sported.

"That deal still stands," Kailani said, staring at Zurah. "I'm sure things are confusing right now. Who to believe, what side you should be on. Let me assure you that assisting me is assisting the orders of the emperor. When this is all over, you will want his gratitude, not his wrath."

"I'm not on anyone's side," Zurah said. "I only wanted to make sure no one else got hurt."

Kailani cocked her head to the side then pushed her chin forward to indicate the gun Zurah held. "How's that working for you?"

"Why don't you just let us go? We don't have anything that you want," Zurah said instead of rising to Kailani's baited words.

"I could let you go. While you're proving to have some survival skills, I'll be honest, I'm not too worried about you. But him, on the other hand"—Kailani turned her focus to Jaks—"he's a bit more of a hot commodity right now. Just the ticket that I've been waiting for."

Jaks took a step forward, ignoring Kailani. "Leif, Daren, you need to know that isn't Mayfield. It's an outsider with tech to disguise herself as Mayfield. No doubt she's killed him and—"

"We know exactly who he… or rather she is," the man standing to Kailani's right said with a grin. "This whole sacrifice routine we're taught is bullshit, and if you were honest with yourself, you'd agree. There are hundreds of worlds out there waiting for us. We deserve the chance to go home, to take back what should have been ours."

"Leif, you can't be serious," Jaks said.

"Deadly," Daren answered for his buddy, lifting his weapon to point its muzzle at Jaks. "We don't have any interest in staying on this godforsaken world. We want out."

"I'm sure you can understand," Kailani told Jaks. "How much has your family sacrificed? Your father then your mother? What about your brother? I'm sure they were all brave but misguided in their efforts, and for what? A species which hides the truth of their past? Of what they are truly capable of?" She spread her arms wide. "I may not have been born here, but I see this world for what it is. You should too. It's an illusion, meant to trap the Kin and the descendants of the *Eagle's Nest*. The Io are lying to you."

"You're twisting everything to suit your own purpose," Jaks snapped. "Daren, we studied together under the Old Mother."

"And I told you, we don't care. If you'd really been paying attention to what's going on, you'd have realized there are only a handful of saps like you left. We see the truth, and we want out."

"There's no need for unnecessary bloodshed," Kailani added. "I want this to be as painless as possible. We can work together, reveal the Io for what they truly are—"

"What would you really know about the Io? Or the Kin, for that matter?" Jaks asked.

"Far more than you think," a new voice answered from behind Zurah and Jaks.

Zurah's heart fell when she heard the voice, and she whipped around in time to watch sand drift across the floor, building upon itself into its humanoid form.

Alex smiled at Zurah, the same lopsided grin she had become accustomed to. "You all right?" he asked. "I really thought I wasn't going to get to see you again."

"What did they do to you?" Zurah whispered.

Alex raised a hand and waved it back and forth. "Nothing like the cryrot, if that's what you're thinking. The Kin shared their knowledge with us and offered us a choice." He let his hand drop then shrugged. "It's not without some sacrifice, but the benefits far outweigh the cost."

Zurah took a step away from him and shook her head. "No. The Alex I know wouldn't have done this. Not after what we experienced on Objer. Not after the cryrot."

Annoyance flashed through Alex's eyes, but he quickly composed himself. "The cryrot—no, excuse me, the *Io*—are the real enemies. You know that. You saw what they did on Objer and what we experienced on the platform. What do you think those crew members were trying to tell us? Or Gregori, for that matter? They were warning us about the Io, trying to get us here so we could find the Kin and be able to fight."

Zurah glanced over at Jaks then back to Alex. "But that's not what—"

Alex smiled softly. "I get this is confusing. And I know I haven't helped matters by not explaining things to you. I really try not to play the game, but after growing up with my family, it's hard not to." He took a step forward. "Just hear me out, okay? I'm not asking you to make the sacrifice that I have. All I want is to make sure we get you back to Objer safe and sound."

"The Kin are lying to him," Jaks said. "When we get to the Old Mother's chambers—"

Zurah stopped Jaks. "You told me that the Io doesn't share their history with you. Why is that?"

Jaks looked taken aback. "It's a delicate matter, about making sure information doesn't fall into the wrong hands."

"That's a bullshit excuse," Alex said. "They're hiding the truth in order to manipulate you. Trust me, I should know. My father's the master manipulator of them all."

"This is all quite touching," Kailani said. "But we're wasting time."

Alex moved at inhuman speed and placed himself between Kailani and Zurah. "You won't touch her."

Kailani smirked. "As I've stated, I'm not interested in your flavor of the month. But I *do* want *him*." She pointed at Jaks.

"And I could care less about him. So it appears we have a deal," Alex said.

Without thinking, Zurah reached out and grabbed

Alex's arm. He flinched but didn't shrug her off. "Don't let her take Jaks. He's been—"

"Manipulating you, Zurah. Come with me, and you'll understand. I promise."

"I won't be bargained over like a piece of food," Jaks growled. "If you want me, then come and get me."

Kailani snapped her fingers, and the two men opened fire. Alex turned and wrapped himself around Zurah to protect her, and before his body obscured her vision, she watched Jaks twist to the side and charge his one-time friends.

"We have to help him," Zurah tried to argue. "We can't let her have him."

"I'm sorry. I really am, but we need to go," Alex said. "This isn't going to feel the best, but hold on."

Zurah struggled against him as he wrapped his arms around her and hugged her tightly. Out of the corner of her eye, she saw Jaks throw a punch at Leif, then Daren grabbed Jaks's arms and twisted them behind his back. She cried out, but it was too late. Kailani stepped up next to Jaks and pressed her hand against his neck. In the next instant, Jaks's body slumped forward, and Zurah's world was ripped apart.

14

Zurah felt as if she were in the middle of a very violent and angry sandstorm that was intent on ripping through her flesh, one grain of sand at a time. There was a maelstrom of swirling colors, tans and reds, intermixed with flecks of black. Through the pain, she could still feel Alex's body—or the impression of his body—pushing up against hers.

Just as Zurah was all but consumed by the pain, it stopped. The sandstorm was gone, and Alex was holding her, grinning down at her like a fool.

"Welcome to the possibilities the Kin offers," Alex said.

Zurah blinked, trying to scrub away the sensation of grit in her eyes. When she dropped her hands, she stared in shock and reached out to grab onto Alex. "What the hell… Are we… dead?"

Alex laughed, throwing his head back in delight. "Not in the slightest. You can let go. It's okay, I promise."

Zurah hesitated, but his wide grin and carefree

manner provided enough reassurance that Zurah pushed back and let go of one of his arms. Feeling a tad bit more confident, she let go of his other arm, her mind trying to process what she was experiencing.

"Isn't it something?" Alex asked, throwing his arms wide and turning in a circle.

The air was warm and full of moisture against her skin, and it carried the scent of something sweet that she couldn't quite place. Wherever they had been taken, there were no physical walls, ceilings, or flooring. To Zurah, it appeared as if they were floating in space, except she wasn't. She could step forward or backward, and although she did not see anything, her feet moved across something solid. The darkness of space expanded all around them, and pinpricks of light from stars long dead decorated the view in the distance.

"Is this an illusion of some type?" Zurah asked, taking another hesitant step away from Alex. She stretched out her arms, trying to see if there were any edges her fingers might brush up against.

"I can't give you any scientific answers," Alex said. "All I know is that this is the Kin, that they offer the infinite possibilities of the universe, and all they ask for in return is freedom. Something that the Io took from them."

"But freedom at what cost?" Zurah asked. "Jaks told me that the Kin would spread from world to world, stripping it bare consuming it."

"I highly doubt that," Alex said. "If that was the case, wouldn't they have done the same to the world they're trapped on?" He moved closer and took her hands. "This partnership the Kin is offering, it's a game changer. There are so many possibilities with what the Consortium could do with the Kin, how they could help the known worlds."

"This seems too good to be true," Zurah said. "Nothing comes without some kind of price tag."

"Look, I understand your doubts. I had them, too, when we were taken. But Captain Ujthout has been a great help. He's been working with the Kin for a long time. Talk with him, voice your concerns with him, and he'll be able to set your worries at ease," Alex said.

Doubt wiggled its way through Zurah's thoughts, and she studied Alex for a moment, trying to see if there was any hint that he wasn't really himself. *Could this be a part of Kailani's trap? What if this really isn't Alex but one of her team members?* "Alex, what game were we going to play on the arcade wall you imported?"

He scrunched up his nose and answered, "Darts of Fire. Why?"

Zurah let out a sigh of relief. "Just checking that you were you." She started to tell him about what had happened with Kailani, then she stopped, watching his face transform into pure rapture as he gazed out past her. Alex might still have been Alex—at least where Kailani's subterfuge was concerned—but that didn't mean he wasn't compromised. And as the awe and impossibility of her situation receded, her mind caught up with what Alex had said. *There are so many possibilities with what the Consortium could do with the Kin, how they could help the known worlds.* Zurah was fairly certain if she had told the emperor what she'd said to Alex, his response would be much the same.

"Are you ready?" he asked. "I want you to meet the Kin. To hear what they have to offer."

Zurah couldn't say that she was eager to meet the Kin—or the Heart of the Io, for that matter. But she needed information. Nodding, she took his hand, and he pulled her in close, wrapping his arms around her. For a brief moment, she let herself rest her head against his chest and pretend that everything was okay, that they weren't trapped on an unknown world and the threat of danger wasn't lurking on the horizon.

The sand still stung, but the sensation wasn't as overwhelming as the first time. And when she opened her eyes, a sense of relief came over her. *At least we're somewhere now my brain can comprehend.* If she didn't know better, it appeared they were in the exact same type of underground tunnel Jaks had taken her to. That made her wonder how extensive the tunnel systems really were.

"I'll give you the quick tour. I'm pretty impressed with how resourceful the crew has been. This all feels… homey, if you can believe it. Probably because the captain and—"

"Alex, why did you come looking for me?" Zurah asked. The surreal sensation of it all was rapidly wearing off, and Zurah knew she had some tough questions that needed answers.

He gave her a puzzled look. "What do you mean? I needed to make sure you were safe. Who knows what they were planning on doing with you."

Zurah hardened her heart. "Not right now, but before.

When you were with the two other men. Were they threatening you somehow? And where are the others? Where's Finn?"

Alex stiffened and scowled. "How did you mask your signal?"

"I don't know, but I did see you, Alex. Why did they want us?"

All of the joy and exuberance drained from his face, and Zurah had a flash of memory of how he had looked when he and Finn addressed the group about going through the gates. This was the Alex Goldsmith everyone feared, the one who would one day run the Consortium. This wasn't the Alex she had come to think of as a friend or possibly something more.

His expression darkened, and he stepped forward, leaning toward her. "Zurah, whatever *he* told you were lies. You need to listen very carefully. The Kin are on our side. The Io are not. Or have you forgotten about the cryrot and what it did?"

Before Zurah could answer, sand swirled around then and formed into Captain Ujthout. Seeing the infamous man up close and personal was a bit of a shock. There were streaks of gray through his thinning hair, and his skin was sallow and deeply wrinkled. Zurah even saw a touch of madness in his eyes.

"I wasn't sure you would uphold your end of the deal. But I see you've only brought half of our agreement." Captain Ujthout was terrifying up close, and Zurah took a step backward. His irises were a pale yellow, and the sclera were bloodshot. The captain's lips were chapped, with dried blood flaked at the corners. Even his skin, what Zurah could see of it, looked horribly dry and scabbed. "Where is the other?"

Alex shrugged. "I'm sure he'll show up at some point. You know she wants to make a deal."

The captain scowled and reached out to grab Zurah. Just as his fingers were about to brush against her arm, she darted out of range, ready for a fight.

The captain's expression changed from disdain to surprise then to outrage. "She's already compromised. She's one of them."

"Impossible," Alex protested. "Zurah wouldn't make a deal with the cryrot. She was there, she saw what they could do."

"You fool," the captain snapped. "The Kin need to be made aware."

Alex stepped forward, glowering at the captain. "She isn't, and she's under my protection."

"That doesn't mean a damn thing," the captain sneered. "You're just the next shiny new toy to play with."

Alex stumbled back as if the captain had struck him. Then he shook his head. "I had assurances I could escort her here, that she would be safe. The Kin told me that she wasn't to be harmed."

"Then ask her," the captain demanded. "Ask her if she's still human."

Before Alex had a chance to do so, Zurah went on the offensive. "Still human? That's a bit like the pot calling the kettle black, isn't it? You're not really human anymore, are you?"

"I'm *more* than human," the captain said. "I'm

everything humanity has the potential to become. A jewel in the known worlds."

Zurah stared at him. "You too, huh? Angling for superiority? Because I've seen that story play out before, and it doesn't end well for the bigots."

The captain shook his head. "No, it's about pushing boundaries of what humanity is capable of. Being able to move throughout the known worlds, able to scout new resources, new planets suitable for colonization. We are spreading to the stars, and we need to be able to depend on ourselves to ensure the survival of the human race."

"In case Alex has failed to inform you, humans have done pretty well for themselves. We've developed competitive tech and businesses, partnered with several different alien cultures, and spread out through the known worlds," Zurah countered.

Captain Ujthout sneered. "And you would have humanity stay at that level? Stagnate while their competitors get the edge?"

Zurah shrugged. "No, but not like this. I mean…" She waved her hand at him. "Is it really worth what you've apparently given up?"

"Says the girl who has given herself to the enemy."

Alex turned to Zurah. "This is nonsense. Just tell him what he wants to hear, and I can give you the grand tour."

"Alex," Zurah said, "this isn't some vacation cruise. What's wrong with you?"

The captain took another step forward. "You're in league with *her*, aren't you? Trying to beat me to the prize."

Zurah was taken aback by the captain's vehemence in his words. "I'm not with anyone."

"But you came here with her. She showed you the way. Even after all this time, I can't be rid of the bitch."

What? "Alex, what is he—" Zurah stopped. She knew the captain couldn't be talking about the Old Mother, because she hadn't traveled anywhere with her. Nor could he be referencing Finn. While Zurah had come through the gates with her, Finn wouldn't have been known to the captain. Not until after they were on this world. That meant there was only one woman the captain was talking about. Angelina.

"That's enough," Alex said. "Zurah isn't a part of this. She simply was caught up in something far bigger than herself. My job is to make sure she gets home safely. But she isn't a part of any of the negotiations. Are we clear?"

The edges of the captain's form blurred as a look of pure fury settled in his eyes. "You don't tell me what to do. *I* secured the deal with the Kin. *I'm* the one who calls the shots."

"Not anymore," Alex growled. His body burst into a tornado of sand and moved straight for the captain.

Zurah backed out of the way but tripped. A fresh wave of pain rolled through her body. She desperately wished she had her suit and could numb the pain.

Alex and the captain fought, whipping around the corridor. Zurah had to turn and shield her face from the particles of sand, and she pulled herself up against a wall, trying to take cover. She wanted to run, to get away from it all. But she had nowhere to go, and a small part of her hoped Alex would have a rational explanation.

There was a howl of outrage, and the sand exploded outward. Half of it vanished down the tunnel, while the other half reformed into Alex. There were minor cuts throughout his body where he had a difficult time trying to pull himself together. When he turned toward Zurah, she shrank back from the distorted features. Sand flowed from his sightless eyes and out of his mouth.

He crouched next to her and extended a hand. The rest of his face settled, and he looked almost human again. "It's okay. I won't harm you."

"What have you done?" she whispered.

"What needed doing," he said as he stood. "Come."

Numb, Zurah stood and followed. "Alex, I'm sorry. I… I don't know what happened."

Alex laughed and shrugged it off, a complete one-eighty of his attitude. "Doesn't matter. I'll fix it. I told you I'd make sure you got back safely, and I will. Besides, I'm sure the Kin will understand once you explain it to them. They've been extremely forthcoming about all of this." He shook his head. "It's really just one giant mess, but you know what? Coming here was the best thing that could have happened."

"Why?" Zurah ventured to ask. If she had been confused earlier, she was completely adrift now.

Alex looked like Alex. He was full of smiles and grandiose gestures. She hadn't seen him this animated before, and a part of her was happy to see him so care-free. But another part of her was uneasy about being swept up into yet another situation she didn't understand. "Where are Finn and the others?"

His mood shifted again, and his shoulders fell forward as he frowned. "I tried to reason with them. But they wouldn't listen."

"Alex," Zurah said, a little more sharply this time. "Where are the others?"

"Come on. It's just up through here." He motioned for her to hurry.

They didn't have far to go until they stopped and turned into a room that had been carved out of the rock. Unlike the places Jaks had shown her, the walls, floor, and ceiling were as smooth as glass, as if someone had taken the time to polish the surface until everything in the room could see its reflection.

Encased behind gleaming walls were humans. But not just humans. There were species encased behind the walls that Zurah didn't recognize. Tall bipedal individuals with arms that touched the floor. Others were short and squat with ears and snouts that reminded her of lunar bats. Still others appeared more insectoid than humanoid. What truly bothered her, though, was the similarity with what she'd witnessed on the platform. Even though those crew members hadn't been behind a wall of sorts, they'd been placed in their own little alcove as if on display.

And here, each individual was encased in a crystalline cocoon. Zurah slowly made her way around the perimeter of the room, recording what she saw. When she stopped, she couldn't help but gasp and reach out to touch the gleaming walls. Finn was encased in one of the cocoons. To her right was Angelina, and to Finn's left was Montgomery. Each one had their eyes wide open, their expressions showing absolute terror.

"What did you do?" Zurah whispered.

Zurah jumped when Alex answered—she hadn't

realized he'd been following her. "Finn's always been too stubborn for her own good. I tried to get her to see reason, that we could figure out a way to come to a compromise. I agree that this knowledge, this partnership with the Kin, can't fall into the emperor's hands. Hiro is unstable at best and crazed at worst. There's no way he needs some kind of supersoldier. He would get humanity embroiled in a war we couldn't win. But the Consortium has checks and balances. We can make sure our partnership with the Kin doesn't become a powder keg with the other worlds. Of course, we'll return all intellectual property rights with whatever tech comes out of this, but we'll make sure it's for the betterment of humanity then the rest of the known worlds.

"I tried to explain all of that. But… Well, my cousin's not known for her ability to give and take. As for the other two, they became a security threat. It was better for them to be neutralized." He laid a hand on Zurah's shoulder, and she cringed. "Don't worry. We can revive them when the time comes. This is just another form of a stasis pod. No permanent harm will happen while they're in there."

Zurah spun around, fear and anger swirling through her. "How could you do that? Are you even you?" She leaned forward, peering at his eyes, looking for some kind of hint or tell that would assure her it wasn't Alex who had done this but something inside of him that had forced him to make this choice.

He smiled, and his eyes softened. "This is a lot to take in. Especially after the pack of lies I'm sure you've been told."

A jolt of disgust swept through her as she looked at him. Zurah couldn't wrap her mind around his attitude, how nonchalant he was acting. Forcing herself to take a physical and emotional step back, she asked, "What are you getting out of this? What's the catch?"

Alex's face scrunched up then fell as he looked hurt by her question. "I told you before that I don't—" He turned his head and sighed. "You're right. Unfortunately, there is a catch. As much as I wish I could be free of it all… I had a deal to make." When he looked back at her, his eyes were bright and earnest. "You have to understand, the Goldsmith Consortium maintains a delicate balance in the known worlds. If it wasn't for what my family has built, a lot of the way humanity lives and the tech they enjoy wouldn't be possible. We've had to make a lot of concessions behind closed doors in order to keep the peace, in order to protect humanity. Nothing is ever given for free."

In that moment, Zurah's heart broke, and she hadn't realized how close she had been to giving it to him. But he wasn't any different from anyone else. She'd been a fool, thrown into an impossible situation, and she'd latched on to the one person who really seemed to care, to be honest with her. She glanced over at Finn. *What was it that she told me? She warned me that his loyalties may be divided.*

Facing Alex, Zurah searched his face. *What did I really know about him? Has he been playing a long con with me or using me as a tool against his cousin? Or is he simply someone caught up in a battle he has no control over?* Either way, Zurah knew Alex had a choice. Everyone had a choice. Zurah had chosen to become a security hack and work with crews who ran less-than-legal jobs. She'd chosen every step of the way, but she'd never crossed the lines she'd drawn for herself.

"What did Captain Ujthout mean, accusing me of working with Angelina?" she asked quietly.

Alex's expression dropped like a kid caught in a candy store trying to sneak out with something. "Caught that, did you?"

"Yes. And I'd appreciate the truth."

Alex straightened up and moved to stand in front of Angelina. "When her pod came up for auction, I bid on it out of curiosity. I wasn't expecting anything. The auction house marketed the pod and occupant as an interesting relic to add to anyone's collection. Of course, most thought Angelina was dead and the pod had simply preserved her. Except when I got her home, and a few of my techs took a look, we realized not only was she still alive, but there had been a massive download into the pod's back storage units right before it had been launched from the ship."

Zurah was able to put together the pieces from there, but she needed to hear Alex's confession.

"While Angelina was alive, there was some damage to her neocortex and prefrontal cortex. I had the best medical docs work with her, but the damage had been sustained before she'd stepped into the pod, and being in stasis for so long... Well, there wasn't anything the docs could do.

"It turns out Angelina was a spy for the Emperor's Seat. She had direct orders to uncover what Captain

Ujthout had been tasked to do by the Central Alliance of World Leaders. Which, by the way, is where a part of the Goldsmith Consortium sprang from."

Zurah sucked in a breath and looked at Angelina. The information fit, from the attitude of Clara and the captain toward her name and even the complicated emotions from the Old Mother. Somehow, when the *Eagle's Nest* had been stranded here, people had discovered the truth. Or at least part of the truth.

"And the intel from her pod?"

Alex shook his head. "An opportunity too good to pass up. Especially when I realized Finn was already sniffing around. I couldn't be sure if she was looking for the same thing, but if she was, I had to make sure I beat her to it. Turned out, working with her was the easiest way to accomplish things."

Alex turned back to face Zurah, and he reached out to grab her hand. But Zurah stepped back and shook her head. A look of disappointment flashed across his face, then Alex schooled his features into dispassionate neutrality. "I wasn't out to get you, you know. You were just… someone outside the system who I thought I could work with. Someone without any entanglements with my father or other corporate dogs. And even though Finn had hired you, you had no loyalties to her. I'd really hoped you wouldn't find all of this out. I don't want you to think any less of me."

This time, Zurah made sure to keep her voice even and calm. "I don't think less of you. On the contrary, I should have realized it from the start. You are a Goldsmith and the heir to the Consortium. This is all you know, and I don't blame you for that. I only wish you could have been honest with me from the beginning."

There was a moment of uncomfortable silence between the two of them, then Alex spoke again. "When we downloaded and ran the decryption keys on the info from Angelina's pod, we found an old assessment document from the Weplies. Turns out, they had done a bit of exploration back in the day, looking for potential business opportunities and data mining. One of their scout ships came across an unknown alien ruin, and the crew ran a risk-assessment data spread. The tech they found held a lot of promising possibilities, but they determined there was too much risk in the business venture. They filed the report, and it was buried. An archivist doing a doctoral research program into Weplie culture ran across the report and sent it up the ladder to the Central Alliance of World Leaders."

"And this supposed tech?"

"The Weplie researchers identified several potential uses despite the large gaps in understanding how the tech worked. Psycho-resonance computing, psionic communication networks, quantum entanglement manipulation, reality manipulation fields, temporal displacement protocols, quantum cognition enhancements, and harmonic frequency shielding."

The list was impressive, and Zurah knew any of those applications would take the current level of tech to a whole new level, not to mention military applications. *What would the known worlds be like if the* Eagle's Nest *had returned with this tech? Where would humanity and other cultures be now?* The possibilities were staggering.

"You're being summoned to the Eye," a man said as he walked into the room. "Both of you."

Alex turned and nodded, then he shooed the man out of the room. "There's a handful of the original crew still running around plus quite a few of their descendants." He paused. "Zurah, I *need* this deal to go through. Captain Ujthout has agreed to work with me. Even though the political landscape has drastically changed since his time, he doesn't want the emperor to get his hands on this tech. Just… I'm asking you to let me do what I need to. I won't go back on my word. I'll make sure you get home safely and that Nissa receives the best of care."

Zurah didn't respond. She didn't know what to say. But despite what her gut was telling her, she believed Alex was here to make a deal. She had a sinking feeling he wasn't interested in understanding the war between the Io and the Kin and that he only wanted to plump up the bottom line for the Consortium. As she followed him out of the room, Zurah couldn't decide if that made Alex more or less dangerous than anyone else.

15

As Zurah followed Alex, the temperature in the tunnels fluctuated. One moment, she was chilled to the bone, and the next, sweat dripped down her face. The only constant was the sweet, almost floral scent that permeated the tunnels. Alex made one last turn, and a blast of air and noise hit them. At first, Zurah could only describe the noise as a massive space station generator on its last legs. But as they crept closer and the air blasted her face, Zurah realized the noise was *different*, and she couldn't quite figure out why.

"We're here," Alex half shouted. "Use these." He grabbed two belts and handed one to Zurah. As she secured the belt around her waist, Alex leaned in close. "This is the Eye. At least that's what the captain calls the Kin."

He tugged at her belt, took a heavy piece of cable,

and secured one end to her belt and the other to his. "Just a precaution. Don't worry. I've got you."

Each step forward became a struggle as the wind battered their bodies. When the tunnel angled slightly to the right, Zurah glimpsed the maw of an enormous cavern. Swirling inside the cavern was the largest tornado of sand she had ever seen. The power the Kin could generate terrified her.

Alex tapped her on the shoulder, and when he had her attention, he pointed to thick pieces of iron embedded in the rock. He grabbed one and motioned for her to do the same. As they slowly made their way closer to the sandstorm, Zurah was sure that her grip would slip any moment, and she would be sucked into the vortex. Alex stopped and tugged on the cable connecting the two of them. He pointed to the floor.

"No," she tried to shout over the roar of the Kin. Alex shrugged and pointed again. Zurah knew she had little choice and gingerly slipped one foot into what appeared to be an old spacing boot half encased in the rock. She slipped in the other, and the instant her foot settled in place, she could feel sand crawling up along her body, twining itself around her, and locking her in place. Panicked, she rolled her eyes to Alex, but he grinned and gave her a thumbs-up. Zurah assumed he was trying to reassure her, but every cell in her body was screaming with terror.

As Alex settled into place, Zurah realized they weren't alone. On the wall across from them were Captain Ujthout and the strange man she'd seen when she tried to steal her suit back. Except now there were two of them. *The Elder Sons! It has to be them.*

The sons were identical twins, and Zurah shivered at the sight of them. One more person had tethered themselves to the wall next to one of the Elder Sons. Zurah didn't recognize them and assumed they were a part of the captain's followers.

A part of the sandstorm broke off from its brethren and whipped through the narrow corridor where Zurah and the others were tethered. Pinpricks of pain broke out along her face and neck as the sand drew blood. But as it passed by her, she once again could smell something floral. When it had its fill, the sand settled into a rough imitation of a human. This one was different from the ones she had seen on the dunes, though. Subtle veinlike lines with a blue tinge wove through its body. *What the hell?*

Despite the Kin not appearing to have a voice, Zurah could hear it loud and clear. The words grated against each other and felt raw. "Where is the one who holds the tribunal?"

Both of the Elder Sons tilted back their heads and howled. Their cries of agony competed with the roar of the sand, and when they finished spilling their grief, they spoke. And despite the Elder Sons' mouths not moving, Zurah could hear them. They spoke in sync, neither voice distinct from the other. "The Old Mother is no more. The Old Mother has been killed. The one who holds the tribunal has been vanquished."

"Who now speaks for the one who was before?"

"We do. We do."

The Kin appeared to leap backward off the edge, returning to the angry swarm of sand. Then, as abruptly as it had disappeared, it returned. "This has been accepted."

"We acknowledge your acceptance," the Elder Sons replied.

"We are hungry. We are dying. Do we have an accord?"

Zurah's heart raced. She knew what was coming, and she had no way to stop any of it.

"We no longer hold to the precepts of the Old Mother. We are our own selves. We, too, are hungry and wish to rid ourselves of this world. We have secured the means to do so."

Zurah turned her head to Alex, who appeared eager and ready to reply, but before she could hear what he wanted to say, someone else spoke.

"You hold the key to leaving this world, and I have the ability to use it," the voice said.

Zurah turned her attention to the man who was strapped in next to the Elder Sons.

"Your prisoners have the ability to signal the next world and open the gates. I will do that, as long as I have your word I will secure the right to the Heart."

"It has been agreed," the Kin replied. "We will not be slaves again. We will be free, and we will have our fill."

"As agreed, provided you don't touch the list of worlds I've given the Elder Sons. If you do, then all deals are off," the man said, except Zurah knew it wasn't a man. *Kailani.*

"Hold on," Alex interrupted. "*I* had a deal with you. You promised me that when we returned, we could—"

The Kin dissolved into a miniature version of the frightening tornado of Kin. It spun itself toward Alex and covered his body. Zurah desperately wanted to clamp her hands over her ears to drown out his desperate screams. When the Kin was finished with Alex, he was covered in blood, and his breathing was heavy and labored.

The Kin reappeared and spoke. "You boast of profit. Of technological riches. We will not be slaves. We have endured enough."

Zurah wasn't sure what came over her, but she turned to stare at the Kin. "That's all she wants too. She isn't what you think she is," Zurah shouted. "She'll use you and trick you into doing whatever the emperor wants." She turned to look at Captain Ujthout. "I thought you hated the Emperor's Seat. Why would you make a deal with one of his Shadows?"

"Lies," the captain hissed. "Lies from an Io host who only seeks to keep the Kin prisoner here."

"I'm not lying!" Zurah shouted. "Test her." She scrambled back in her memory, to when she'd studied the schematics for the masking tech.

"I don't know what she's talking about," Kailani protested. "I'm here to help you. To relieve you of your—"

The masking tech had an interface that was implanted at the base of the skull, with units extending into the motor cortex. But the masking tech required a small unit to be clipped near the face somewhere outside of the body. This unit carried the nanotech that created the mask. Zurah frantically searched Kailani's outfit and realized there was a band around her neck. *That's it.*

"I can prove I'm not lying!" Zurah shouted. "Target the band around her neck. Rip it off, and you'll see I'm telling you the truth."

"Don't you dare!" Kailani shouted back. "This violation will nullify our agreement. I won't stand for this. Release me!"

If they hadn't been securely tethered in place, there was no way she would've been able to reveal Kailani for who she really was. But Kailani had nowhere to go.

She turned to stare at the Elder Sons. "I brought you what you wanted. We have a deal. You know what I'm offering."

But the Elder Sons were mute as a second Kin appeared in front of Kailani. Its swirling hand of sand reached out and ripped the band from her neck. The mask disappeared, revealing her true self.

Kailani glared at Zurah. "You foolish girl. You don't understand what you've done."

Captain Ujthout was thrashing against his restraints, yelling obscenities at Kailani. Despite the shouts and the sandstorm, Zurah heard a cough then a raspy voice.

"I haven't lied to you about who I am," Alex said. "My offer still stands."

"Alex, you can't do this," Zurah tried to say, but he spoke over her.

"Honor our agreement, and I'll help you leave this world. The Goldsmith Consortium wields more power than the emperor. We will be a more powerful partner. And I can guarantee you will not be a slave but brought in as a sentient race, granted the full rights of any other race in the known worlds. You have my word."

"We do not acknowledge this man," the Elder Sons said. "For whom does he speak?"

"Silence!" the Kin roared.

The floral scent overwhelmed Zurah's senses, making her nauseous from the sickly sweet smell. Both of the Kin returned to the maelstrom, and the captain, the Elder Sons, and Kailani all started to argue among themselves.

Zurah rolled her head to the side. "You can't let them off this world without understanding the threat they might pose. Don't you want to know why the Io trapped them here?"

The blood had already begun to crust on Alex's skin, and as he turned to look at her, Zurah could see the pain the movement caused. "The cryrot have lied to you. Or don't you remember what happened on Objer? Because I do. I can't forget their voices, the screams…"

"The cryrot doesn't speak for all of the Io," Zurah protested. *Or at least I hope it doesn't.* "We need to understand what happened between the Kin and the Io before you make any rash decisions."

"Rash?" Alex coughed. "You think I'm being rash? We've had this intel for over three years. The best in the Consortium have weighed the benefits against the cost. The technology we can gain is incalculable. You're just worrying over nothing. If anything goes wrong, the Consortium has the ability to contain it. Thanks to you and what we discovered on Objer, we can control the cryrot. And if it doesn't want to cooperate, then we'll destroy it.

Besides, it isn't like there haven't been bumps along the way before. There's always pain in growth."

"Are you hearing yourself right now?" Zurah asked. "You sound exactly like her."

"I'm nothing like—"

But his protest was cut short as the Kin reappeared. Everyone went silent as they waited.

"We are not pleased, and yet we are hungry. The Old Mother held the sway of the Io, preventing the Kin from satiating their hunger. The Elder Sons have made promise after promise, only to bow and scrape to the Old Mother. The man who is not a man has brought the memory of deceit, and the captain, who brought us hope of being free from our prison, has done nothing. We are not pleased, and yet we are hungry."

The Kin walked until it was standing in front of Alex. "We have shared our gift with your flesh and are not pleased. Yet we are hungry. You will provide us the means to leave this prison."

"Then we have a deal?" Alex asked.

"We have reached an agreement." The Kin turned to Captain Ujthout and the Elder Sons. "We are tempted to consume what is left but feel it will be needed in the effort to free us from this prison. Do not fail us again."

The Kin disintegrated into sand and left to join the swirling mass of its brethren. The scent of flowers lessened, and the roaring of the maelstrom quieted, yet the roar left an echo in Zurah's head. Even the terrifying winds that had threatened to sweep them away had significantly diminished. The sand that had twined around their bodies was swept away, and Zurah watched as the others disengaged from the boots.

"I want them taken to the cells," Captain Ujthout ordered. His look was murderous as he lunged for Zurah, and the Elder Sons went for Kailani.

But Kailani was prepared, and a knife flashed in her hand. With three quick movements, she had one of the Elder Sons lying in a pool of blood on the floor, while the other hissed and snarled as he lunged for her. But Kailani was fast—Zurah bet she had bioupgrades laced throughout her body—and she disappeared down the tunnel. All of this happened in the blink of an eye, and Zurah was too overwhelmed to resist the captain's grip. He all but pulled her out of her boots and threw her to the ground.

"She's still under my protection," Alex groaned, and he pulled free of his own set of boots.

"I don't care what you think she is," the captain snarled. "She's a threat."

"And that threat exposed the enemy." Despite his apparent pain, Alex placed himself between the captain and Zurah. "I'm in charge now. And that means you'll take orders from me. Or do you wish to argue this point with the Kin?"

Whatever was left of the captain must have seen the logic in Alex's words, because he stepped to the side and didn't protest. But the madness swirling through his eyes made Zurah wonder how the captain was going to try to get back at Alex.

"What are your orders?" the captain ground out.

"There still remains the problem of her relationship with the Io."

Alex took a long look at Zurah, and she shrank back under his scrutiny. "Have you joined with them?" he quietly asked.

"I don't know." Zurah was too afraid to lie to him at this point. Not without a plan in place. "Something happened when you were looking for me, but I didn't seek them out. Whatever it was, it was an accident."

Alex nodded. "I see." He took a deep breath and exhaled slowly. "I find myself repeating my promise to you over and over again, which makes me wonder if it's worth much. As long as you don't get in my way, you'll return to Objer. You and Nissa will be taken care of, and you'll enter into a contract with the Consortium. You'll make far more working for me than you ever would with freelance jobs."

Every inch of Zurah wanted to scream in protest, to fling the truth in his face that she had destroyed the way home, but she was out of options. Instead, she bowed her head in submission.

"Good, then it's settled. Captain, I agree with your recommendation that she be taken to the cells. But I want her made comfortable. She isn't a prisoner; she merely needs to be kept safe until it's time to go home. Do you understand?"

"Yes, sir," the captain said. He swooped down, grabbed Zurah's arm, and hauled her to her feet.

She wrestled her arm free of his grip. "I can walk on my own, thank you."

"Then move," the captain said.

When Zurah made a wrong turn, the captain snarled and made a snide remark, correcting her. When they reached the cell, he flung open the door, bowed mockingly, and extended his hand toward the small room as if being a gracious host. Alex hadn't followed them nor had the other Elder Son. She didn't know where they had gone or what they were doing, but she was sure it wasn't good. None of what had happened was good or right. Alex had completely transformed into something Zurah detested. *Or that was the true him all along, and I was played as the fool.*

Disgusted with herself and the situation, Zurah stepped toward the cell then glanced at the captain. An idea flashed through her head, and she didn't hesitate or stop to think through the consequences. Instead of meekly obeying and walking into the cell, Zurah rammed the captain.

He toppled into the door as she grabbed her gun. *Fools, they never even took the time to disarm me.* Without wasting a moment, Zurah fired and turned away as the captain sank to the floor. She fired two more times then held her breath as she waited. Zurah didn't know if a bullet would wound the captain or if it would merely serve to irritate him. The sound of the shots had echoed through the corridor, and Zurah was sure someone would come running to see what had happened. But she needed to know if those who'd gone over to the Kin could be stopped.

Captain Ujthout looked down at his chest then up at her. He snarled as sand trickled out from his wound.

Pushing himself away from the door, he staggered toward her, then there was a look of shock as he fell to his knees. The sand continued to pour from his chest, and he scooped his hands through the growing mound on the floor, frantically trying to stuff it back inside his body.

Zurah was both disgusted and relieved. *Jaks didn't mention the weapons had been modified.*

The captain's movements gradually slowed down, and the wounds grew in size and consumed his entire body. Before long, the captain was nothing more than a pile of sand. Alex had underestimated her. He'd seen her as nothing but a cog in the great machine of the Consortium. A tool to be used. Someone who wasn't going to fight back.

He should've known better after what had happened on Objer. *Or did he think I'd fallen for him? Some kind of star-struck-lover scenario?* Zurah no longer cared. Alex was now the enemy. Her original mission stood—no one was going to get through the gates. She was here to protect the known worlds.

Racing down the corridor, she looked for a place to hide. But these corridors all had lights. There were no darkened passageways or offshoots from the main tunnel. She tried a few doors, but they were locked. Bringing up her SeeClear tech, she retraced her way to the chamber where Finn and the others were being held, but as she was about to round the last corner, she heard voices.

"Release Finn. I need the intel in her suit," Alex was telling someone. "But give her a neural dampener. We don't need her to be aware when we go digging around for the information."

Zurah came to a stop and pressed up against the wall. *Shit. I've got no allies. No schematics of this place. What's my next move?*

Zurah had completely forgotten about the crystal tucked away in her pocket, and she felt its warmth seep through the material of the suit and into her skin. Once again, Zurah didn't hear any words but understood what the Io was trying to communicate. It was asking her for completion, as long as Zurah would stand on the side of doing what was right.

If that means protecting Nissa and the known worlds, then yes. I'm in. The warmth flooded her body, and purple webbing danced its way around her, weaving in and out to create a similar version of the knots that Zurah had witnessed at the gates. Light flooded her vision, and in the blink of an eye, Zurah vanished.

16

When Zurah was able to see clearly again, she yelped in surprise and leaped back. Jaks was stretched out on a rather tattered-looking mattress, his eyes closed, and his chest evenly rising and falling. Zurah spun around and took note of the small cell she had landed in. As she came full circle, nausea abruptly overwhelmed her, and she fell to her knees, emptying the meager contents of her stomach. Acid burned her throat, and she started coughing. When she was able to take a breath without triggering another round of coughs, she sat back and wiped her mouth. She was alarmed to see a smear of blood on the sleeve.

"You should not have used the Io to transport," Jaks said, then he added, "Palm trees."

"I didn't do it on purpose," Zurah replied as she turned around.

Jaks had sat up and scooted up against the wall.

"You look a little rough around the edges. Oh, and Gambler's Rift."

"Right back at you," he said. Purple blotches were beginning to appear on various parts of his face and arms. He had dried blood in his hairline, and his left eye was starting to swell. "What are you doing here?"

"That's all I get?" Zurah asked. "No, 'Gosh, great to see you. Thanks for trying to rescue me'?"

Jaks raised an eyebrow. "Is that what this is?"

Zurah huffed. "No. I don't know what this is."

Jaks's expression softened, and he got up and moved to sit across from her. "Then tell me what happened."

There was a faint glow within the depths of his eyes, and his expression was earnest and open, waiting to learn what had transpired.

Zurah was pulled in two different directions. She had trusted Alex when she needed an ally, yet he had turned around and… *Not betrayed. I don't think I can call it that. Because he never promised me anything but being able to safely go home. But he definitely played me for the fool.*

Jaks drew back, and the glow in his eyes dimmed. His expression hardened.

But what do I gain by staying silent? Or telling selective bits of what happened? I need people who can help me stop Alex and the Kin from going through the gates.

Another wave of nausea overwhelmed her, but there was nothing left in her stomach except for bile. She leaned to the side, her stomach cramping again and again. The pain wrapped around her torso, and for a brief moment, the sensation was unbearable.

"The Io need to complete their bonding process,"

Jaks said quietly. "The fact that you transported here will only escalate the breakdown within your body until the process is finished."

"That would have been great to know before," Zurah muttered. "But it's not like I had a choice. I wasn't going to end up a prisoner nor at the mercy of any of them."

"Then tell me what happened. Let me help you," Jaks said.

As Zurah pushed herself back into a sitting position, she cringed at the twinge of pain in her side. "I've trusted before, and it isn't working out like I'd hoped."

"I want to make sure the Kin are not released from this world, and I want Kailani and those who've followed her to be punished for what they've done," Jaks said. "Why don't we start there?"

"And what if the Io have truly been lying to you? What if they're the real threat?" Zurah asked.

"I"—Jaks glanced down then back at Zurah. "I can't answer that."

"Good," Zurah said. "Then until that time comes, we're partners, agreed?"

"Agreed."

Zurah knew the risks, but she was well aware of the reality that she wasn't going to be able to do anything on her own. Especially not on a world with no tech she could hack and very little understanding of how it all fit together.

She told Jaks what had happened, and by the time she finished, he was furious. Despite limping, Jaks had gotten to his feet and was pacing, cursing Alex and the captain for their stupidity and slinging a slew of other hateful statements aimed at the Elder Sons.

"Are you done?" Zurah finally asked, feeling a little exasperated.

"Yes," Jaks snapped then regained his composure. "Yes, I'm done. For now."

"Great. Then it's your turn," she said. "What happened to you? I thought for sure Kailani was going to kill you."

"I'm fairly certain she wanted to, but after they'd… subdued me, they dumped me here. From what I gathered, she must have thought I could be used as a bargaining chip with the Elder Sons."

While that wasn't the great breakthrough Zurah was hoping for, she agreed with Jaks's assessment. It was always wise to have an ace up your sleeve, and Jaks had obviously made enemies with the Elder Sons. If Kailani had needed to persuade them, being able to offer up someone whom the mark hated was a definite ace.

Shakily, Zurah tried to stand, but her legs were weak, as if she'd run the whole circumference of a Lunar base—twice. Jaks moved to help her, and with his support, she was able to stand.

"The first thing we need to do is get you to the Old Mother's chamber," Jaks said. "You won't do me any good if you're dead."

"Great," Zurah muttered. "O, great crystals, would you pretty please be able to take us to the Old Mother's chambers? That'd be great, thanks."

"This isn't a joke," Jaks said, but he tensed as if waiting for something.

Nothing happened. No subtle glow of lights weaving their way around their bodies. No unspoken messages. Nothing.

"Well, it was worth a try," Zurah mused. "But that leaves us with a bit of a problem. How *are* we going to get out of here?"

"I was waiting for confirmation of the Elder Sons' next move. Now that I have it, I can contact Clara," Jaks said. "You okay?"

Zurah nodded as Jaks let go and reached down to his right boot. He quickly slipped his foot out of it then twisted the heel off the boot. A small object dropped into the palm of his hand. After replacing the heel then his boot, Jaks stood. "Now, this is old-school."

"What is it?"

"A short-wave radio."

Zurah pursed her lips and studied the object. It was dull black and boxy in shape, with dials on the front. Jaks pulled up an antenna and grinned.

"Told you it was old," he said. "Of course, there have been a few minor upgrades." He flipped it over and popped open a panel to reveal a small crystal. It was white and perfectly spun into a small cylinder, exactly like what she'd seen in the room Kailani had thrown her into.

"I don't get it," Zurah said. "You've told me that the Io are a sentient race, and yet you must have ground this down for its shape and size to place it in there. How can you do that?"

There was a flash of confusion on his face, then Jaks laughed. For a moment, Zurah was horrified she'd made a terrible mistake and feared the worst—that the descendants of the *Eagle's Nest* had enslaved the Io and mutilated the crystals in order to suit their own needs.

"I'm really glad to hear the disgust in your voice. That tells me quite a bit," Jaks said. "No, we aren't monsters. We haven't done anything to the Io. These crystals are… waste products. There's a lot we don't understand, but what we do know is that the Io gave us permission and assured those who doubted that these crystals are not sentient."

A wave of relief washed through Zurah. "Wait. Waste product?"

Jaks shrugged. "When you're thrown onto a world with barely anything to survive, cut off from anyway of returning home, you use what is available to you."

"Uh-huh." Zurah unconsciously wiped her hands on her jumpsuit at the thought.

Jaks put the panel back in place, flipped the radio over, and adjusted the dials. When he flipped it on, there was a burst of static then a steady crackling noise. "Clara. Come in, Clara. This is Jaks." He paused then tried again. But there was still nothing but static.

"Are you sure Clara hasn't switched sides?"

"No. But I highly doubt it. Her mother was executed by the—"

"I'm here. Jaks, all hell is breaking loose. Where are you?" Despite the static, Clara's words were clear.

"Long story, but the short of it is I need a jailbreak. Think you can manage?"

There was another pause, then she responded.

"I've tagged your location. I've got a couple people I trust in that rim. It'll take a hot minute, but hold on."

"Understood," Jaks said. "We're running out of time, though. So as fast as you can—"

The door to the cell burst open, and Alex marched into the room. His expression was cold and calculating as he surveyed Jaks and Zurah. "I figured Finn had given you a few assignments she wasn't going to share with the rest of us, but I hadn't thought my cousin foolish enough to want to destroy our way off this planet," Alex said. "You stupid woman. I made you a promise, and I would've kept it. But now, you've forced my hand."

As he turned to focus on Jaks, he spotted the small radio and lunged for it. Jaks pushed Zurah to the side then rolled away in the other direction. Alex quickly regained his footing and went for Jaks again. This time, he made contact, and they hit the floor with a sickening thud. The radio flew out of Jaks's hand and slid across the floor, coming to rest beside the door.

Despite the injuries both men had sustained, neither was giving in. Jaks flipped Alex off, then he rolled on top of him and landed two solid punches to Alex's right kidney before Alex managed to punch Jaks in the jaw. The momentum of the punch was enough to throw off Jaks's rhythm and allow Alex to gain the upper hand.

Alex threw another solid punch to Jaks's side then kicked him off. But Jaks managed to find his feet and stumble back before Alex had a chance to pin him down. The two men rushed each other again, and as they struggled, Zurah got to her feet and raced over to the radio.

As she grabbed it, she spun around, unholstered her gun, and pointed it at Alex. "Let him go."

Alex glanced up and grinned. "You're not going to shoot me, and even if you did, your bullets can't do anything to me anymore."

"I think Captain Ujthout would disagree with your assessment," Zurah replied. "Alex, let him go. I don't want to hurt you, but I will if you leave me no choice." Her grip tightened around the gun's handle.

Alex raised his hands, stepping back from Jaks, and said coldly, "And here I thought we were friends."

"We were temporary partners," Zurah responded. "And when our agendas went in different directions, our partnership was dissolved."

"Spoken like a true thief," Alex said.

"You'll let us go," Zurah replied, ignoring his little jab.

"No, I don't think he's going to." The muzzle of a gun pressed against the back of Zurah's head. She glanced at Jaks then back to Alex. If she fired, she might wound Alex, but she would be dead. Then Jaks would die. She had no choice but to surrender, drop the gun, and raise her arms.

"Looks like you're in the market for a new partner," Kailani said as she stepped to the side.

"I have no interest in getting into negotiations with the emperor," Alex commented dryly as he reached down to pick up Zurah's gun.

"Neither do I," Kailani replied. "My son is a fool. A scared little boy grasping at straws as his empire collapses around him."

Zurah jerked her head to the side and stared at Kailani in shock. *The Empire is collapsing? What?*

"Why do you think my father has been so adamant about this whole damned mission?" Alex asked. "I wasn't aware of the stakes until Finn let it slip that the emperor had sent a team through the gates. If I'd known, things would have happened differently. But why go through with your mission then? If you have no interest in helping him?"

"Because when I return, I plan on making a tidy little sum of credits off this enterprise, enough to rebuild the emperor's Seat the way it should be. Not the caricature my son has turned it into."

"Ah, so this is a coup," Alex said. "I shouldn't be surprised, really. You lot have a bad history of trying to usurp each other. You really should take a page out of the Goldsmith family handbook. That type of insubordination isn't tolerated."

Kailani laughed. "Your father told me the same thing. Now, back to business. I'm quite certain my clever little daughter has encrypted the more important files on her suit. But who do you think taught her those tricks? Have you tried to access it yet?"

Alex's face darkened. "We have."

"And?"

A wave of panic washed through Zurah. *The gates must have been destroyed. I did everything right, the blind, the melting codes… all of it. What could be so important in Finn's suit? Did she play me?*

"You wouldn't be offering your services if you didn't already know the answer to that question." Alex glanced at Zurah then swung the gun to point it at Jaks. "But I happen to know a very good security hack."

The blood drained from Zurah's face as she realized the choice she was being forced to make. If she told Alex she would help hack Finn's suit, then she would save Jaks's life but allow Alex and the Kin to go through the gates. That was against everything Zurah had set out to accomplish on this mission. But she would be forced to watch someone else die, someone who had risked their life for her, even when they hadn't known who or what she was.

Zurah closed her eyes for a brief moment. Oddly enough, her mind calmed, and her body relaxed. When she opened them again, she looked at Jaks. "No, I won't help you."

Once more, Alex had underestimated her resolve. He looked shocked then sneered at her. "I'll shoot him."

"I understand," Zurah replied.

Jaks smiled and gave Zurah a small nod of respect, and she didn't take her eyes off him as Alex marched over and pressed the muzzle of the gun to Jaks's temple. Time slowed as Alex's finger moved to the trigger and started to pull it back. Jaks mouthed "Thank you" and closed his eyes, waiting for death to take him. Zurah forced herself to watch, fully understanding the conse-quences of her decision and the choice she had made. But something behind Jaks caught her attention.

Streaks of light, deep greens and purples, raced across the room. Then came reds and blues along with vibrant yellows and oranges. The lights danced with each other, twining back and forth, until they grew so bright, Zurah's

SeeClear tech had to adjust. Then, just as the light grew too bright even for her bioupgrade to handle, it burst into a thousand different hues, raining down color all around them. Alex and Kailani were thrown back against the walls. Their bodies slid down before coming to rest on the floor at unnatural angles.

Jaks's eyes widened, and his jaw dropped open as he stared at Zurah. He took a step forward, but before he could reach her, the lights formed their intricate webs around each of them. Once more, the Io transported them to safety.

Zurah stumbled as her feet hit something solid but uneven. Jaks reached out to support her and let her lean against him. A fresh wave of nausea flooded her body, and he patiently held her until the trembling and dry heaves stopped. When she wiped her face, the jumpsuit came away soaked in blood.

She turned to stare at Jaks. "What is happening to me?"

Jaks's expression was grim, but his eyes danced with the strange green light. "You proved yourself worthy to the Io. And they are giving you a chance to live. Look."

Zurah blinked and saw jagged stalagmites and sta-lactites throughout the cave the Io had taken them to. A light shimmered toward the back of the cave, and as Zurah zoomed in, she realized she was staring at a wall of gleaming crystal. Its surface was a honeycomb with a myriad of different-colored crystals tucked up within each section of the honeycomb.

Jaks tugged on her arm gently and led her across

naturally occurring bridges and under delicate archways stretching across the cavern. The view was breathtaking.

"As I said before, the Io do not share their history with us. But there are some things that we know. The Io are connected, like a hive mind, and the heart of their race is here, in this cavern. There is only one way in and out, and that has been a secret closely guarded by the Old Mother. Not even the Elder Sons know about this place. They suspect, but she never told them."

"So how do you know?" Zurah asked.

"The Old Mother knew she was dying, or rather that she wanted to die. The Io and the Kin could have kept her alive for hundreds of more years, but she was tired of carrying the burden of the tribunal. She wanted to pass on the responsibility to someone else. Someone who understood what the Io were fighting for and why."

Zurah forced them to stop and stared at Jaks. "She had chosen you, hadn't she? That's why the Elder Sons want you, and they've kept you alive."

Jaks nodded. "The Kin are powerful, but so are the Io. And the Elder Sons are greedy. They want what the Old Mother had. They want both transformations for themselves. But I… I've resisted what the Kin offer even though the Old Mother assured me that I would remain in control. That was one of the reasons she chose me— she believed I wouldn't succumb to the Kin's whispers, their invitations of power."

"And now, you're going to? Is that why we're here?" Zurah felt as if the answer were on the tip of her tongue, but she couldn't quite find the right order of events to fully understand it.

"No. We're here in order to make sure you survive. I told you it had been quite some time since the Io chose another host. There are always a handful in each generation, potential candidates for the Old Mother. But my generation was the last. No one understood why they stopped except the Old Mother, and I suspected it was because the Io knew she had selected me. But now, they've chosen you, and the bonding process needs to be completed."

"But wait. That doesn't make sense. If no one else knows about this place except the two of you, and yet several others have been chosen, wouldn't they have been brought here too?" Zurah asked.

"No. There is another, smaller version of the Heart in the Old Mother's chambers. That is where I had planned on taking you, but it would seem the Io have something else in mind. I believe that the Io have chosen you to take the place of the Old Mother."

17

Zurah's heart swelled with pride and gratitude as the weight of what the Io were offering settled over her. Out of all the different possibilities, the Io had *chosen* her. She was valued and wanted.

Letting go of Jaks, she slowly headed toward the crystal wall, careful to watch her step, but at the same time feeling lighter and more carefree than she had in years. She couldn't stop the grin as she approached, mesmerized by the shifting colors and the opalescent gleam to the honeycomb-riddled crystal. As she grew closer, the warmth she had felt from the crystal in her pocket surrounded her and filled the cavern. She reached into her pocket, drew out the crystal, and carefully unwrapped it. As she held it up in front of the Heart of the Io, the crystal's inner light gleamed with abundance. Instinctively, Zurah knew what to do. Carefully, she approached the Heart and located an empty part of the honeycomb. Gingerly, she placed the crystal within the Heart then felt a surge of joy move through the cavern.

But there was one other item Zurah needed to take care of. She turned to Jaks, who had followed her, and smiled. "This is a gift beyond anything I've ever received before, and I'm grateful for the Io's trust in me." She turned back toward the Heart. "I never fully realized how unwanted I felt all these years after my parents left me, and for the first time in a long time, I don't feel that way. I feel like I belong, that I've found something precious that I'd lost. But finding that feeling, knowing that you have so graciously chosen me for this honor, has also helped me realize something else. Because I also chose *myself*."

The crystals lit up in a dazzling display of twinkling lights, and a gentle hum of contentment resonated from the Heart.

"I've been home wherever I go. It isn't about a certain place or a certain person making me feel wanted; it's about me accepting me for who I am. For all of the trials I've faced, the victories I've won, and the quiet moments where I've found a few moments of contentment. I'm a security hack and a damned good one. But I don't need anyone else's validation. I *know* what I am."

Jaks had moved to stand next to her, and he reached out to squeeze her hand. "Are you ready?"

Zurah shook her head. "No. I'm honored, please believe me, and I would take this opportunity if I was the only candidate. But I'm not. You are of this world, Jaks. You understand the dynamics between the Io and the Kin, the suffering of the descendants of the *Eagle's*

Nest, and the unique ways each generation has had to make sacrifices while on this world. You should be the one to take the place of the Old Mother, not me. I promise to help you navigate what comes next, but this honor is for you."

"Zurah, the Io have chosen you," Jaks tried to protest.

"Just as they've chosen you," Zurah said. "Trust me."

The lights of the crystals grew with intensity. The sensations of warmth and joy only increased, twining around the two of them.

With a deep breath, Jaks released Zurah's hand and stepped toward the Heart. "If you'll still have me, I will gladly accept."

Zurah started to take a step back out of the way, unsure as to what exactly was going to happen. The lights from all the different crystals combined into one blinding array. She lifted her hand, shielding her eyes from the blazing glory of the Heart, then she heard a voice.

"The pair of you are about to try my patience."

The words were decidedly not what Zurah had expected.

"Old Mother?" Jaks stammered.

"Yes. Who else would it be?"

Jaks shook his head. "I don't understand."

A sigh whisked throughout the room, tickling the back of Zurah's neck. "I know you don't. And frankly, you're not supposed to, not yet. Everything would be far simpler if my sons hadn't become so greedy, so caught up in what they perceived we were missing and not recognizing the wonders that surround us each day. The

Io have stayed silent on so many things for good reason, and it has taken a long time for me to convince them to share their history. The truth of their relationship with the Kin and this world, that will be the key to defeating the Kin."

"Then I am ready," Jaks said. "Please help me understand."

"You were always my best pupil, and I recognized the goodness in you the first time your mother brought you to me. If I could snap my fingers and gift you with everything you need to know, I would. But the Io are concerned about the consequences of learning the truth in one fell swoop."

"Old Mother?" Jaks questioned.

"Each of you will be gifted with the sight I've carried all of these years. To see the true nature of this world. And in doing so, you'll start your journey to finding the key to stop the Kin. For I fear this world will not hold them for much longer."

"What?" Zurah asked in surprise. "Dammit. Kailani. She must have been able to hack Finn's suit."

"Know this: even if you succeed, the Kin are now aware and will find a way off this world, whether it be through your gates or by another means. Their sight has never been blinded."

"We've got to go," Zurah said, trying to reach out to grab Jaks's arm.

"Old Mother, how could the Kin leave this world without the gates? Without a way to transport away? You've always taught us that the Io removed the Kin's ability to move from world to world," Jaks said, ignoring Zurah.

Another sigh moved through the room, but this one carried the sounds of regret and pain. "My sons. My poor sons. When I gave birth to them, I held so much hope for their future, but I didn't understand the ramifications of how the changes made by the Io and Kin would affect them. As they grew and I realized the evil intent tucked away in their hearts, I pleaded with the Io to help me blind them to the truth of this world. In time, the Io agreed, but it was too late. There are secrets they know which should never have been revealed."

Zurah reeled back as if she'd been struck. *The white eyes of the Elder Sons. Their own mother had had them blinded.*

"Do not judge me too harshly. I did what I believed to be right in protecting the tribunal."

Jaks knelt and bowed his head. "I do not. You are the Old Mother, the keeper of our wisdom, the light which guides our way."

"The Io will complete your bonding and provide the sight to both of you. Once that's done, the rest is up to you," the Old Mother said.

Zurah would've sworn she could feel the Old Mother standing in front of her, staring right at her. Jaks shivered as he stood and moved back to stand at Zurah's side.

There was another intense flare of light, then it gradually dimmed to the level it had been when Zurah first approached the Heart. She glanced over at Jaks and frowned. "Is that it?"

"I believe so," he said.

"I don't feel any different."

"Well, it's not like you were going to sprout crystals from your face or anything," he commented dryly.

Zurah frowned and huffed. "That isn't funny."

Jaks stared at her for a moment then blinked. "Oh. Sorry."

Zurah glared at him and couldn't decide if he was truly sorry or not. He raised his hands in defense. "No, I really am. We don't have anything like what you described with the cryrot here. No one sprouts crystals or forms a crystalline body. Really."

"The pair of you…" a voice whispered through the cavern.

"All right, then," Zurah said, glancing back at the Heart. "We don't have any time to waste. I thought I'd succeeded, that I'd made sure there was no way they could use the gates. But Finn must have had another damned contingency plan. Whatever it is they're trying to do, we've got to stop them."

Jaks nodded and grabbed Zurah's hands. She tried to shake him off. "What are you doing?"

"Just trust me," he said, and in the blink of an eye, they vanished.

Zurah rocked back and forth as her feet touched the floor. "A little warning would've been great," she muttered. Taking a quick look around, she frowned. "And where exactly are we?"

"I accompanied the Old Mother as her security detail on a few occasions when she was required to visit the Kin. If I'm remembering correctly, we should be a few rooms down from where you described the rest of your team was being held."

"How did you do that?" Zurah asked.

Jaks shrugged. "I'm not entirely sure, other than it

just felt… like the right thing to do. We don't have time to hash out the mechanics of it all. We need a plan."

That was easier said than done. Zurah stared at Jaks then looked away, her mind tumbling through several different options. If she had access to tech, she would set up a diversion. But that was off the table. If she still had her gun, she would suggest going in hot. *How are we going to be able to create a distraction without getting ourselves killed or captured in the process?*

Zurah was well aware they needed access to not only the room but Finn's suit as well. Without understanding what surprises Finn might have had in store, Zurah was operating in the dark. If her message hadn't gone through and the gates were still active, she would have to try to shut them down from this side, even though she had no idea how she was going to accomplish that. All she knew was that she had to try.

"I'll go in. I can be the distraction," Jaks said. "The Kin will know what's happened to me, and I'll be a target. I can lead them away from the room while you do your security hack thing."

"That's not a great plan," Zurah commented. "Your odds of making it through that alive are going to be pretty slim."

"I understand that. Sacrifices are needed in times of hard decisions. If I don't survive, you can still do as the Old Mother instructed and find a way to stop the Kin."

Zurah really didn't like his plan, but she was coming up empty with any better ideas. Without time to really hash out anything better, Zurah finally gave in. "Fine, but for the record, I'm not going to be happy if you get yourself killed."

"Likewise." Jaks grinned, then his expression sobered. "We don't know each other, and I know you've taken a big leap of faith in trusting me right now. And I want you to know how much I appreciate it. If you hadn't shown up, I would never have known what was really going on, and all would've been lost. So thank you."

Before Zurah could say anything else, Jaks vanished. Grateful and annoyed at the same time, Zurah went to the door and peeked out. Not seeing anyone, she slipped into the corridor and quietly stole down the hallway. Everything looked the same, and there were no handy signposts along the way, but Zurah's instincts told her she was heading in the right direction.

When she heard shouts and the sound of weapons fire down the hallway, Zurah froze. She held her breath, praying no one would rush her way. Luck was on her side. She heard feet running away from her, with more shouts and weapons fire. Slowly releasing the breath, her heart pounding against her ribcage, Zurah crept the rest of the way down the hallway to the cavern where Finn and the others were being held.

There was no door to the cavern, and Zurah cautiously looked around the curve of the archway and let out a sigh of relief. She didn't see anyone inside. She slipped around the corner and headed to where she had seen Finn. As she approached, her heart sank. Finn wasn't there. A surge of anger moved through Zurah as she looked to where Angelina and Montgomery had been. The smooth surface had been cracked. Each had a bullet wound to the head and chest.

Zurah whirled around then fell back as she was punched in the face.

"I told him you'd show up," Kailani said. "But he didn't believe me. Sometimes, I'm amazed at how stubborn the Goldsmith men can be when it comes to women. They think that just because they smile and throw some kind words around, it makes them invincible. Tell me, did you think Alex was your friend? That he was on your side?"

Zurah threw a punch, but Kailani ducked then turned to kick Zurah square in the gut. Zurah stumbled back, almost losing her balance.

"He might've been. I'll give him that. Alex always had a soft spot for wanting friends, but at least that never stopped him from following through with his father's orders." Kailani moved with lightning-quick reflexes, and Zurah was helpless against her.

Hand-to-hand combat had never been one of Zurah's strengths, and now, she was facing someone with Kailani's training and bioupgrades. The Shadow landed blow after blow, driving Zurah back up against the wall where so many unsuspecting individuals had been entombed. Zurah was desperate; she knew she was trapped. She tried to fight back, but Kailani was able to either dodge or block all of Zurah's moves.

"I shouldn't have doubted my daughter, though. When I hacked her suit and looked at her files, I can see why she let you come. Zurah Winters, a renowned security hack. Wanted by the IGJ for several charges.

You were good at what you did, but it's too bad Finn didn't give you some other skills to help you stay alive," Kailani said right before she landed a devastating blow to Zurah's right ear.

Zurah cried out at the pain in her ear, which traveled down her throat and wrapped around her head. She reached up to clutch at it as Kailani stepped back. Her body started to tremor, and the world tipped to the side. She crumbled to the floor, writhing in pain. She looked up through the haze and watched as Kailani drew her weapon. Kailani was saying something, but Zurah wasn't able to catch the majority of the words.

So much for helping to stop Alex or the Kin. Now, it's up to Jaks. She half joked with herself that she wished she'd kept the crystal with her instead of returning it to the Heart. *Wait, didn't I return it?* Zurah felt something poking her hip, and she grunted as she rotated her body. Then she remembered it wasn't the crystal but the screen she'd taken from her suit.

She felt a rush of hope and glanced up at Kailani. Zurah couldn't help but let a small smile of satisfaction lift the corners of her lips. Curling in on herself to hide her face from Kailani—the cryrot hadn't known about her SeeClear tech when she'd used it to help defeat him, but Kailani would undoubtedly recognize what Zurah was doing. *Thank the universe for Finn's paranoia.*

Working quickly, she opened several different programs and sent a ghost ping, marking Kailani's tech. The security walls around Kailani's system had been expertly modified from the standard base model. But thanks to Finn's resourcefulness, Zurah was already familiar with how the suit's basic systems were set up. She only needed a few seconds to hack into the system.

She glanced up, noting Kailani had taken a step closer and prepared to shoot. Zurah pushed her legs out, catching Kailani by surprise. Kailani lost her balance and crashed to the floor. It was the few seconds that Zurah needed to unleash the whole barrage of hacking worms. As Kailani quickly got back on her feet, she began a series of blinks. No doubt, Zurah's worms had triggered a hefty number of alerts—hopefully so many that the messages were piling up and obscuring Kailani's vision.

Zurah scrambled to her feet, wincing as a fresh wave of pain struck the right side of her head, but she raced across the room, still sending out her worms and working on getting through Kailani's security walls.

The Shadow tackled her, forcing her to the ground, and with an expert maneuver, she flipped Zurah onto her back and pinned her.

"Nice try," Kailani hissed. She pressed the muzzle of her weapon against Zurah's head. "But not quite good enough."

Zurah smiled and blinked. She'd bought herself enough time to bring down Kailani's first security wall, which was all Zurah needed. She sent in her unique brand of melting codes, targeting all control nodes. Having multiple bioupgrades did have its disadvantages. When they were implanted to increase muscle control and other physiological processes, catastrophic overload could freeze them out. Zurah's particular brand of melting code sent a false cascade failure matrix into the system. Kailani's body jerked then started twitching as she fell backward and off Zurah.

Zurah grabbed the gun and tucked it into her holster. Then she stood and finished her hack. Kailani wouldn't die, but she wasn't going to be a threat either. Not bothering to look back, Zurah left the room.

"Please, take me to Jaks," Zurah whispered then squeezed her eyes shut. A tingling sensation spread across her body, then in an instant, she felt the change in temperature as she was transported from the underground complex to the surface. When she opened her eyes, she sucked in a deep breath out of shock. The surface world had completely transformed. It was no longer covered in just sand dunes, but interspersed among them were ruins of a great city stretching out across the horizon. Everywhere Zurah turned, she saw more ruins and great megalithic structures.

"What the hell?" she muttered. The Old Mother's words came rushing back to her. *Each of you will be gifted with the sight I've carried all of these years. To see the true nature of this world.* Zurah couldn't believe that all of this had been here and none of their scans had picked up on anything. It helped her realize just how advanced the technology everyone was competing over was—and how deadly it could be in the wrong hands.

Off in the distance, Zurah spied a cluster of individuals walking across the sands. She had no doubt where they were headed. She raced after them.

18

Zurah didn't catch up to them before the group came to a stop. She zoomed in with her SeeClear tech and noted Jaks and Finn were being held by the two men who'd stood with Kailani when she'd cornered Zurah and Jaks. Alex was arguing with an Elder Son, and a handful of other individuals were standing guard. She hunkered down and took a better look. Finn was still in her suit, with one of the other individuals keeping a firm grip on one of her arms.

Finn must have not agreed with Alex's plans.

Jaks was trying to break free, but the way his arms were twisted behind his back, he wasn't having much luck. As she watched the argument between Alex and the Elder Son, the Elder Son was gesturing to the east. Zurah zoomed in and wasn't surprised by what she saw. Two more gates towered over a cluster of smaller structures. It made sense that an alien civilization advanced enough to build the gates would have made more than one.

Then she took a look at the supplies next to Alex. *Shit. One of the probes.* And when she took another look, Alex was holding one of the white cylindrical crystals. *I bet they're going to use the crystal to somehow boost the probe's signal. Then use whatever Finn did to get through to Objer. Dammit. Why didn't I think of that? But better yet, how do I stop them?*

If the gates still worked, Zurah had to stop Alex. Zurah considered pinging the probe and shutting it down. But if she did it now, then it would be a dead giveaway she was still alive. She was reasonably sure Alex would believe Kailani had taken care of her, no matter what the Shadow had tried to say in order to confuse Zurah.

The ultimate goal is to trap the Kin on this world, but the immediate problem is preventing them from contacting Objer.

An idea started to form, and Zurah ducked back down, using the dune as cover. She sent out another ghost ping, but with Finn's comm markers. *Thank goodness for paranoid Finn wanting her own private comm line.* There was a return query, and Zurah breathed a sigh of relief. Zurah crept back up the sand dune and focused in on Finn.

"Finn, it's Zurah. I know you can't respond, but can you signal me with your free hand?"

There was a tense moment before Zurah caught Finn's hand open and close.

"Good. I can stop the probe, but we still need to neutralize the others. The man called Jaks is working with me; he's on our side," Zurah said. *Well, at least you need to think he is. Zurah wasn't sure where Finn was going to line up with everything, except for the fact she wouldn't want Alex to win.*

Finn's hand moved back and forth, indicating a no-go.

Frustrated, Zurah replied, "It's the only way I can stop them from here. I don't have any other support. I'm going to fry the probe."

Again, Finn tried to signal a no-go, but Zurah felt she was out of time. If she waited, Alex would finish his modifications to the probe. She scanned the area, caught the probe's signature, and sent the hack. The walls fell within seconds, and Zurah shut it down. She hadn't expected any resistance from the probe; its systems hadn't been designed with a lot of security in mind. As she watched the group, there was an angry shout, then Alex whirled around and dropped the probe.

Zurah moved to the top of the dune and stood, watching and waiting for him to turn around and look for her. But he never did. Instead, the entire group—except for Finn and Jaks—burst into a cloud of sand.

Oh no. Zurah took off at a dead run, closing the distance between her and the others. The small sandstorm swept across the dunes then headed directly for the gates. As she reached Finn and Jaks, there was a crackle of electricity in the air, along with the distinct smell of flowers. Her stomach dropped, and she turned to stare at the gates. A great sandstorm appeared, a malicious swirl of the Kin, hovering like a predator at the mouth of the gates. There was another jolt of electricity, and Zurah caught the flash as the strands of light flowed toward the two pillars, revealing something suspended between them. Before anything else could be done, the great storm that was the Kin flowed through the gates.

"I told you not to disable the probe," Finn snapped.

"What the hell happened?" Zurah asked as she closed the last bit of distance between them.

"The whole group was camouflaged. Seems they took a page out of Gregori's book," Jaks said. "We were the decoy to lure you away from their real target." He gestured toward the gates. "The Elder Sons have been working with the Kin on activating the gates for years, and it turns out all they needed was the information stored in her suit." He pointed at Finn.

Zurah paled as she realized what they'd done. Finn and Zurah had had copies of Gregori's information in their suits—everything he had provided in order to activate the gates. She had succeeded in ensuring no one could return to Objer, but she'd never considered the possibility of there being more than one set of gates on this world.

"Then we've got to stop them," Zurah said. "Come on, we can't waste time."

"Zurah." Jaks reached out and grabbed hold of her arm. "It's too late. Look."

The strings of light were dimming and, within seconds, were gone.

"But we can't—"

"What the hell are the two of you looking at?" Finn demanded.

Zurah glanced at the woman then realized what

was wrong. Before she could reply, Jaks stepped up next to her.

"It's all right. This isn't over," Jaks tried to assure her.

"You're damn right it isn't over," Finn said as she dusted herself off. "I never trusted my cousin more than absolutely necessary. Do you really think I'd let a Goldsmith just take all of my work out from under me?"

"What did you do?" Zurah asked.

"I set a secondary rendezvous time." She paused. "In thirteen hours, the gates will activate on Objer's end. I'll send for reinforcements, then we'll hunt my cousin down. There can't be that many places he could hide here."

"First, they won't be on this planet. What you can't see is that there is another set of gates to the north of us, and Alex and the Kin have just activated them and left. Second, I did what you said. I made sure the gates were destroyed by sending a blind through the probe's transmission when the gates were activated. Plus I mimicked your code—just in case—and sent an emergency broadcast telling them to destroy the gates."

Finn stared at her then burst out laughing. It was the first time Zurah had seen Finn do so, and for a moment, she wondered if Finn had lost her mind. "I knew I hadn't gone wrong when I let you come with us." She took a deep breath. "All right. We'll have to figure out another way to get back to the known worlds."

Again, Zurah shook her head. "We can't do that either. Or at least I can't. We don't know where these gates have taken Alex and the others, but the Kin are free of this world now. They said over and over again that they were hungry. I think we can safely assume that only means one thing, and I can't let that happen."

"Then it's a good thing I hacked my cousin's bioupgrades, isn't it?" Finn said. "I've got a tracer embedded in a few of his bioupgrades. All we need is something strong enough to interface with, and if they're in range, we can track him. Even if he isn't, when—" She stopped then stressed the word *when* again. "*When* we make it back to the known worlds, we'll know if he's there."

Jaks cleared his throat. "I don't think anything that's left of the *Eagle's Nest* is going to be able to help you. The power cells we use have been repaired countless times, and none of the major equipment still works. Everything is funneled into basic support and security systems."

"I know how," Zurah suddenly said. "When we were in the room with all of your family's stash, what was it that was behind the quilt?"

"A mainframe unit," Jaks said, confused.

"Exactly. I told you that people don't hide junk. There's a reason it was tucked away. And I would lay bets on the idea that if one family hid a unit, there were others as well. We find them, use the power cells, and we'll be able to rig something together."

"But what?" Jaks said. "There isn't a ship left. Everything has been torn apart years ago for scrap."

Zurah gestured at the ruins around them. "The Io changed us and allowed us to see what this world really is. You can't tell me there won't be something some good old-fashioned human ingenuity can't put together. No matter how long it takes, we'll figure it out, and we're going to go after Alex. We're going to stop the Kin."

Zurah started walking, and when the other two didn't follow, she turned around and huffed. "Jaks, you have people who are loyal to you, and you've also taken on the role of the Old Mother… although perhaps we should say Old Father?"

He scowled, and Zurah threw him a sickly sweet smile. "Anyway, you can help use your influence to get people on board. And whoever doesn't help, then it's their loss." She climbed to the top of a dune and took in the breathtaking scene. *If I'd been a xenologist, I'd be salivating at this kind of find right now.* But she wasn't. Zurah initiated a scan and started taking notes of anything that the system pinged that might be useful.

"What else are you seeing?" Finn asked as she joined Zurah.

"This world is a grave, littered with the ruins of a long-lost alien civilization," Zurah said.

"Poetic," Jaks said.

Zurah shrugged. "Maybe, but it's true. Something happened here that wiped out a very advanced civilization. And I have a guess or two as to the cause."

Jaks nodded. "The Kin."

Zurah didn't correct him. She had a feeling there was far more to the Io's involvement in all of it. The Io had hidden their history for a reason, and they wanted Zurah and Jaks to take their time and piece that history together instead of saving time and telling them. But whatever the truth was, tucked away on this forgotten world, Zurah was bound and determined to find it.

"Finn, I rather think you owe me quite a bit," Zurah said.

"Perhaps."

"Alex promised that Nissa would receive the very best in medical care, and now that he's out of the picture… well… if you make it back to the known worlds, will you make sure she's taken care of? Not just medically but also set for the rest of her life?"

"Done. You have my word."

Zurah had heard that promise too many times, but each time she did, she decided she would start anew and hope that it would come true. *Nissa, I'm sorry I'm not going to make it back, but I have to see this through. The Io chose me for this. They saw something in me that spoke to them, just as you did. Even though I was your niece, you didn't have to hire me. You could have kept your distance and never made yourself known. If there's a way I can stop the Kin, then I have to try.*

Something inside of her told her that Nissa would've understood, and it was a bit of comfort.

"So where do we start first?" Finn asked.

Only a handful of days ago, Zurah would've cringed at the idea of Finn asking her for directions, but now, it felt natural. She glanced over at Jaks. "The first thing we need to do is gift sight to those who are willing to help. The rest of your people have a right to know."

He shook his head. "I don't think that's what the Io intended, or else why wouldn't they have done that generations ago?"

"Timing. Timing is everything on the job." A small bud of warmth bloomed in Zurah's chest, and she felt the soft brush of a hand against her cheek. "Something tells me the Io are going to be willing to. If we're going to stop the Kin, then we need everyone we can get."

The three of them stood on the dune, gazing out over the horizon, for quite some time, and Zurah took a deep breath. The air still carried the hint of something floral along with the dry heat of the desert. Determination welled up inside her. She would figure out what the Io wanted them to know, and she would stop the Kin. No matter what it took or what sacrifices would have to be made along the way.

Thank you for embarking on this adventure with Zurah in *Echoes of Revenge!*

Zurah's adventures will continue in the third and final installment of the Black Gates of Objer series:

Corrupted Echoes

If you haven't checked out the other adventures within the Embedded Universe, or if you'd like to explore my other titles, and stay up to date with what's happening, visit my website and sign-up for the newsletter!

elizabethknollston.com

You can also follow me on social media at:
facebook.com/elizabethknollston
twitter.com/EKnollston

Thanks again for going on this journey with me and all the crazy characters in my imagination!

Acknowledgements

Life is difficult.

Zurah's story has been difficult to unravel. She's led me down several different paths, only to pull back and force me to reconsider. There are large chunks in her story that have been rewritten and thrown out multiple times in order to uncover the complexities of her journey.

Yet through all of this, there has been one constant, the support of my family and friends. My parents were my biggest cheerleaders, and after their passing, I was blessed with the time and opportunity to deepen my relationship with my aunts and uncles who have stood by me through my adventures with writing and publishing. I'll never be able to adequately expression my love and thanks for all that they've done for me. Thank you, always!

Nor can I ever say thank you enough to Naomi who continues to challenge me and provide grace in understanding the ups and downs of writing, publishing, and health.

And as always, the editors at Red Adept Editing continue to help me learn and grow. Challenging me with their feedback and help with working to make my stories the best they can be. I am so grateful for their expertise and advice.

Also, thank you for taking a chance and reading this book! I'm so grateful for each one of you, with your kind words of reviews and encouragement. I hope to bring you more stories of far off adventures!

About the Author

Elizabeth Knollston collects dragons. No, they're not real. But if you know of a mad scientist or genetic engineer who's working on the real deal, be sure to let her know. She would dearly love to collect star ships too, but those won't fit in her garage.

Her (overactive) imagination is credit to her parents, who outrageously encouraged her poor spending habits of buying too many books. And just a side note—if you ever plan on moving, book collecting isn't helpful.

In another life, Elizabeth dreamed of becoming an archaeologist, but a fascinating and rewarding job as a therapeutic horseback riding instructor derailed those plans. When Elizabeth isn't wondering about being on a manned mission to Mars, she enjoys bugging her dog, battling the weeds in her garden, and being a productive member of society.

www.ingramcontent.com/pod-product-compliance
Lightning Source LLC
Chambersburg PA
CBHW061119310726
48974CB00002B/599